Families First A Post-Apocalyptic Next-World Series

Volume 5 Homecoming

Lance K Ewing

COPYRIGHT

***Families First ~ Homecoming A Post-Apocalyptic Next-World Book Series* Volume 5**

www.lancekewingauthor.com

ISBN: 978-1-7350305-9-3 (trade paperback)

First Kindle edition: October 2020

First paperback edition: October 2020

Printed in the United States of America

Dedication

Dedication

To my wife, Hannah, our three awesome crazy boys, Hudson, Jax and Hendrix, and to my mom, Shareen, for her tireless editing.

To the readers who took a chance on a new author without knowing if there would be a second volume.

Thank you to all readers who left honest reviews on Amazon and Goodreads, making this continued series possible.

To all my Beta readers, thank you for your contributions and support: Chris S., Judy R., Larry R., Pam W., David E.

Dear Reader

Dear Reader, If this is your first look at my *Families First* series, please consider reading Volumes One, Two, Three and Four first.

This is a planned series of 7 volumes, depending of course on you, the reader. Thank you for purchasing and, most of all, for reading the first four books in the series.

In this day of Internet publishing, I realize you have many other choices in this genre, and I am honored you would spend your money and time with me.

As writers, we now more than ever are judged by our reviews online. If you enjoyed this book, please leave an honest review on Amazon.

For those of you interested in this series, please consider keeping in touch by visiting my website at *lancekewingauthor.com* for upcoming books and projects, as well as weekly updates on what I am up to. I will not distribute your e-mail anywhere.

In return for your e-mail, I will forward you my Quick Guide e-book (free of charge and not available for sale) with more information on the characters of *Families First*, including their backstories, much of which you will not find in any of the volumes.

Lance K Ewing

WHAT READERS ARE SAYING

5 ***5.0 out of 5 stars*** **Good family approved reading**

Really enjoyed all four books! Good character developments with some surprises that I didn't see coming. Enjoyable read that will be read again.

5.0 out of 5 stars **What a story**

This is the 4th of this series and all have been so well written, flowing seamlessly one into the other. A quick recap at the beginning, in case you need a refresher, is nice. Now I have to wait till the next release for answers to the cliffhangers! Hopefully soon!

5.0 out of 5 stars **Action and great characters**

I have really enjoyed this series. The characters are really well developed and lots of action and suspense—I can't wait for the next book!

5.0 out of 5 stars **Review**

The plot gets thicker. What will happen with the Judge? James and Jason are trying to be neutral. Maybe they can get support from the townsfolk. Lance and his group still have not reached their destination. David and his group are at peace for the moment. Will the Military be able to stop the groups from taking over the Ranch and the Valley? Looking forward to the next book. Love the references to the songs and the movies in the dialogues. Love the humor as well in the story.

5.0 out of 5 stars **Great story**

What a great story—well thought out and keeps you on the edge of your seat!

5.0 out of 5 stars **Providing for your own is essential**

Greatly enjoyed the perspective and the energy of this story. So many values and virtues are on display. Good read.

5.0 out of 5 stars **Very comfortable and believable stories!**

These books are so much more than 5 stars! I have books 1 and 2 and am just beginning number 3. I can hardly wait to find out what happens to Lance, Joy and their adorable boys. All the characters feel like I've known them for years. Very comfortable reads of an uncomfortable but highly likely subject. Keep them coming, Lance. They are wonderful books!

5.0 out of 5 stars **Wow!**

This has been by far one of the best post-apocalyptic series I've read. *Families First* was like reading about your own neighborhood and hoping it would turn out the same way. Kudos to Mr. Ewing!

5.0 out of 5 stars **I'm there with the characters in the storyline!**

I have read many apocalyptic books from a number of authors and find Mr. Ewing's writing style to be as well developed as some of the best writers. His ability to keep the storyline moving along at a pace that has you flipping pages as fast as you can read is phenomenal!

After reading all 3 of the books so far within a week, I can hardly wait for the next book! The storyline is realistic with the struggles people will face when the SHTF, but not gory with in-depth details. The characters' personalities are real and complex, revealing the types of internal struggles expected when blending them together. He uses their personality differences to enhance the dynamics of the groups in very realistic ways that keep the reader intrigued. For heaven's sake! Read this series!!

***5.0 out of 5 stars* Fabulous series, can't wait for the next book!**

I love this series, *Families First.* What a great theme. Families are not always about blood but include friends who would die protecting each other. A must-read!

****

Foreword

Recap of Volumes One, Two, Three and Four

In Volumes One, Two and Three of *Families First ~ Post-Apocalyptic Next-World Series,* we were introduced to a cast of characters spanning multiple locations across the United States, all with diverse points of view and hardships to overcome.

We learned that North Korea dropped an EMP in the center of the United States, knocking out power to all states except Hawaii, as well as parts of Canada and Mexico. With no electricity, food or running water, and few working vehicles, the country is instantly reduced to the hardships of days long gone. It's every family for themselves in this new and hostile world.

Lance and Joy, along with their children, like-minded friends and neighbors, embark on their journey, headed to Saddle Ranch in the Colorado Rocky Mountains by way of Raton Pass, on the Colorado/New Mexico border.

The first leg of the trek to Raton Pass would prove more difficult than they could ever imagine, plagued with injuries and losses along the way. Relying on faith, and loyal to the group, they soldier on and finally arrive at their destination.

Vlad is transferred to a FEMA camp, and eventually to Trinidad, Colorado, for surgery following a life-threatening injury.The sons of Lance and Joy each face hardships and potentially catastrophic situations.

Former McKinney police officer, Mike, proves to be a hindrance to the group as well as an invaluable help when safety is on the line.

Lonnie and Jake keep everything running as smoothly as possible.

Joy, Nancy and Tina earn MVPs on the first leg of the trip.

Mac, on Saddle Ranch, falls in love with a beautiful medical doctor, but the relationship is complicated from the very start.

Crossover has begun between the communities of Saddle Ranch, led by John, and The West, led by Samuel.David and the Jenkins family in Raton, New Mexico, suffer a devastating loss after an accident involving mistaken identity.

James and Janice, in Weston, Colorado, start their new family, taking in a young orphaned boy named Billy. With both James and Jason in new town government posts, they try to remain neutral as the Sheriff and Judge passively battle for control of the town.

It is clear to all that Ronna is working with the US Military, and always has been.

Volume Three finds our main group held up at Raton Pass longer than they had planned, but their assistance will prove invaluable to David Jenkins and the Raton Pass Militia.

The battle for control of the town of Weston, Colorado, heats up, with both the Sheriff and Judge vying for the allegiance of the town Mayor, James VanFleet.

On Saddle Ranch in Loveland, Colorado, old foes unexpectedly turn into allies and the security detail is gutted and put back together, piece by piece, for the imminent battle for control of the pristine Valley.

The Colonel takes a shine to Lance's group and forges a friendship with the always-boisterous and joking Vlad that may prove life-saving for many others. As they learn new information about Ronna's and Baker's intentions, they become more concerned with getting to Saddle Ranch in a timely manner.

Volume four continues with James VanFleet being shot and subsequently paralyzed from the waist down, but that won't keep him from his family or his town's responsibilities. The rivalry between Sheriff Johnson and Judge Lowry is heating up, and the only thing they agree on lately is that one of them has to go. With the death-defying show right around the corner, the Sheriff becomes distracted, and even his girlfriend Kate thinks he is becoming increasingly irrational.

Mac and Cory, on Saddle Ranch, have their hands full with Ralph once again, but they aim to make this the last run-in. They have bigger fish to fry and need the entire Valley focused on the threat that is literally walking towards them.

Lance and group are teaming up to help David and the Raton Pass Militia defend the mountain against only a small part of Baker's group. They are counting on the Colonel's help if things go badly, but there are no guarantees in this Next-World. Either way, they have outstayed their welcome and are back on the road to Saddle Ranch. Every town and pit stop they go through is an opportunity to help those most in need, even when it puts the group at risk.

* * * *

Contents

Chapter One ~ Weston, Colorado

Judge Lowry stood still, arms at his side. He clutched the first pistol he had owned, purchased only days before. The instructions from the lead deputy surrounded him like a cloud of smoke, dulling his senses. Everything before him slowed as the commands seemed to come from miles away.

"Drop the weapon and lie facedown on the ground," came the command again.

This time the Judge dropped the pistol and slowly crouched over, lowering himself to his knees.

"Now, hands behind your back, sir," called the lead deputy.

Doing as instructed, Judge Lowry succumbed to arrest.

"What are the charges?" he spat out as his wrists were tightly cuffed. "I have rights, you know," he continued, as his voice grew louder and angrier. "You deputies all took my moonshine gladly, and this is how you repay me? I'll have your necks in a noose by week's end, all of you!" he yelled.

"Let's put him in the back," called out the lead man, "and don't talk to him. This thing is between him and the Sheriff, and nobody else."

Judge Lowry kept mostly quiet on the way back to town, after asking a few unanswered questions.

* * *

Sheriff Johnson made a point to not be at the jailhouse when the Judge arrived. He wanted to give him some stew time before having to answer questions. After talking with his girlfriend, the Sheriff was sure he had made the right decision.

"It was going to be him or you," she told him. "If his secretary hadn't told me about his trip to see James," she continued, "we would already be at a disadvantage."

"Why would she do that?" he asked, surprised. "She betrayed Judge Lowry's trust after all these years?"

"Well, it's like this," she said. "*You* see things in front of you, whether good or bad, and act accordingly. Maybe someone says something you don't like and you lock them up, or you get an idea for, let's say, a wheelchair and you go full throttle to get it done. Does that sound right?"

"Yeah, I guess so."

"We've been dating now for three years, two months, and twelve days—right?"

"Um, I don't know, but it sounds right," replied the Sheriff.

"It is, and I always knew you and the Judge were going to have it out eventually, so I've been a friend to her the whole time. See, I'm a planner and a plotter; I always have been."

"But you couldn't have seen this coming—the power failure, I mean," he said.

"That's true, but now it just makes the decision even easier. How long are you going to make him wait in the cell?" his girlfriend asked.

"Overnight, I guess. I want to see if he talks to any of my deputies."

"How will you know?" she queried.

"Ken will tell me. He's my eyes and ears in there, and he believes he's about to go free."

"Is he?"

"We'll see. We will see."

* * * *

Judge Lowry had calmed down, and he didn't ask even one of the dozens of questions he wanted to.

"Where's the Sheriff, and when will he be here?" were the only ones he would voice aloud.

"Last open cell, Judge," said the lead deputy. "Unless, of course, you want to share one with Richard? No, no...I didn't think so. Eat your dinners, and the Sheriff will see you all in the morning."

Judge Lowry spent the first part of the night plotting his revenge and the second half accepting his defeat. He would broker a deal of sorts with his old friend. *Surely, it's still possible*, he thought. The other jail mates didn't dare speak to or about him, each still hoping for a chance, however slim, of walking out of jail alive. Only Ken listened intently, as he always did now, for anything that may help the Sheriff.

* * * *

"I hear you're going to be jumping my courthouse," called out Judge Lowry at first light.

"Yes, sir, that's the plan," Ken replied quickly.

"And I'll be fighting the skinny boy across the hall," interjected Richard. "Unless, of course, the Sheriff puts the three of us in the arena together."

"Screw you," came the call from James' shooter, and "I don't think so" from the Judge.

"It would make it interesting is all I know," replied Richard, laughing and feeling more confident every minute.

"That may not be a bad idea," said Sheriff Johnson, quietly slipping into the jailhouse.

"We need to talk and right now," called out Judge Lowry, unable to see him yet.

"Oh, we will in good time, old friend. I just don't have all the charges on you yet."

"What charges? I was just going for a drive when your boys started in on me."

"A drive to where?"

The Judge was silent as Sheriff Johnson continued. "Maybe a drive out to the VanFleet ranch?"

"Who told you that?" the Judge asked angrily.

"Why, your secretary, of course. Who else knew?"

"Why would she do that, after all the years we worked together?" asked the Judge.

"You didn't work together. She worked for you, just like I did. But my girlfriend set her straight, and me too. Now I just need to figure out the best use for a defunct courthouse. Maybe a gymnasium of sorts for the schoolhouse or a new office for the Mayor," he said, sliding breakfast trays under each cell.

"I run that courthouse!" screamed the Judge, seeing where this was heading. "I make the rules for it and this town."

"Not anymore, old friend...not anymore. And besides, now you are eating up all *my* food."

"Keep your crappy food," he spat, throwing the full tray through the cell bars. It crashed onto the floor with a bang.

"I'm not so sure that was a good idea," said Ken after the Sheriff left the building. "He keeps a clean jailhouse, and he does it himself."

* * * *

Sheriff Johnson walked home with a grin he couldn't wipe off his face.

"What do I do with him now?" the Sheriff asked his girlfriend.

"Let me think on it... We have all the time in the world," she replied.

* * * *

Sheriff Johnson decided to check on Ken. He wanted to see if the Judge had said anything important in his cell and if there had been any progress on James' chair.

"You won't be seeing the Judge here anytime soon," he told the shop owner without elaborating.

"What about the chair his guy Cam is working on?" asked the shop owner.

"How close is it to being done?" asked the Sheriff.

"A week at best, but more likely it will be two or three. He gets in late and cuts out early, and sometimes he doesn't make it in here at all."

"Okay. Let the old-timer finish it; we will still beat him fair and square and present ours first. Right, Ken?" he called out.

"Yes, sir, and I'm almost finished. We should be able to take it for a test run tomorrow."

"Ha! That's great news!" replied the Sheriff. "I'll be honest. I didn't much care either way at first if you made your upcoming jump, but now I'll admit I'm rooting for you. Hold tight. I have a gift of sorts for you, but don't let it go to your head. We still have a long way to go, you and me."

"Yes, sir," replied Ken, wondering what it could possibly be.

He got back to work, and minutes later heard "Heads up! Catch!" as he turned just in time to see the round object twisting in the air.

"I hope you're a large," stated the Sheriff as Ken smiled broadly at his new, used bright orange motorcycle helmet. "It's got a couple of scratches, near as I can tell, but she looks in good shape over all."

"This may just be the best gift I've ever received. Thank you, sir."

"Keep your ears open for me in the jail, and I'll be back at, say, noon tomorrow for the chair test."

"I'll have her ready," replied Ken. He attempted to fight off daydreams about being back home with his girlfriend and dog on Saturday night. *Only if you survive the jump and he decides to keep you around*, he thought.

"Oh, last thing, Ken," added the Sheriff. "I'll send my girlfriend by later today. She wants to meet you."

"Ah, okay, sir. Sure."

* * * *

"Hi, Ken," came the call a few hours later.

"Hey, Kate. It's been a long time. How are you?"

"I couldn't be better, considering the circumstances. The chair, it's looking good," she added.

"How did you know about this?" Ken asked.

"I know a lot about you, actually—about the chair and your upcoming jump."

"Oh, now I get it. The Sheriff said his girlfriend would be by today. I guess that's you."

"That's right. Let's get a few things straight, though," she added, closing the door to the side room and lowering her voice. "Sheriff Johnson and I have been together for a few years now. I'm sure the new addition to the jailhouse yesterday didn't go unnoticed by you or the other men there."

"No, you're right. It was something I didn't expect, that's for sure."

"Have you heard the phrase 'A man is only as good as the woman who stands next to him?'" she asked.

"That sounds familiar," Ken replied.

"That's what we have here in this town now. It was the Sheriff's idea to let you jump the courthouse, and it was mine to save you from the noose. Do you think it was just a coincidence that I handed him the *1974 Guinness Book of World Records*, featuring none other than Evel Knievel at the exact moment he was wondering what to do with you all?"

"I'm not sure I follow," said Ken.

"Here it is. I've known it was you inside since the beginning. You ran for City Council—and I voted for you, by the way."

"Oh, that makes sense. And thanks for the vote!"

"Anyway, if I could have got you out of there by winning a motorcycle race, I would have done it, but the Sheriff loves the death-defying stunts, so I pushed him towards something I thought you could walk away from alive... What do you think of the helmet?" she said with a wink.

"That was you, too?" Ken asked.

"A little of both, I guess. You're growing on him too."

"What about Richard and the other guy?" he asked.

"Ha! I don't give a crap about that slob Richard or James' shooter. Nope, he came up with the gladiator thing on his own. Do you talk to those guys?"

"Hell no. I keep to myself."

"That's what I thought. There's one more thing," she said, moving in close and whispering in his ear "It doesn't matter who wins their little fight; neither of them is getting out alive. We, you and I, just drifted apart. I know that, and I don't blame you for it. But he doesn't know about us, and I'm not sure what he would do if he found out. Does that make sense?"

"Completely."

"So, the short of it is, you keep that our little secret, and I'll do my best to keep your head on your shoulders. I also expect complete loyalty to the office of the Sheriff moving forward, assuming you make the landing."

"And if he decides to keep me around, right?" he asked, only half-joking.

"Nope, you just make the jump and I'll make sure you get to stay in town. Besides, I hear you have a dog and a new girlfriend to get back to."

"I, uh...well, I mean..."

“Don’t worry about it,” she said, with a smile. “Make the landing, and you will be home on Saturday night. Are we agreed?”

“Sure, Kate. It sounds like you’re the one doing me a favor.”

“I am. See you around, Ken.”

She kissed him on the cheek and opened the door to leave, giving the shop owner a mind-your-own-business look.

* * * *

“What did you think about Ken?” asked the Sheriff as soon as he saw her at home.

“You should keep him around. You can trust him; I know that much.”

“That’s what I thought you would say, honey.”

* * * * * * *

Chapter Two ~ Second Chances Ranch Weston, Colorado

James had a visitor later in the day. He was looking at the gate through his binoculars when the man arrived on horseback. James recognized him immediately.

"Jason, can you let him in through the gate?"

"Sure, but do you know him?"

"Yep, he's one of the Sheriff's deputies; he's got a small farm a few miles towards town."

"Why didn't he just drive up here?" asked Jason, as he headed down the front porch stairs.

"Well, he either is just out for a ride on his day off or is not looking to draw any attention, and I'm guessing the latter, so let's see what he has to say."

"Howdy, James."

"Deputy, how have you been?"

"Better than most, I have to admit. Oh, I didn't mean..."

"We've known each other a long time," said James. "You're not going to offend me with anything you might say—and besides my legs, I'm better than most!"

"Point taken, old friend," replied the deputy. "Time to state my business, I guess... I heard you had a visitor yesterday."

"Maybe," replied James. "What are you asking me?"

"Well, I'm not askin' as much as I'm only giving a heads up to an old friend and one of the few men I trust in this town. Judge Lowry was arrested on Sheriff Johnson's orders shortly after leaving your place. I wasn't there, but it seems there was a long chase before they apprehended him."

"What's the charge?" asked James, trying not to act as surprised as he was about the news.

"That's just it! I don't know. Our guys were just told to arrest him and bring him to the jailhouse."

"Hmm, that makes things interesting, for sure—any word from the Sheriff on what he plans to do with him?" asked James.

"Nope. There's been no word, but he's been in a cell since yesterday and refusing to eat, from what I hear."

"Thanks for the heads up, and let's just keep this little conversation between us. Agreed?"

"Yes, James. I was hoping you would say that."

Jason showed him out, locking the front gate behind him.

"Who is that, Daddy?" asked little Billy, jumping up into James' lap.

"Oh, just somebody Daddy works with. How about you get your mom and Aunt Lauren? Uncle Jason and I need to talk to them."

"Okay, Daddy. I'll find them."

* * * *

James, Janice, Lauren and Jason sat on the front porch sipping iced tea, minus the iced part, and discussed their options.

"Jason, what do you think?" asked James.

"I don't...well, I don't really know. This is all just a shock—something I wasn't expecting."

"Let's start at the beginning," suggested Janice, "so we are all on the same page."

James told her and Lauren everything they knew so far.

"Hmm," said Janice, without elaborating.

"Hmm, what?" asked James.

"To be honest, I'm not surprised at all about this," she replied, with Lauren nodding in agreement. "We knew things were headed south between those two, and it was bound to come to a head. What I'm concerned about is that the arrest happened at some point between our ranch and Weston. I wonder who all knew he was coming here to talk to you guys."

"That's a good point, honey," said James.

"Jason, you and I will head into town tomorrow morning and stop by the jailhouse."

"Are you sure you're up to that?" asked Janice.

"I'll have to be. You know I always want to know upfront what's headed our way. Plus, we owe it to the girls and Billy to always make sure we're one step ahead of everyone else."

All agreed with a head-nod while watching the four young children play a game of tag out by the main barn.

"In fact, let's make a day of it," James continued. "We will head to town together, and you all can drop Jason and me off at the jailhouse. We will meet you at the restaurant for breakfast when we're done."

* * * *

At 7 a.m. they were off and headed to town. Jason drove and Chance stayed behind to keep an eye on the ranch.

They pulled up in front of the police station at 7:20, and Janice, Lauren, the girls and Billy headed on to the restaurant.

"You need a push?" asked Jason.

"Nope, this chair is not the best, but I'll be the one to roll it."

"Hopefully, we can fix that sooner than later," replied Jason. "Maybe it's locked," he announced, as he tried the front door.

"Give it a couple of knocks; maybe the Sheriff is inside."

Jason knocked on the door, getting a loud response from more than one man inside.

"Sheriff, are you in there? It's James VanFleet and Jason Davis."

The announcement set off a chain of overlapping responses, the loudest one announcing he was Judge Lowry.

"Well, there's our response to the Sheriff when he asks how we knew about the Judge being here," said James.

"James!" came the call again from the Judge. "You need to get me out of here. He's going to kill me! You owe me that much after all I've done for you."

Jason was getting nervous. James didn't respond.

"Aren't you going to say something?" Jason asked.

"No, Jason. This is where we stay quiet and don't say another word."

There was ten more minutes of Judge Lowry's ranting before Sheriff Johnson pulled up in his truck.

"James VanFleet," he said, smiling as he exited his truck with his lead deputy. "Already back from the dead, I see. Hello, Jason."

"We stopped by to say hi," said James in a casual tone.

"Did you now? Have you heard anything interesting this morning?" he asked, as Judge Lowry continued shouting in the background.

Jason's stomach tightened, but he did not speak. He would not speak unless James needed help, he thought.

"Just that," replied James, pointing inside the building.

"Yeah, that's complicated for sure, don't you think, James?"

"I couldn't say, sir, because I don't have all of the facts yet."

"Spoken like a true politician!" replied the Sheriff, laughing. "The funny thing is, I haven't even talked to him yet."

James gave Jason a look that said let's take it slow and only reveal what he thinks we already know.

"What do you think I should do with him, James?"

"I don't know; I'm not sure why he's even in there."

"That's a fair statement, I guess. Maybe you have an idea, though, since he was at your ranch right before we picked him up."

"Excuse me," said Jason, exiting through the front door and running towards the building's side with his hand over his mouth.

"I'm not sure he's got the stomach for all of this business," said the Sheriff, laughing.

"He'll be all right," replied James. "So, what now?" he asked, wanting to get to the nuts and bolts of the issue and how it would affect their families.

"Well, now... What's next is up to you, James...well, partially. Come on in, and we'll talk a bit. Can I help you inside?"

"Nope," replied James flatly.

James rolled in, following the Sheriff. "Let's talk in my office," the Sheriff suggested.

"Sheriff, is that you?" called out Judge Lowry.

"Yep, just me and James having a little talk about the future of *my* town," he replied, knowing it would set the Judge off.

He was right. Judge Lowry started hollering and threatening both him and James.

"All right, James," the Sheriff said over the shouting down the hall. "Today is the day. You knew it was coming one way or the other, didn't you?"

"Sir, with all due respect, everyone in town knew this day would come."

Sheriff Johnson smiled without a response, pausing briefly to listen to Judge Lowry's rant.

"When I told you, Sheriff, that your election was a landslide victory, it was true. What I didn't tell you was that Mr. Grimes got all the votes," said the Judge. "Do you hear me? He beat the crap out of you. Do you know the one man who could have beat Grimes? Do you?!" he screamed. "He's sitting right next to you. That's a man who can win an election. That's a man who has the respect of this town. That's the man who should have your job. And that floozy girlfriend of yours is nothing but trouble for this town. She might as well be the Sheriff because she runs you around like her little monkey, and you don't have the cojones to do crap about it!"

Sheriff Johnson turned red and called to his deputy to quiet the Judge.

"You shut him up, or I will," the Sheriff called to his deputy. "I need a minute, James," he said, stepping outside.

"Were you coming to find me, sir?" asked Jason when the Sheriff exited the jailhouse.

"No, not exactly. I'll have James back out in just a few."

* * * *

"James," he said, walking back inside, "did you know about the election results?"

"I heard it just yesterday from Judge Lowry. Before then, I had no idea."

"Who else do you think knows? His secretary, I'll bet," stated the Sheriff.

"I don't know of anybody else who does, except maybe Mr. Grimes. But he left town, never to return. Right?"

"You know better than that, James."

"Yeah, I guess I do," replied James.

"Bring Ken back to the office," Sheriff Johnson told a deputy. "I want him to meet our new mayor...

"Ken, this is our new mayor, James VanFleet."

"Hello again, sir," said Ken, shaking James' hand.

"You know each other?" asked the Sheriff.

"Yes, the city council had one meeting with him and the deputy mayor right before... Well, you know."

"Oh, I forgot about that," the Sheriff admitted.

"Anyway, James, I'm sure you already heard about the jump he'll do on Saturday over the courthouse."

"I did hear something about that," replied James.

"He's also been working on something else that I won't go into right now, but I think you will like it. You'll see it on Saturday. So, my point is, assuming Ken here doesn't fall off the roof or completely miss the landing, there is a good chance that he will be joining my team. He fixes things, is a good way to put it. Isn't that right?"

"Yes, sir. Whatever you need fixing, I'm your guy."

"He's loyal from what I can tell so far, and that's exactly what I need right now," the Sheriff said, once Ken had left the room. "Are you, James?"

James paused, being careful of his next words. He was glad Jason was outside.

He rubbed his scruffy chin with his hand and nodded his head. "Sheriff, I am loyal to this town and its citizens. I always have been, even when I was technically outside the city limits."

"Okay, that's good enough for now," he replied, patting James on the shoulder.

"I'd better check on Jason," said James, "unless we have more to discuss."

"Not today. I would see what you thought I should do with the Judge, but I remember you don't particularly have the stomach for that. Thanks for coming in, James. We'll see you on Saturday for the exhibition. Don't be late."

* * * *

James rolled out of the jailhouse with his head feeling heavy, like every time after meeting here.

"What happened?" asked Jason. "Are we all good?"

"I'm not sure we're all good, but we showed our faces and that's enough for now. They have a surprise for me on Saturday, I guess."

"I've got to make a quick stop downtown," Jason blurted out, "before breakfast!"

"All right," replied James, not asking why.

"Be right back," Jason told him, ducking into the hardware store.

"I haven't seen you in a week, son," said a scruffier, somehow slower Cal.

"I know. It's been busy is all. The chair—is it done?"

"Nah," he said, laughing. "It's going to be another two or three weeks, near as I can tell. Plus, I'm over budget now, so tell the Judge I'm going to need more coins to continue."

"We had a deal," said Jason. "Judge Lowry and I both gave you money, and the other guy is nearly done with his chair."

"Well, he's a jailbird. Got nothin' else to do all day. I've got other things I'm responsible for, and most of 'em are higher on my priority list than this here chair. I'm clocking out by noon today, and if you want me to continue, I'll need six more silvers."

"Six? I don't have that many," said Jason.

"Judge Lowry does, so pass on the message."

Jason put his hand up to his face and walked out before saying something he wouldn't be able to take back.

* * * *

"Everything all right?" asked James. "Anything I should know?"

"I was just trying to do something good, and it seems harder to do nowadays."

"You're right about that, but it's still always worth a try. Let's get some breakfast, Jason."

"We're Shakin' Our Bacon for a Limited Time" read the sign on Weston's Grill and Tavern storefront.

"I hope that means sausage, too," remarked Jason.

"You found some pork, I see," James said to the restaurant owner.

"Sure did, Mayor, at least for now. I'm glad to see you're up and running...well, I mean..."

"I know what you mean, and it's good to get out of the house," replied James. "Now tell me about your specials this morning."

* * * *

Breakfast was the real deal, and Candice, Carla and Jenna each had six pieces of bacon. Little Billy was full after his head-sized biscuit and four slices of bacon.

"Oh, and before I forget," said the owner, "your family, all of you, have a reservation here Saturday night after the festivities, compliments of Sheriff Johnson. It's been pre-paid, so please show up and help support our restaurant. It's steak night, so don't be late."

"All right! We'll be here! Thank you," replied James.

* * * *

Meanwhile, back at the jail, the Sheriff was interested to speak with Ken. "It's Thursday, Ken. I hope the chair is done."

"It is, sir. Care to take her for a test run?"

"I do. Deputy, you two get it loaded, and I'll meet you down by the river at the old fishing spot. I don't want anyone to see it before Saturday. Be there in an hour," he commanded. "I've got to take care of something first."

Sheriff Johnson readied the breakfast trays. "Only a couple more days, gentlemen," he called out. "I trust you will put on a good show for my citizens. Judge, let me know right now if you're going to throw another tray of food. It won't go over too well next time."

Judge Lowry didn't respond. He scowled but did not overturn his tray this morning.

"We need to talk," he told the Sheriff after accepting the food tray. "Just us in your office."

"You remember Kate, my girlfriend. Right?" asked the Sheriff.

"Yes, but what does that have to do with us talking?"

"She will be here soon, so we can all talk together."

"That's bull. Why would I want her opinion?" said the Judge.

"Because I do. Sit tight and eat your breakfast."

* * * *

"Hey babe," said the Sheriff as Kate walked through the front door minutes later. "Thanks for coming in today."

"Oh, I wouldn't miss this for anything—except maybe a trip to Hawaii!"

He called to his deputy to bring the Judge to his office.

"You want him cuffed, right boss?"

"No, I don't," he replied after seeing Kate's head go back and forth. "Give us a few minutes, then bring him in."

* * * * *

"Why no cuffs?" he asked his girlfriend.

"It's more fun this way. I'm not worried about him overpowering you, or even me for that matter. But bring him up with no cuffs on, and he just might think he's walking out of here, back into his old role. That's the hope I want to take away from that dirtbag that always put you second over the years. Put the cuffs on at the end of our meeting, and the look on his face will be priceless."

"Okay then. It doesn't matter to me either way, so let's get this done," he replied.

The meeting started out friendly under the circumstances, with Judge Lowry pretending he didn't tell the sitting Sheriff he had badly lost the election or that he told him his girlfriend ran the show.

"What we need," started Judge Lowry, "is a path back to where we were before this whole misunderstanding happened."

"There is no misunderstanding, Judge," Kate jumped in. "You've been running my fiancé around like a dog on a leash for too long. And then you try to get James VanFleet on your side against us?"

"Not against both of you, and not even against you, Sheriff... What is she doing here, anyway?" he said, pointing to Kate. "She speaks for you now?"

The moment was awkward, and for the first time in a while, Sheriff Johnson could feel his stomach tighten. He thought of Jason leaving a room whenever things got heated. Now he was the one needing a break.

"Excuse me!" he blurted out, calling for his deputy to go into the office until he returned.

The Judge continued with Kate, sensing an opportunity and hoping to negotiate a peace treaty of sorts before the Sheriff returned.

"Cuff him to the chair," she told the deputy.

"But the Sheriff told me to..."

"I'm telling you now," she snapped.

The deputy did as instructed, cuffing his prisoner's right hand to the chair, and stepped out.

“I’ll be right outside the door; just knock if you need me,” he said.

“I always figured it would come down to this someday,” started the Judge.

“Down to what?” she asked.

“You and me reaching some sort of agreement without him here.”

She smiled without a response.

“Okay. Here’s the deal,” she said. “You agree to leave this town and never return, and I’ll do my best to keep your neck out of a noose.”

“Why would I agree to that?”

“Because if you don’t, you will hang or maybe be thrown into a mix with the two soon-to-be gladiators back there, or following Ken jumping on a motorcycle over your own courthouse.” She paused, letting the words sink in.

“Oh, you mean the Ken in the back cell, who used to help with maintenance projects around the courthouse maybe five or six years ago?”

Kate kept her composure and didn’t acknowledge the accusation she knew would come next.

“Yes, the same young man,” he continued, “that was dating a local girl named Kate, I believe. You two were talking about getting married, if I remember right. I’m sure that’s hard for your new boyfriend...I mean fiancé...pardon my mistake. I just get confused when the Sheriff refers to you as his girlfriend, but you call him your fiancé. I’m sure there is a logical explanation. I’m sure it’s also hard for the Sheriff having you two former lovebirds so close to him now. Am I being obtuse?”

Kate paused, not being able to remember the last time she was at a loss for words.

“Oh, now I see,” he continued. “The Sheriff doesn’t know you two were lovers, so much so that you almost got married...”

She turned a fiery red and wanted to choke him to death with her bare hands. Without hesitation, she reached back her right hand, bringing it swiftly across his cheek, leaving four finger markings.

"I'm the only reason you're not dead yet, Judge. If you breathe a word of this to anyone, I'll have your head in a jar on my dining room table. Do you understand me?" she called out louder than she wanted, grabbing the collar of his shirt. "Do you?" she screamed as the door opened and Sheriff Johnson came back inside.

"I told you to stay inside!" the Sheriff spat to his deputy.

"We're done here," said Kate. "Judge Lowry has a lot to think about. Come on, honey. You promised me lunch at the Tavern and dessert at home," she said, with a sassy yet flirtatious smile.

"That I did. Okay, let's get him back in the cell, Deputy, and I'll take it up again later."

* * * * * * *

Chapter Three ~ Weston, Colorado

Sheriff Johnson drove them to the river and let Kate have the first crack at James' new chair. He was talking with his deputy as Ken showed her the controls.

"He knows," she whispered. "Judge Lowry knows about us."

"You know that I worked for him, and maybe I said your name way back then, but believe me, I haven't said a word about it since then. Anyone else know?" he asked quietly, glancing back towards the Sheriff.

"No, not yet. Let me handle it and don't speak a word to anyone in jail, not one word."

"I can do that," he replied.

"We're okay," she whispered. "Just follow my lead."

"So, about this chair," he said, speaking up as Sheriff Johnson walked up. "She's ready to go. This way is forward, backward like this, and the steering is smooth. Watch out, though. She's quick!"

Kate took off fast and navigated the off-road trail, winding next to the river with ease.

"You have to try this, babe," she called out, laughing.

"Okay! Hold my pistol, Ken."

"Really? Wait. Really...are you sure, sir?"

"Yep. Just don't drop it."

"See. I told you, Ken," said Kate, smiling. "He trusts you now."

"Then why not just let me go? I told him I would be happy to work for the town."

"He could let you go now and probably wouldn't mind, but it's about perception. He needs to be both respected and feared by the citizens of this town. Your little stunt is a compromise. He ordered the best architect he could find and the best materials for the ramps. But you have to earn it. Show the people what they need to see to toe the line. That's what the hangings did."

* * * *

"This is the chair—exactly what I wanted! Good job, Ken," said Sheriff Johnson, patting him on the shoulder, "and thanks for watching my gun."

"Now, good to my word I'll give you time to inspect the jump ramps and take the bike for a spin."

"Sure, that sounds great. But why would you let me hold your gun, sir?"

"Well, I didn't want it digging into my side," he responded, taking the magazine out of his vest pocket and slamming it back into the pistol.

"You didn't think I was going to give you a loaded weapon, did you?"

"No, sir. I guess not."

* * * *

Ken rode the motorcycle—a modified 1995 Yamaha YZ 450—around the courthouse, gauging the handling and acceleration. He was given a 30-minute meeting with the architect, who proceeded to weigh him and the bike to determine the amount of gas needed to jump the bike, but not fully loaded. She handwrote the speed needed to mathematically clear the roof of the courthouse.

"Okay, Ken," said the architect. "You want to hit the center of the ramp at 82 miles per hour, according to my calculations. We have the speedometer dialed in, and the top speed of the stock bike is 80 mph. The mechanic was able to boost that top speed to 94, but this is a dirt bike, as you know, and it's going to be hard to control. So, on Saturday morning we will do some practice run-ups, making sure you can hit the 82 mph before you hit the front ramp. The landing ramp is over 200 feet long. Overkill, in my opinion, but that's what the Sheriff wants. We have stacked hay bales at the end of the ramp, should you make it that far. Have you jumped before?"

"Yes, ma'am, but never anything like this."

"That's what I thought."

"We'll have Doc Walters and his group waiting at the landing ramp, in case they are needed," the architect added. "Any questions?"

"Where do I start?" asked Ken.

"See that American flag hanging above the bank there? You will start right under the flag, giving you enough time to get into fifth gear at the launch, with about five seconds to spare."

"What about the wind speed—if it's gusty or something else?" asked Ken.

"That's the only thing I can't calculate precisely. See, this is a rain-or-shine jump. The Sheriff has been adamant about that from the beginning. I'll be praying for a good day."

"Me too," replied Ken, thanking her for her hard work.

Ken was both excited and nervous about his jump in just two days' time. His ribs hurt as he turned the bike in a large circle with sprint starts and stops. The finger splints would have to be removed Saturday morning for practice, as his grip on the handlebars had to be tight. Kate flagged him down as he was test-riding the motorcycle.

"Hey, Kate," he said, lifting the visor of his helmet and killing the engine. "What do you know?"

Kate had never been at a loss for words, until now.

"We have a problem, Ken," she started.

"What's that?" he asked.

"What Judge Lowry knows about us. He remembers you talking about me when you worked at the courthouse."

"That was a long time ago. Does it really matter?"

"Yes, and it's the only thing right now that does," Kate replied. "I never told him about us. I kept meaning to gauge his response before he could hang you or put you in the fight with Richard and the other guy. Then everything worked out, and you were given a stunt that you have a good likelihood of completing, in my opinion, and I thought we could just keep the secret between you and me. Both you and I have a lot to lose if he finds out."

"Don't you think he will eventually anyway? This is a small town, and people talk."

"I understand that," said Kate, "but I've been dating Sheriff Johnson for three years now. Even through the City Council election, nobody put it together...except for Judge Lowry."

"But they will know when I jump," Ken replied. "I mean, surely they will recognize me."

"Nope. You'll never take your helmet off, and I'll make sure he doesn't announce your name or have you run for office after. You will just be a close ally of his and mine who works behind the scenes, moving forward. If you keep quiet, I know I will."

"So, what about the Judge?" asked Ken nervously.

"I threatened to put his head in a jar if he told anyone."

"Ouch," said Ken, starting to laugh and catching himself. "So, he'll keep quiet?"

"Probably until right before he's hanged or otherwise. Then he'll sing like a sparrow because, well, why not?"

Ken paused... "I thought the jump would have my stomach all tied up in knots. But nope—turns out it's this talk."

"What do we do?" Ken asked.

"I'm glad you asked. I'll make this quick because people are starting to stare over here. There are three sets of keys to the jailhouse and every cell. Sheriff Johnson has one, his lead deputy another, and the last set is right here," she said, pulling a ring with six keys attached out of her purse, just high enough for him to see. "So, the short of it is, if you want to save your skin and mine, we have three choices. You kill him tomorrow night; it has to be before Saturday. Or we set him free in the cover of night, and if he's smart, he'll never return. In this scenario, the Sheriff and his men will be so focused on Saturday's events they won't have time to go looking for him for at least another day."

"Wait...that's it? What's choice number three?"

"There isn't a number three," she said, with a sigh.

"Kate, I don't like this at all. None of it."

"Neither do I, but it's him or us. I can control everything else, but not this unless the Sheriff decides to let him walk, and I highly doubt that now. It's the only way, unless you have a better suggestion."

"Can I think about it?"

"Sure, but don't take too long. I'll make sure I serve dinner tonight, so I can let the Judge know I'm serious. All I need from you is an answer of one or two when I ask how many ketchup packets you want."

"Then what?" asked Ken.

"The note I pass you when I pick up the plates will have the next instructions. Eat it when you've read it."

"Eat it?"

"Yes, there can be no trace of it, and it will go down in small bites. Understand?"

"Yes, Kate. Unfortunately, I do."

She dropped the keys back into her purse, making a mental note not to forget to hide them in her special spot inside an old high-heel shoe in the back of her closet.

The third set always stayed in the home safe, but she had made two duplicate sets more than a year ago, taking an entire day and traveling up to Denver to use an anonymous locksmith. He questioned her at first, stating they looked like jail cell keys. She said, "That's not your concern," slipping him a crisp $100 bill before paying the flat rate charge per specialized key.

"Not bad for a high school dropout," she said aloud, to no one else as she walked out to her car. Kate was never book-smart but she always considered herself streetwise, and she never once felt she was selling herself short.

* * * *

Friday came quickly, with everyone anticipating tomorrow's happenings.

Convincing her fiancé to let her serve tonight's jail dinner was easy with the promise of his favorite smothered pork chops when she returned and "whatever happens after that," using the classic line she had heard once in a movie.

"Just slide it under the cell," he called out as she walked out the door, "and don't get within arm's reach of any cell, no matter what."

"Got it, babe. Just relax," she said, handing him a jar of James' finest. "I'll be back in no time."

"Don't forget the keys," the Sheriff called out. "You will need them for the front door."

"Oh, silly me," she called back. "Can you get them for me? I can never remember the combination to the safe." The lie rolled off her tongue so smoothly she almost believed it.

"You should really know it," he replied.

"That's why I have you, my strong man," she flirted as he retrieved them. "I'll be back before you miss me," she said, with a smile.

* * * *

Kate would take the truck down to the jailhouse with the meals she had prepared at home. She needed something that went with ketchup, and she opted to serve something quick and easy. After all, she was due to cook a special dinner for the most powerful man in Weston, and probably the county. Hotdogs and tater tots were on the menu at the jail.

The town general fund was paying for the meals, but the Sheriff's budget was slowly draining. Ken was the exception, reminding him of a younger self. Or maybe the younger man he wished he had been. Either way, he was resolved to clear the jailhouse in one fell swoop, dreaming of a few days off, fishing at the lake his dad took him to as a young boy—Trinidad Lake Park. He would mention this to his girlfriend at least twice a week for the last three years.

"We leave on Monday," he told Kate before she left.

"I'm not going fishing at some god-awful lake thirty miles away," she responded.

"It's 18."

"What?"

"I said it's 18, and that means it's within our 20-mile town radius. I've been thinking of doubling that to 40 miles before some other Sheriff, or Judge, beats me to it with their town. Anyway, I aim to go fishing in *my* town. Besides, I haven't met my citizens on that side. Technically the entire lake is mine, anyway. How cool is that?"

"It's cool, all right," she responded, "but only if they already know it. You had better take some backup if you want to make it back home."

"Maybe I should just take Judge Lowry with me! He loves to fish, you know," he told her.

"I know you're joking, honey, so I won't even respond to that. Speaking of him, what are your plans?"

"I don't know. Wish I did, Kate, 'cause man, I need a break."

"You could..." she started to say, before pausing and not wanting to give away anything she may be planning.

"Could what?" he asked.

"Oh, I don't know," she said. "I was just thinking out loud, but I've got nothing. Anyway, I'll be back in just a bit," she added, carrying the container of food with four trays.

* * * *

"It's me, everybody," she called out as she unlocked the front door to the jailhouse. "Now. I know you can't all see me right now, but I have your supper here. When I slide it under the cell, I am going to ask you how many ketchups you want. Your answer will be one or two. And don't even think of reaching through the bars towards me or I'll see you're shot this very night. Understand, gentlemen?"

"Yes. Yes, ma'am," came the response from everyone besides Judge Lowry.

"You okay, Judge? I don't hear your response."

"I'm here," he said.

"Good, and I hope you've been a good boy since the last time we spoke."

There was a pause before Ken broke the tension with "He has," getting a look from the others.

"Well, now. That's what I like to hear," she responded. "One or two packets of ketchup?" she asked, starting with Ken.

"Ah, I guess... Well, ah..."

"Just answer her!" shouted James' shooter. "I'm hungry over here."

"Okay, okay," said Ken, taking in a deep breath. "Two, please."

"Good choice," she replied, giving him a wink only he could see.

She moved down the hall with two cells side by side, housing Judge Lowry and Richard.

"One more to go," she said, after sliding Richard's plate under the door.

"Boo!" called out Richard, as he ran up to the cell door, slapping his large mitts on the bars in a slamming motion.

Kate was ready for some attitude or maybe a sexist remark, but not this.

She stumbled backward, like after the car wreck she had been in at age seven. The very same one that killed her mother and put Kate on a rollercoaster of physical and mental rehabilitation. As she grew older, a relationship developed with her father that no thirteen-year-old girl should ever have. Falling backward, she tried to turn and catch herself.

"Gotcha, darlin'," said James' shooter, reaching his arms through the bars, with one around her waist and another around her throat. His breath, hot and sticky, hit her neck like a firehose trying to cool off a midsummer Arizona sidewalk. One breath after another and another, as she squirmed to get free.

"You let her go now!" commanded Ken.

"Or what? the Sheriff will kill me? You intend to do just that, don't you, Richard?"

"That I do, my fine opponent-to-be," replied Richard.

"Stay calm," Ken called to her intentionally, not using her name.

"Let me go, you bastard!" she screamed. Her heavy breathing slowed as she realized he was not squeezing her throat. Not yet, at least. But the breathing reminded her of everything wrong with her daddy before he left town, for the last time, when she turned fourteen.

"What do you want?" she asked, as calmly as her trembling voice would let her.

"You're shaking, lady," he said, laughing. "So, either you're scared to death or mad as hell. Which is it?"

"Let me go, and you'll find out quick, you poorest excuse for a human being."

"We have a winner!" he announced to his audience, with the Judge now starting to pay attention.

"So, I'll ask you again," she repeated. "What do you want?"

"I just want to talk, darlin'...at least to start. I ain't been this close to a woman in quite some time, and even longer since I was around a girl as pretty as you. Whatever you're wearing, it's working," he said, inhaling deeply through his nose resting on top of her head.

Kate struggled to get free but could not.

Judge Lowry offered no support for either side but stood at his cell door, observing intently as Ken continued to scream, "Let her go!"

"Okay, you have options," she stated calmly. "You let me go in ten seconds, and maybe we pretend this didn't happen. And you, Richard—don't forget you started this!

"Or you kill me right now, and when the Sheriff finds me he makes an example of you both for everyone here in this jail."

"Let her go!" called out Richard. "Do it right now."

"Or what?"

"Or come Saturday, I take my time with you, real slow like, with no mercy."

The man hesitated for only a few seconds before loosening his grip, allowing Kate to slip away. Without a word, she ran up to the office, past the keys she would need to get to Ken, and grabbed her pistol.

The silence in the back was thunderous as they all strained to hear what was next. She racked the slide of her compact Ruger LC9 pistol. The snap echoed throughout the building.

"Hey now, wait just a minute," the man who was in control only moments ago called out. "We had a deal!" he yelled.

Kate couldn't hear him; she couldn't hear anything. Never in her life had she felt such utter terror and blinding rage, at least not at the same time.

Without a word, she walked back, her hands shaking as she held her pistol out. Pointing it at the man she had come to hate deeply in a matter of only a few minutes, she steadied one hand with the other and pointed toward his chest.

“Ma’am, Ma’am!” called out Ken, again not wanting to say her name in front of the other men. She was unfazed, not hearing his pleas.

“Kate! Kate is her name,” called out Judge Lowry from around the corner, “but you know that already, don’t you, Ken?”

“Kate,” called Ken, not responding to the Judge.

“What?” she replied, without taking her eyes off the target.

“You don’t want to do this,” he continued. “It’s dangerous.”

“I think I’m good, and I’m ready to send this piece of crap back down where he came from.”

“What I mean is, it’s dangerous to fire a gun in here. If you hit one of the bars or miss him, there’s no telling where that bullet could end up.”

James’ shooter took six steps back, cowering in the corner, with his back turned.

“Come on up to the front, tough guy. I don’t want to shoot you from behind. Where’s the sport in that?”

“It’s okay, Kate,” said Ken calmly. “It’s over. This is done.”

She slowly lowered the pistol towards the ground and started back towards the office.

“Eat up, boys,” she called back behind her. “I’m picking up trays in fifteen minutes.”

Kate breathed deeply, wiping the tears from her eyes. She would never let them see her cry. “Focus,” she told herself, pulling a sheet of blank typing paper out of the top desk drawer.

“Option #2,” she wrote across the top. Then underneath, she wrote this note:

Tonight, after midnight, when all are asleep, you will take these keys and open your cell door, Judge Lowry’s, and then the front door.

The Judge will need to keep the keys, locking you back in your cell before leaving. We don’t need the keys back, so tell him to keep them.

If he refuses to leave, tell him he will be the third man in the gladiator contest this Saturday.

He is to leave town this night, never to return. He must stay off the main roads out of town. If he's picked up tomorrow, I won't be able to help him.

Last, eat this note, every bit of it.

Love, Kate

She hadn't yet figured out how to get the note and keys to Ken without being seen by the others.

Think! Think! she told herself. *This is too important to screw up.*

"Trays down in five," she called out.

Kate still hadn't figured out how to pull off the next step and briefly considered pulling Ken out of his cell quickly for the exchange.

Glancing up at the old poster she had seen hundreds of times before, hanging above the front door, she had an idea. Not a great one, or even a good one, but one that could possibly work.

The poster showed a man from behind, cuffed and turned away from the photographer. The slogan didn't matter, and she had her idea.

"Trays on the floor," she called down the hall. "Push them outside of your cells and turn around facing the back wall of your cells. Anyone turns around or looks at me, and I'll risk letting a bullet bounce around this jailhouse. Understand, boys?"

She only got a couple of responses, but it didn't matter. They were all faced away, with trays shoved into the hall. She made a clanking of the trays intentionally to cover the sound of the paper with keys wrapped inside sliding across the floor of Ken's cell. He was quick to recover the package and stuff it under his mattress.

"All right, gentlemen. It's been interesting, for sure," she said, with her confidence back. "And I'm just as excited as you are for Saturday's entertainment. Sleep tight," she called out as she locked the front door behind her.

Ken made a point of crouching in the corner to read the note before the light outside faded to dark. Reading the note over three times in a row, one thing stuck—"Love, Kate."

* * * *

"How did it go, honey?" asked her fiancé. "Did the guests behave themselves?"

"They are fed and still alive. Now relax, and I'll get started on your favorite dinner," she said with a smile.

"What did I do to deserve all of this?" he asked.

"Everything," she replied. "Everything you do for us and this town, day-in and day-out."

"Well, I do try, and thanks for saying that."

* * * * * * *

Chapter Four ~ Weston, Colorado

Ken was worried that he would fall asleep and miss his opportunity to complete "the mission," as he called it.

A bright and nearly full moon filled the windows of each cell with enough light to navigate basic objects.

He sat with his back to the bars and front door of his cell, listening intently. It had been totally dark for about three hours, near as he could tell, and he could separate the loud snoring from Richard and the heavy breathing, with occasional fearful outbursts from his soon-to-be rival. *It's now or never*, he thought, wishing he only had to worry about his jump tomorrow. He vowed to get this over with and try to get some sleep for the big day.

There were three keys on the ring. He guessed one was the front door; one was universal for the cells...and the third? *Maybe the office*, he thought, although it didn't really matter, he decided. Reaching out through the front bars, he used the skeleton-type key he had seen every time his door had been opened. His hand shook and cramped as he fumbled to insert the key from the outside.

"Let me go!" screamed James' shooter, startling Ken enough to drop the keys.

A clang echoed through the halls as they fell on the hard cement floor... Ken froze, holding his breath and straining his ears like a big buck on the first day of hunting season. Richard was still snoring, so that was good, and only minutes later he heard the other one breathing hard once again.

"The second time is a charm," he mumbled, reaching through the bars for the keys. Streaks of light through the window distorted his perception.

"No, no, no!" he whispered, realizing he was six inches short of reaching the keys. Trying again, pressing his body against the bars and exhaling deeply, he gained three more inches in reach, but it wasn't enough.

This isn't good, he thought. *Tomorrow morning they are going to know it's me!* He scanned the room, looking for the broomstick or coat hanger he knew wasn't there. Sitting on his cot, he wondered if he could take it apart, cut a wire maybe and make some fashion of a hook. With his head in his hands, he nearly laughed out loud.

Laces, he heard, as if someone were standing next to him. With this having been his first-ever stint in the big house, he thought he might not have them in a larger jail. But this was Weston, and things were different here.

Tying both laces together to a single shoe, the retrieval process was less than a minute. He quickly unlocked his cell before something else, with his luck, could derail the mission.

Operation Get the Judge Out of Town resumes, he thought.

Judge Lowry's cell was between the other two, and he hadn't heard a peep out of him since last night. Lacing his own shoes back up, he hoped the good Judge hadn't done something worse with his own laces.

Opening his cell door, the creak went unnoticed and he stared down at the Judge. *What now?* he thought, feeling dumb that he hadn't already thought this through. I mean, he had enough time, hours to be exact, to plan this out. He could shake him awake or cover his mouth, but they would need to talk in the end.

At the last minute, he covered the Judge's mouth with one hand while shaking him with the other. Two shakes and Judge Lowry jumped up, red eyes glaring in the moonlight.

"Easy Judge. I'm just here to talk." Judge Lowry pushed his intruder back, almost screaming out loud. "What happens next is your future, good or bad," Ken whispered.

"What is this about, old friend, or should I say 'employee'?"

"This intervention is about your freedom if you choose it, and it's the only reason you're getting a chance not to hang from a rope. So, listen closely. You are going to take these keys, lock me back in my cell, and leave the front door unlocked. You have until sunup to gather what you can from the courthouse and disappear, never to return. Stay off the main roads...or, even better, off all roads on your way out of town. If the Sheriff sees you, you're done. You know that, right?"

There was a pause for too long...

"Do you hear me?" Ken asked, waiting for a response.

"All right, don't threaten me," the Judge whispered. "I'll leave for now."

"Do I get a thank-you?" asked Ken, with a hint of his former snarky self.

"I'll give you 'You're welcome,' but that's it."

"Okay, whatever... Let's get you going," Ken conceded.

* * * *

Judge Lowry played the game, locking Ken back in his cell and walking out the front door a free man. The smell of rain coming was in the air—his favorite smell in the whole world, launching him towards his new life.

* * * *

Keys to the courthouse's back door lay under the same fake rock where it had been for the last 23 years. His bug-out bag hid inside the secret room he called home since the day.

"I know," he yelled at the clock on the far wall. "It's 1 a.m. I get that," he continued, "but I'm not going to let them win," pointing to the wall of pictures, including Sheriff Johnson, James VanFleet, and other town higher-ups. Minutes later, they were all ripped off the wall. "I'm going fishing, you bastards," he yelled loud enough for nobody to hear in the empty courthouse.

The large pack was heavier than he remembered, and he was now regretting having not picked up another running vehicle. His old truck had surely been impounded by now, and he didn't have time to go gallivanting all over town looking for it. "Tires are shredded anyways," he said, laughing. "I gave those boys a hell of a chase, though. They will be talking about that, I'll bet, for years to come," he said, exiting the courthouse for the last time. "South or east," he said aloud. "South or east, south or east? Would James hide me out if I head south? Maybe, maybe not. Head east to the cabin?"

The cabin was a secret from almost everyone, including Sheriff Johnson. He had owned it for sixteen years this coming fall. He had only ever told one person about it, and he hoped she had long since forgotten the conversation. The neatly kept cabin was a place he could call his own, close enough to drive to in thirty minutes, but far enough away to warrant calling it a true getaway. In all this time, not a single other soul had stepped inside since his agent did the final walkthrough with him before the purchase. He would go up for long weekends, careful not to commit to working Friday afternoons at the courthouse. His secretary saw to that. It was off the lake, maybe a half-mile, but so were all the others in the area. He remembered telling his realtor he wanted something on the water.

"Not at a state park, Your Honor," was the reply. "Nobody gets that right, not even the Governor."

Judge Lowry kept the small cabin stocked with food, both in cabinets and refrigerated, and always parked his truck, which didn't start now, under the attached carport, not wanting to grab attention from his neighbors. He was a loner up there at least ten weekends a year and liked it that way. The last time he was up was right after it happened. It was around election time and Sheriff Johnson had loaned him one of the patrol vehicles that still started. Now he would have a long walk, as he had to stay off the main roads. *At least I cleaned out the refrigerator last time,* he thought.

* * * *

Exiting the courthouse he had called his own for more than 20 years, he headed east, ducking behind buildings and cutting up back alleys.

"I never did get a chance to use this," he said aloud, as he patted the revolver in his right front jacket pocket. He picked up the pace, with his slight build straining under the weight of the nearly 70-pound backpack.

It's two hours before sunrise, he thought, *and I need to be far up the road by then.* The plan was simply to get out of town within a few hours and hide out until the early afternoon.

The Sheriff would be too busy with trade days and the afternoon's exhibition to do a full-on search. He would lay low at a secret fishing spot seven to eight miles out of town, and continue the remaining ten miles in the mid-afternoon, hoping to get to the cabin by dark.

* * * *

"What the hell?" said Sheriff Johnson as he put the key into the front door of the jail and tried to unlock it.

"What's wrong," asked Kate, who had practically forced him to let her help serve breakfast to the inmates this morning.

"The lock...it was already open!"

"I'm sure it's just a deputy," she said, trying not to smile.

It's fine, she thought, but in a panic, she wondered who knew. Had the others seen or heard something? She was about to find out and soon.

Reaching her hand into her purse, she felt the smooth barrel of her semiautomatic pistol that her fiancé had given her just over a year ago and taught her to shoot with confidence. She wasn't planning to use it, but she was not going down like the rest of the people in here if it went bad. After all, she had watched a woman hanged only a few short weeks ago.

"Piece of gum?" she asked him. He was staring at her fiddling with her purse.

"Huh? Ah no, but thanks for last night," he said, with a wink.

"It's just what I do, taking care of my man," she said, smiling flirtatiously.

Let's get this over with, she thought, following him inside.

"Sheriff, is that you?" called Ken from the back.

"Yeah, I'm here. Just getting breakfast ready. Have you seen my deputy this morning?"

"No, sir. Can you please check on Judge Lowry?" Ken asked. "I can't see him, and I haven't heard a word out of him since last night. None of us have. I hope he didn't do something stupid to hurt himself...or worse."

"Be right there," the Sheriff said, picking up two trays, not wanting to waste a trip on this most important day.

"Judge, you all right?" he asked, as he put two trays under the other men's cell doors. "You all right?" he called again, while Kate slid one under Ken's cell door, getting a subtle thumbs-up.

"What's going on here?" called the Sheriff loudly, resting his arm on the cell's front door, fumbling for his keys. The door shook enough to see it was unlocked, and he entered in a rage, tossing the keys across the narrow room. "What the hell is going on here?!" he called out again.

Kate came running up behind, with her shocked face already formed perfectly on her high cheeks.

"Where is he?!" she gasped.

"That's what I want to know. He was here last night for supper, right?" The question was directed at Kate and the other prisoners. Everyone nodded their heads yes.

"Where's my lead deputy?" the Sheriff called out.

"I'm here," the deputy called back from the front door, unaware of the situation. "Thought I would come in early to help get these guys ready for the show today," he added, walking towards the back... "Is everything okay?" he asked when he received no reply.

"What do you think?" asked the Sheriff, pointing into the empty cell.

"Oh, no!" said the deputy.

"Unbelievable!" replied the Sheriff. "Let me see your keys," he added, pointing to the man he had trusted for more than five years.

"What for?... Wait a minute! You don't think I let him out?"

"He's a Judge, not a ghost, so I'm sure he didn't just float out. Besides, both his cell and the front door were unlocked, replied the Sheriff.

Ken was now officially more nervous about this than his jump, only hours away. He was happy Kate had thought to have his cell door relocked, and the paper he had consumed last night was digesting nicely.

"There are three copies of these keys. Only three. Yours, mine, and the set at home in my safe. When was the last time you heard him speak, Ken?" he said, realizing the last person in here was his girlfriend with the spare set.

"A few hours after she left," Ken said, pointing to her but not saying her name. "He seemed fine last night. It was just this morning I didn't hear him."

"You locked the front door?" he asked her.

"Of course," she replied, intentionally acting annoyed.

"I done heard it," said James' shooter. "Plus, she didn't come near any of the cell doors, I can testify to that."

"Your testimony I don't need!" yelled the Sheriff.

James' shooter realized she hadn't said anything about what he did last night, and he still had a better chance of fighting Richard than just being killed. Besides, he had a plan.

"Let's go up front," said the Sheriff, still upset. "You—in my office," he added, pointing to his deputy. "Kate, please wait outside."

"Now, show me your keys," Sheriff Johnson demanded from his right-hand man. "Did you let him out last night? Form some sort of deal with him?"

"No, sir, I didn't."

"So that just leaves Kate?" the Sheriff questioned.

"Well, sure, Yeah, I guess."

"What would you do?" asked the Sheriff.

"I don't know, sir. Maybe talk to her or me, I don't know."

"How many sets?" asked the Sheriff.

"How many what, sir?"

"How many sets of your keys did you have made?"

"Why, I'm not sure what you..."

"How many?" he screamed.

"Three, sir. Three more sets."

"Why?"

"It's just...well, I'm working a lot, way more than the other guys. I was always the one to open the jailhouse early in the morning and lock up at night. My wife was upset, and I hardly ever got to eat with my kids. So, I had a couple of other sets made on my day off a couple of years back and gave them to a few of my guys to help out, and even out the load a bit."

"You made sets of my keys to my jailhouse without my permission?"

"Yes...well, yes, sir. But I'm really..."

"Lay your pistol on the table and your badge next to your keys."

"Wait a minute. Just wait a minute!" said the deputy.

"Do it!"

Reluctantly he did as he was instructed, laying both his firearm and badge on the desk before turning to walk out the front door. He caught Kate's eye, and his expression said it all. The trusted man was defeated, caught in a lie, and still had no idea what happened.

"You're going the wrong way, deputy," said the Sheriff from behind him, taking the safety off his weapon. "Back," he motioned with his pistol. "We have an open cell that needs an occupant."

"Please," the deputy begged. "Please give me a chance to make this right. Kate, don't let him do this," he called out.

The deputy was led back to the cell and there was a clank as the door was locked.

* * * * * * *

Chapter Five ~ Weston, Colorado

"I need some air," said the Sheriff, brushing past Kate and out the door.

Getting on his radio, he called the rest of his men. "We've had a breach of the jailhouse. Judge Lowry has escaped. Check the courthouse and main roads around town, and don't forget what day it is. Trading starts in one hour."

Ken was feeling bad for the lead deputy, as the deputy had always been fair with him. He hoped he would be released eventually.

"How is it that I can't trust anyone?" asked Sheriff Johnson.

"You can trust me," Kate said, hugging him.

"That's not what I mean," he replied.

"I needed to trust the Judge before, and James and my deputies now. Everyone is against me in my own town."

"No, babe. It's not like that at all. To be honest, Judge Lowry didn't betray you until the very end, and James didn't help him with his plan. And your deputy."

"What about him?" he asked gruffly.

"He may be guilty of making some extra keys for a little time off, but I think that's it. Today is a huge day for the town; you need him out around town, helping to keep everyone safe. The Judge is gone. So what? Isn't that what you wanted? I mean, you didn't have any plans for him anyway, and after today the jailhouse will be cleared out. He won't show his face around here again. Why, I'll bet he's headed back to Pennsylvania as fast as he can get there. Besides, I thought you wanted to go fishing, just you and me... The old couple two doors down...the ones with the airstream trailer..."

"Yeah, what about them?" he asked.

"Well, I talked to them about a week back, and they offered to let us use it for a few days. We could take off Sunday after church and be back on Wednesday by lunch. What do you say?"

"I could use a vacation, but who do I trust while we're gone?"

"You trust your lead deputy, James, and as long as that Ken guy you think so highly of makes it over the courthouse, you can count on him as well."

"Wait here," he said, walking back inside. "Come on out," he called to his deputy as he opened the cell door. Walking to the office, he said, "Look at me in the eye, and tell me you had nothing to do with the Judge's mess."

"Sir, I had nothing to do with it and zero knowledge about any of it," he said, looking the Sheriff square in the eye.

"Okay, I believe you. I don't have any more time to waste on this. If you see him in town, shoot him on sight. Tell the other men the same."

* * * *

Sheriff Johnson got the trading under way without fanfare, just like every other Saturday before. He spoke briefly with James VanFleet and Jason Davis about the Judge, ending with the statement that it might just be the best thing, after all.

"I'm betting he tucked tail back to the East Coast; and besides, I wasn't really sure what to do with him anyway," remarked the Sheriff. "I'm glad not to have him oversee any future elections in this town. He can't count for crap. And James, today is your day. I'm sure you will enjoy it, and after church tomorrow me and my girl are taking a few days off to give the fish over in Lake Trinidad something to worry about. Happy trading, and I'll see you in front of the courthouse at 4:15... Don't forget the family dinner right after the strongman event!"

Ken was given as much time as he wanted to test the bike, and he inspected both ramps. He was never asked about the Judge by anyone and spent most of the morning riding start-and-stop sprints. He glanced every now and then at the overcast sky.

"Stay dry," he said. "At least until 4:30. Then you can dump all you want," he repeated a few times each hour.

Sheriff Johnson could hardly contain his excitement for the upcoming events. "Screw the Judge," he told his girlfriend. "We have a show to put on, and it's going to rival any town in the whole country. Who else would do all of this for their citizens? No one, that's who! The people will talk about this for generations to come. And don't even get me started about James. That old-timer Cam isn't even half done with his chair, and I'll be delivering mine today."

"You're a proud man," she said, taking his hand. "Don't stop."

* * * *

Trading was getting bigger every week, as news traveled to the new borders of the once-tiny town. The booth count was up to 210, as everyone tried selling odds and ends from their houses and garages. Setup was free and required only a table and five percent of goods sold to be returned to the town, on the honor system.

"Are you ready, James?" asked Janice.

"Ready to go back to work? Yes, I am," he replied.

"Not ready for an entire city program dedicated to you?"

"If it was you, honey, throwing the party, then of course I would be ready and excited, but it happens to be one of the two most powerful men in town, and I don't trust either of them. But we will show up, accept the new chair, and I'll be back to work on Monday."

"Are you sure you're up to it?" asked Janice.

"If I can sit here, I can sit in town. Besides, we're behind on the greenhouses, and winter has a way of sneaking up on the ill-prepared."

* * * *

James was happy to be getting around again. Jason helped him roll over a few dirt ruts to get to the family trading booth. "It seems everyone in town wanted to come by and say hi today," pointed out Lauren.

"Yeah, Daddy. You're real popular around these here parts," said Billy, testing out the new cowboy shtick he had practiced over the last week.

"It is nice to be liked, son, I suppose," he replied.

"What do you think the strongman competition is all about?" asked Jason.

"I'm not sure. And better we don't ask when the Sheriff comes over here to make an appearance. I'll bet it's not what any of us are expecting. I am looking forward to the motorcycle jump, though, if I'm honest," replied James.

"How do you know he'll stop by here?" Jason asked, feeling uneasy.

"Because he's a politician first...and Jason, you need to work on that."

"What?"

"That expression like you have to take a crap every time you see or even hear anything mentioned about Sheriff Johnson."

"Oh, that. Yeah, I'm trying."

"I know you are," replied James.

Sheriff Johnson did stop by, as advertised, dragging Ken around to each booth and bragging about the upcoming jump.

So much for the masked jumper, thought Ken. Nearly everyone knew by noon that he was the one who would be jumping this afternoon.

"I think you're going to like what we've got planned, James," said the Sheriff, pulling him aside.

"Oh, and before I forget. I let Judge Lowry go," said Sheriff Johnson.

"Really? How did you decide that?" asked James.

"We just came to an understanding is all. He won't be back, and if he stays away he'll get to die of old age, if he's lucky. He did give my deputies one hell of a car chase, though, in that old truck of his."

* * * *

Ken had the afternoon to tool around on the bike but would need to end on a quarter tank of gas for the jump.

The Sheriff had two low-ranked deputies doing the last-minute preparations on the rodeo arena. The others were busy ensuring fair trade, but all would be on the clock this afternoon to ensure the guests' safety as well as the containment of Richard and his opponent.

The air horn blew, as was the new normal to start and end the trade days, and traders packed up quickly, setting the required town donation on the ground in front of each booth, to be collected by truck and trailer.

"Everyone, please find your way to the front of the courthouse," came the announcement over the loudspeaker. "Remember, the exhibitions will continue, rain or shine," was heard as the first drops of rain splattered on the top of Ken's helmet.

"Are you kidding me right now?" he asked, looking up to the sky. "All day nothing, and thirty minutes before my jump, you drop rain down on me." *Stay the course; it's not all about you*, he heard in his head—or maybe he said it out loud.

* * * *

People gathered around the front ramp on both sides, pointing to the top.

"Please, everyone. You will get a better view from the building's side," the Sheriff called out, "or you might just want to go around back to see if he sticks the landing."

He nodded to Ken, signaling it was warm-up time.

"Come one, come all!" Sheriff Johnson called out, as if he were about to ride a lion around the town square. "We have two spectacular events coming right up, with a special surprise in the middle."

The Sheriff made his way to where James was sitting and asked him to come up to the front.

"Ladies and gentlemen," he yelled through the bullhorn. "Today honors our Mayor for his heroic protection of some of our citizens a couple of weeks back, and our first death-defying stunt was one of my favorites growing up. In the spirit of the late, great Evel Knievel, I give you Ken, the Highflyer!"

The crowd cheered as Ken took a couple runs up to the ramp in classic jumper-style, waiving to the crowd.

"Eighty-two miles per hour," he said to himself in a low voice... "Eighty-two...eighty-two."

"One more practice run, and then let's get to it," called out the Sheriff as he passed by.

"Oh, that's interesting," Ken said only inside of his helmet, looking over at the Sheriff flanked on both sides—on one side was Kate and the other Ken's current girlfriend. *I need to get this done,* he thought, *before they all get too chummy and start talking about one couple getting invited over to dinner.*

Vroom! He revved the engine, waving to the crowd. *Vroom!* He took off like it was the real deal, accelerating from first to second gear, pulling a quick wheelie for the enthused crowd, then shifting into third and fourth before slowing quickly, using both the front-hand and back-foot brakes... Seventy-three was the last speed he saw on the second-hand speedometer. *That's not bad,* he thought. He was expecting to slip a bit in the light, steady drizzle.

Okay, Lord. This is it! Ken silently prayed. *I know we don't talk much, but you saved me the first time when I had a gun sighted on my chest, and ironically, I let the very same man go free that stopped it from happening. I guess what I'm saying, Lord, is that I'm a changed man, a better man than before you helped me out last time, and hopefully that's enough to keep me alive. I do want to meet you eventually, but not today. Amen.*

* * * *

“We’re ready!” called the Sheriff over the loudspeaker, startling Ken.

“Oh...uh...yeah,” he said, taking two deep breaths and checking his helmet chin strap. *I can do this*, he told himself, waving a final time to the hyped crowd of nearly 500. He took off smoothly, switching between gears, letting his anxiety out a breath at a time. Fifty-six, sixty-three, seventy-two...as he shifted from a strained fourth into fifth gear. Seventy-eight...as he closed in on the ramp’s center mass.

Forty feet...thirty. Twenty-five...fifteen...ten, as he looked down at the speedometer for the last time. Eighty-six miles per hour, it read.

Too fast! he thought, as he hit the center of the ramp, rising higher and higher.

“Steady,” he yelled out when his front tire left the structure’s safety, slipping on the top that was slick with rain.

Boom! Streaks of color lit up the afternoon sky and crackled ziggy-zaggy around him. They hadn’t told him about the fireworks, but he should have expected it, as it was a part of nearly all big jumps in the past.

Then there was the moment... All stunt riders must feel it—the moment of full commitment, no matter what. Like a newborn leaving the womb’s safety, having been surrounded by fluid for nine months, and in the blink of an eye going back to that environment would surely end in drowning.

He thought about everything and nothing, gliding through the air...and ultimate freedom he would never feel again.

Boom! This time it came from the other side, taking his attention for a split second. The crowd was cheering, “He’s going to make it!”

But he wasn’t. His back tire couldn’t clear the back of the building’s roof.

Wham! The knobby tire skimmed the top like a flat rock skipping across a glassy pond.

The hit wasn’t enough to stop the bike in its tracks, but dozens of conversations would be had over the next days and weeks about whether or not he could have pulled it off with a less-profile street-bike tire. The nays and yeas would be almost even, with a slight advantage going to the "He would have cleared it" camp.

Not that it mattered much now, with the rider's nose down farther than it should be. Ken stayed calm, as this wasn't the first time he would land on his front tire. He only wished the drop weren't so far.

Arching his back, he pulled the bike up just enough to avoid flying over the front handlebars.

Still, it wasn't enough, and the smooth landing he had envisioned over the last week over and over in his mind was no more. The front tire hit the dirt landing ramp just before the back, with the impact more of a bounce than a landing. The angle was all wrong when it hit again, hurling Ken and the nearly three-hundred-pound hunk of shiny metal far to the right.

He had seen the hay stacked on both sides of the landing ramp during practice, but imagined only hitting the ones at the end, and hopefully at a slow speed. Ken was thinking to check his speed when he hit. Hay bales stacked six-high, like a dam holding back a raging river, collapsed under the force of the impact.

The crowd, who had been cheering and hollering only seconds ago, went quiet.

Even Sheriff Johnson was at a loss for words. He ran around the building, breaking through the crowd, followed closely by two women with concern on their faces.

Kate was athletic. She always had been and was somewhat of a track star, if it could be called that, in such a small town. Maybe she was just the best out of two or three, but she took the lead this day, beating both her fiancé and new rival before realizing it didn't look good. She slowed, pretending to catch her breath and not appear as concerned as she was.

The Sheriff got there first out of the three, but the doctors had already surrounded him.

"Is he alive, Doc Walters?" the Sheriff asked.

"Well yes, technically he is. Took a good hit to his head, though. You can see right here," holding up Ken's helmet.

“Aren’t you supposed to take that off later, in case he has a neck injury?” asked Kate, without thinking.

“Before, yes... We would leave it on if he was breathing normally and transport him immediately to the hospital. As you are aware, I’m sure,” he said, trying hard to be respectful in front of the Sheriff, “it’s just that we don’t have access to one is all. And we’re all here, every doc and nurse in town, so things have to be done a little differently. Does that make sense?”

“Yes, Doctor, I see your point, I guess,” replied Kate.

“He’s unconscious but breathing normally, and that’s better than the alternative. We will let you know, Sheriff, when we hear something. Should I send a couple of medical people from here for the next event?”

“No need, Doc. This next one won’t be requiring medical attention...”

“It looks like Ken’s going to be okay!” called the Sheriff over the megaphone. “What a jump! If it hadn’t rained, I think he would have stuck the landing!”

****

Chapter Six ~ Weston, Colorado

Sheriff Johnson nodded to his deputies to get Richard and James' shooter ready for the exhibition. The plan was discussed two days earlier. Each would be given one weapon, and only one man would be left standing. The Sheriff, having feelings for both—equally bad—would personally make sure spoils would not go to the victor.

"Gladiator-style, gentlemen, like Marcus Aurelius," the Sheriff told them in the holding pen an hour before. "This should make it fair," he added, showing them the lances. "Lastly, try to run and you will be shot on sight. Now, let's put on a good show for my guests. Your very life depends upon it."

Richard's confidence waivered with the introduction of the weapons. "I thought this would be a fair fight," he argued—"man to man."

"It is now," replied the deputy. "It's like that kid in the Bible up against the giant, whatever his name was. At least it was fair."

"So, the winner walks?" asked Richard

"That's what I heard."

"So, you can't guarantee it?"

"Nope," replied the deputy. "But I know one thing for sure—the loser is not going home. And lastly, don't run or you will forfeit the contest and be shot on sight, as the Sheriff said."

* * * *

Next to the Bike Jump, Sheriff Johnson was coming up on his favorite part of the event.

"Go get it," he whispered to Kate.

She disappeared around the side of the courthouse and took the large green tarp off the wheelchair. She brought it around slowly, so as not to give away the surprise too soon. Parking in front of James and family, the Sheriff did the honors.

"Today we honor our new Mayor, James VanFleet, for his dedication, both former and future, to this town. On behalf of Weston, we present you with this motorized marvel, handcrafted by an expert in the field. Take her for a spin!"

"Thank you, Sheriff, and everyone! I am very thankful for this wonderful gift," James replied, saying he thought he should try it out later.

"Later!" the Sheriff called out over the megaphone. "The Mayor wants to try it out later. Maybe we can convince him to try it now. *Try it now!*" he said, getting into a chanting rhythm. "*Try it now!*"

One after another, the townsfolk joined in. "Try it now!" they hollered.

."Okay! All right! I'll give it a try. Want to hop on?" James asked little Billy.

"Sure, Daddy! It looks like fun!"

"Forward, back, left, right, fast, and brakes," said the Sheriff, pointing to the levers.

"It seems simple enough," replied James.

James started slowly as the path opened before him. Within a minute, he was speeding around, kicking up dirt and smiling as much as Billy.

"Oh, we're going to have some fun with this back at the ranch!" he told his son.

"They're jazzed now!" said the Sheriff to Kate, watching the townsfolk cheering and hooting. Time for the big show!" he added.

He was able to get James on the megaphone, with everyone chanting "Speech!" as one might see at an office retirement party, where most people were only there for the free food.

"I would like to thank Sheriff Johnson and all of you for this kind gesture and support of my recovery. Enjoy your weekend, and I'll be back to work on Monday!"

Most cheered at the news. Only a few were concerned that he was coming back too soon.

* * * *

"They are ready for everyone over at the arena," the Sheriff called into the megaphone. "This will be the last event of the day. Thank you all for coming and enjoy the show. Please, no hands or other parts on the railing or inside the arena. Enjoy free popcorn and sodas on your way inside. And lastly, let's cheer on our boys!"

"This half," waving his arm across a section of crowd, "cheer for the Red Team, and everyone over here cheer for the Blue Team. Let's go!"

* * * *

They piled into the arena, shoving popcorn into their faces and wiping butter-soaked hands on dirty blue jeans and cargo shorts. Both men were given the simple rules only minutes before going to opposite corners of the arena, and each with designated armed guards.

"The Sheriff's rules are as follows," one of the deputies read. "One, try to escape and we are ordered to shoot you dead. Two, this is a fight to the death. There is only one winner, and your opponent must not be left breathing. Three, you will each receive an identical dagger, called a lance. If it is thrown, dropped or confiscated by your opponent, you will not have a resource to get it back—basically, no time-outs. Four...well, it's crossed out, so I guess that's it. Any questions?"

"The winner gets to walk out a free man, right?" asked Ralph.

"That's the Sheriff's call—above my pay grade, I guess you might say."

Each participant was led to the arena's center with handcuffs, leg shackles, and a two-deputy team. One lawman to undo the restraints and the other to cover him, twelve-gauge style. The crowded bleachers seemed to strain under the weight. Even the rodeo had never once drawn this big a crowd. Sheriff Johnson stepped out into the middle of the arena, working up the crowd.

"In the days of the Roman Empire, once the most powerful civilization on this Earth's face, they were known far and wide for their warriors—the men who fought in battle and the condemned needing punishment for their crimes. They were strong, wild and cunning, and they were known as Gladiators.

"Today we have brought Rome to Southern Colorado. I introduce you first to the Blue Team," he called out like a boxing announcer, raising his arms to get the cheering started. "This man hails from out of town, stands five feet, nine inches and weighs in at 158 pounds." Cheers from about half of the citizens erupted, with most forgetting about the children sitting next to them.

"Now the Red Team!" the Sheriff announced, pausing for the fans and being drowned out by the chant 'Blue Team! Blue Team!'"—on their feet and stomping one foot after the other on the hollow-sounding metal bleachers.

"Now for the Red Team!" he said again, smiling at the raucous crowd. "This man hails from right here in Weston. He stands in at a giant's height of six foot, seven inches and weighs in at a staggering three hundred forty-three pounds." Red Team chants now rivaled that of the Blue, with more than a few switching to Richard's side only on account of his size.

"This is what I've been missing!" said the Sheriff, with his bullhorn turned off. "We didn't have this kind of excitement at the hangings," he told Kate.

"They're scared," said James to Janice, both watching the commotion.

"The men?" she asked.

"No, the citizens. The rabid fans are scared of tomorrow and the day after that. There are no more distractions like we used to have. No movies, social media, or even a drive in the country on a Sunday afternoon for most. This is how things like this, as bad as I imagine it will be, get confused for entertainment."

"Anything for a diversion," added Jason.

"That's right," replied James. "And tomorrow they will forget all about what happened here tonight. Can you gals please take the little ones to the restaurant and we'll meet you in just a few, I'm guessing. They don't need to see this."

"Sure, but we're ordering the jalapeño poppers for an appetizer, and they aren't good cold," Janice replied.

"Point taken; I don't think we'll be too long."

"Let's get up front, be seen, and leave as soon as it's over," said James. "And thank you, Jason, for the chair."

"This one wasn't mine, and I don't even know when or if it will be completed," replied Jason.

"They said it was from the town," said James, "but it was your idea from the start. That's all that matters. So once again, thank you."

"You're welcome, James."

* * * *

Sheriff Johnson gave the nod to his deputies as he backed away from the men he had already sentenced.

"Your weapons will be placed twenty feet behind you," he said to the two men. "Whether you choose to use them or not is up to each of you. Once unshackled, you will remain still until the air horn signals the start of the battle. Good luck, gentlemen, and may the best man win."

With that, the Sheriff turned and walked back to the excited and agitated crowd.

* * * * * * *

Chapter Seven ~ Weston, Colorado

The leg shackles dropped to the ground, and the cuffs were removed.

"Easy guys. Easy," said the head deputy, as if he were talking to a penned bull before opening the chute. "Nobody jumps the gun."

"Let's make this a fair fight—no weapons," offered Richard as his hands were uncuffed and he walked around in a semicircle. "I'll even give you the first punch, he offered."

His opponent circled slowly but didn't speak.

"You know, I told you I would make this quick, but seeing all of my fans on the bleachers over there, I feel like I need to give them a show!" said the big man.

With this last statement, he raised his arm, fist punching the air to the Red Team's chants. The crowd, now stomping on every level of the twenty-three rows of seats, didn't seem to notice how they shook.

Richard's opponent made the first move, catching the big man off guard. It wasn't particularly hard, not knockout power he was sure, but it was fast and it stung, drawing a small amount of blood from his nose.

"Good shot!" yelled Richard as his rivals yelled "Blue Team!"—thirsty for more blood.

The Sheriff smiled, thinking that this could not have gone better.

"My turn," said Richard, still the only one talking.

He swung a heavy right arm, arcing around in a semicircle and catching his opponent in the left rib cage with a thud. "That had to hurt!" he called out, forgetting where he was.

He moved forward, as his man had fallen five feet back, landing in a fetal position. "No bell here," he laughed. "No rounds, no referees, and absolutely no decisions. Winner takes all!" he called out, raising his fist to the raucous crowd. "Come on in; I'll give you another free..."

This one came fast again, but harder as the foot-shorter man sprung up from the ground, getting in close for the uppercut landing just under Richard's chin. He stumbled back two steps when the next two shots hit him in the gut and liver, buckling him over. A right knee to his chin finished the onslaught as he dropped facedown onto the ground.

The smaller opponent took several precious seconds to pander to his base, raising both arms and turning in a circle. The stunt gained him most of his fair-weather fans back, and then some.

"It's not over," said Sheriff Johnson to James. "That slob Richard still has some fight in him. I'm sure of it."

The man danced around Richard, as if the fight were over minutes ago...

A swung leg from the big man caught his opponent on the left knee with a pop.

"Oooh," came from the crowd of nearly 500 as he fell to the ground, screaming in pain.

"Get up," his fans cried. "Get up! Get up!"

Richard gave him a chance to rise again, and he did on one leg. Richard walked in a circle around him as a once-young Mohammad Ali would do to his opponents while talking to them about how great he was. "It's not bragging if it's true," said somebody somewhere, and the champ was arguably that. Richard could have stayed all night. *Who hates a large audience calling for blood, after all?* he thought. If it wasn't for the popcorn's smell wafting down from the stands, tempting his near-empty stomach, he might have dragged this out.

He thought about his favorite MMA fighter, "Country Roy Richard" he called him, since he couldn't remember his last name. The fighter was big like him, a heavyweight, and usually underestimated by both fighters and fans for his lack of a chiseled exterior. He did, however, hit like a mule, could stay in a full five rounds, and had a signature move. Once his opponent was on the ground, he would lay all 360 pounds on him and just count the punches to the face and head until the referee had no choice but to stop the fight. *He usually got to fifteen or twenty*, thought Richard, *before they would call it.*

"Down you go, boy," Richard called, sweeping his opponent's good leg in another devastating kick. He went down hard, turning away from Richard.

The crowds on both sides of the aisle were yelling and taunting the fighters. A few small fights broke out between Red and Blue rivals. "Finish him!" came a chant, nearly drowned out by something he couldn't quite make out.

"Finish him. Pick up the...! Finish him—pick up the..."

"Pick up the...the what?" Richard kept asking, not being able to hear above the raucous crowd.

Clarity was cold as a slap in the face as he saw his opponent reach for the blade he had been falling back towards the whole time. The fans knew where it was all along, but Richard had forgotten.

"How did I forget that?!" he yelled, when he first saw the shiny silver blade lift from the ground.

He took a step back as his opponent swung like a rope, bringing the blade across Richard's right upper thigh, cutting through his jeans and deep into the flesh. Richard gasped, having never felt that much pain.

"Big trees fall hard," was the first thing his opponent said, catching him on the same side calf with another slice.

Richard screamed out in pain and stumbled back, with his head spinning and feeling faint. The crowd on both sides was yelling so loudly that neither opponent could make out what was being chanted. He fell back hard onto the dusty arena floor. Both men looked at each other, crippled and broken.

Richard's man, not wanting to get into a grappling war with his opponent, threw the knife in a last-ditch effort, spinning over and over and careening handle-side off of Richard's head with a thud, opening a large gash and landing another ten feet behind him. "No more swords," said Richard, smiling as best he could through the pain. "Just me and you on the ground. You're in my house now."

Richard began to crawl on his hands as his opponent shimmied away, dragging both legs.

"Run him down! Run him down!" called out the crowd. "Run him down!" they cried, stomping their feet and raising fists into the air. The twenty-year-old bleachers creaked and moaned under the weight of the crowd. Most didn't seem to notice or care.

"Look at that!" said James to Jason. "Their energy, fear and rage are making a mob mentality out of the lot of them... Wait a minute!" he said, as he fixed his sight on a woman bursting down the bleachers' side stairs with her three children, followed by more people on all sides. "What's going on?"

Snap! Screams came from the far-left bleachers. James and Sheriff Johnson looked up to see the crowd falling into the middle of the bleachers from both sides, dropping like a high-rise building detonated precisely so as not to cause any damage to other structures around it.

"Oh, no!" shouted James, getting caught up in the sea of spectators around him headed towards the sounds.

Richard's attention was diverted, and he wondered if the fight was over, as his opponent dragged himself lightning fast around and behind him.

"Got you now, big guy," he called out, wrapping his right arm around Richard's throat. He let out a war cry, drowned out by the large crowd running to help their fellow townspeople.

Richard buckled and gurgled as his rival laid him on his back. It took longer than the last time he had done this, since he had no use of his legs to secure the bear of a man. But after three minutes it was done.

“So, what do I get?” he asked the deputy, still laying in the dirt. “Some kind of reward? Maybe a medal or...I know! How about a Key to the City, presented by the Mayor himself?”

“I’ll send the Sheriff over. Don’t go anywhere.”

The deputy headed over to Sheriff Johnson, amidst the chaos.

“Get Doc Walters and any other medical people here now!” said the Sheriff, out of breath. “Are they done?” he asked the deputy.

“Yeah, the big guy went down hard. The other is asking about some prizes, like a Key to the City.”

“Figures,” replied Sheriff Johnson. “I’ll take it from here. Be right back. You get the medics.”

“Sheriff,” said the last man standing, or lying. “I’m going to need some help over...”

Sheriff Johnson pulled his pistol without a word and shot him in the forehead. “And one for you, big guy,” he added, as he pulled the trigger.

No one seemed to notice, with the chaos going on—no one but James.

* * * *

“All hands on deck!” called out the Sheriff to his deputies, medical personnel, and citizens he directed to check on the injured.

The following weeks would be filled with quiet conversations, both indoors and out, about what really happened that night.

James sent word with Jason that they wouldn’t be joining the family for dinner. The restaurant owner carefully packed a prepaid dinner for eight into travel containers with a sincere “I’m-so-sorry-you-couldn’t-stay” speech.

“Me, too,” replied Janice. “It’s just so sad about those people,” she added, as they walked outside and headed home.

* * * *

Jason returned to join James. "I need you both here," said the Sheriff to James and Jason. "I'll drop you guys off at your ranch when we're done for the night."

"What do we know, Doc?" asked the Sheriff two hours later.

Doctor Walters sighed.

"Your motorcycle man is awake and talking some. He re-broke two ribs, along with his right scapula—the shoulder blade," he replied, sensing the Sheriff's confusion. "Anyway, he should recover fully, but we will know more in the coming days. He got a boxer's lump on his forehead somehow," he added, being careful to use common language with the Sheriff, "but it's improving."

"Yeah, I saw one of those on George Foreman, the boxer and grill guy. Can't remember the fight, but the lump over his eye was baseball-sized and he recovered okay," replied the Sheriff.

"We have 52 citizens from the bleacher incident that have passed through here or are waiting to be seen," Doc Walters continued.

"How many dead?" asked James, standing next to them both.

"Fourteen—six of them under age ten, and seven or eight more that could go either way in the next day or two."

"Oh, my god!" said Jason, gasping at the news.

"The others are not so bad. A few broken bones, cuts and bruises," added the doctor. "Except for the other two."

"What other two?" asked Sheriff Johnson, having a good idea of the answer.

"Your fighters, the gladiators, one with a bullet to the head."

"Well, there's that. Let's keep that between us. Understood?" said the Sheriff.

"Yes, of course, sir. My job isn't to question how they died, just to save them if I can, and those two are beyond that... Well, I had better be getting back to my patients," he replied as he turned to leave.

"Doc Walters!" the Sheriff called out, stopping him in his tracks.

"Yes?" he replied, nervously turning back around.

"Thanks for taking care of my motorcycle guy and all of the others. You do good work for my town. Now show me around here. James and Jason and I want everyone to see us checking on the injured and families."

"Okay," replied the doctor. "There are a few in surgery. We were able to get hold of the hospital in Trinidad and had a few of the injured transferred up there. Just temporary, you know."

"Sure, that's a good call," replied the Sheriff, "as long as they come back."

They stopped in to see Ken, who had his own room for about an hour but now shared it with four others.

"How you holding up, Evel?" asked the Sheriff.

"Oh, you know..." Ken replied groggily. "I still have a few hundred bones to break, but I'm getting a good start on taking the record." He laughed at his own joke, quickly returning to a less painful, stoic demeanor.

"It was a solid jump," said the Sheriff.

"I just caught my back tire is all."

"I know. I saw; we all did. If it hadn't rained, I think you would have made it. Let's try again next week."

"Uh...you're joking—right, sir?"

Now the Sheriff was laughing. "Yeah, I am. When you get out of here," he whispered, "you can go home."

"Really?"

"Yes, but I want you on my team and back on the City Council. You will draw a small paycheck from the town fund, like all of my deputies, but we will have you on other projects."

"How would I get back on the Council now?" asked Ken. "Don't I need to be voted in?"

"You already were. I'm just reinstating your former position. I need your eyes and ears there. Understand?"

"Yes, sir, I do. What did he think of the chair?" he added quietly, looking over at James across the room.

"He loved it. Even took his son, Billy, for a victory lap in front of everyone!"

"That's good; I'm happy to hear it."

"When he's released, take him home," the Sheriff told his relieved girlfriend. "I'll be by to check on him soon."

* * * *

"You did good with that one," said James, as they made their way through the hospital. "I guess you now have an empty jailhouse."

"That I do...for now, at least," replied the Sheriff. "I was going to get away fishing for a few days with Kate before...well, before all of this happened. Now it's probably not the best idea."

"Oh, I don't know. By the middle of next week, most should be well on their way to recovery. It's not your fault, you know," added James. "Those bleachers never carried that kind of weight, and nobody stomps around on them at a rodeo. It was just an accident, tragic as it is."

"Yes, but it's my accident on my watch."

"Thank you also for your tribute to me today, Sheriff," added James, changing the subject.

"Why, you're welcome, James. I'm just glad someone appreciates all of the hard work I put into it. Now let's get a check on the others here and get you gentlemen home to your families."

* * * *

Jason kept quiet on the way home, holding his question just behind the tip of his tongue. He opened the front gate and let James get settled before locking it back behind the Sheriff.

"All right, Jason. Ask it," said James, as they met back on the front porch and settled in with the first glass of Scotch they had since James was shot.

"Okay. Why did you thank him for the stuff he did today, mostly for himself?"

"Because he effectively eliminates his competition, as I'm sure you have noticed by now," replied James. "He is not my friend or yours, and that's why we keep him close...real close," he emphasized, patting his chest. "Nothing he did today was for me but he thinks it was, and that's all that matters for now.

"You and I will volunteer to watch over the town and suggest he take the fishing trip he was planning. If he goes, it won't be relaxing for him, by any stretch, but when he returns to things just like they were, we will have gained more trust in a few days than we have up to this point, everything accounted for. Now, let's get some sleep. We've got chores in the morning before church."

* * * *

Both men slept like only an exhausting day can yield, waking to the sunrise coming through the bedroom windows.

Four more died in the night, and all the others were expected to make a recovery of varying degrees over the next days and weeks. All would be honored on Sunday morning at the largest mass the small church of Weston had ever recorded.

"We will have an additional service at the cemetery tomorrow at 3 p.m. for those who have left us for eternal life with our Creator," announced the pastor at the service.

The Sheriff reluctantly agreed with James' and Kate's assurances to leave for a few days the day after the services.

* * * *

Jason brought James' tractor Monday morning to help dig the cemetery plots and meet with other ranchers. Some on the Council lobbied for one mass grave but were quickly overruled by the Mayor-elect.

"They each deserve a proper resting place," James directed, not asking for anyone's agreement.

Most families had lost someone they knew. Once the sting of losses left the forefront of everyone's minds, the quest began for answers to what happened and how.

****

Chapter Eight ~ Lake Pueblo State Park ~ Pueblo, Colorado

The pit fight went about as textbook as Mike imagined it would. One man, seemingly the champion from the night before, or maybe consecutive nights, emerged with his hands in the air after only a few minutes.

Mike waited another ten minutes, as the men he had watched moved from tent to tent, like some kind of check-in. A few fired shots into the air, maybe blowing off steam or keeping the camp fear factor high. The band of settlers danced around as the music was turned louder. Mike couldn't place it, as he was more of a country music guy, but it sounded like what he knew of death metal. The kind where young men would go down front into the mosh pit, dancing with no pattern or rhythm, just running into each other and occasionally throwing a wild fist or elbow.

Time to go, he thought, as the crowd surrounded him closer on all sides. "Hey man, watch it!" he yelled, as a young teen ran square into him, followed by another from the other side, and two men grabbed his legs.

"Hey, what the hell?!" he said, as he swung his arms, connecting with anyone close to him. He looked down to see his legs wrapped with rope and thought *This isn't good!* as he was pulled off his feet. He covered into a fetal position, protecting his head as best he could from the punches and kicks slipping through the pile of people on top of him.

"That's enough!" he heard from somewhere far away. "That's enough!" was shouted again, followed by two shots in the air.

* * * *

"Do you think he needs help?" asked Lonnie, with all of us concerned, sitting around a small campfire but unaware of Mike's current predicament.

"I don't know, but he didn't want us to come, no matter what. We have to believe he has everything under control," I replied.

* * * *

Mike felt the rifle barrel poking into his back without needing to see it.

"There are four more," the man said, "so don't try any funny business. Hands behind your back."

Mike did as the man ordered and felt the zip tie tighten around his wrists.

"You're a spy," said the man, striking Mike below his left eye before spitting in his face.

"You're a big man when you have your target tied up," said Mike, smiling. He didn't mind getting spit on; it happened to both him and his brother, Arthur, numerous times growing up. This was just an older bully now, but all bullies eventually got theirs—this he was sure of.

"You have a mouth on you," said his captor. "Maybe we have time for one more pit fight tonight."

"Sure. I'll fight you," said Mike without hesitation.

"Not him," said one of the Gatelin brothers, walking up. "I've got something better in mind," he said, holding one arm up.

Two other guards brought out a struggling man wearing a gag and blindfold.

"I'll bet you recognize my brother. Am I right?" he asked.

Mike had a pit in his stomach, which was rare. He wasn't worried about fighting a man, any man, but he saw where this was headed and wanted no part of it.

"How about I fight your last champion?" suggested Mike. "I win, and my group heads out immediately. Same if I lose."

"I don't think so. You see, my brother tends to have a mouth just like yours sometimes, and it has come to our attention that he may be planning a coup with your help. Isn't that right, little brother?"

There was no response from the frightened sibling, who showed visible signs of a beat-down.

"You two will meet in the pit as soon as we get the torches back on. Fight to the death. And Michael—that's your name, right?"

"Only my mother, sister, and women I've cared about ever called me that. Mike is fine."

"Whatever you say, Michael," he spat, drawing out the end like a Northerner trying to re-create a Southern drawl. "Refuse to fight, and either or both of you will be shot where you stand."

Mike waited to be led down into the earth without another word. He learned two things from watching the first fight. The two men had been left down there alone, with only one walking back up to the rim unassisted, and handcuffed again at the top. It was almost of as much importance that he could see one, the champion presumably, taunting the other but couldn't hear what was being said.

The brother was led down first—shaking, sobbing, and calling out to let him go. He called to Mike to show him mercy. Mike shook his head back and forth, not saying a word. He was shoved the last few feet as his hands were unbound. Mike circled his opponent slowly—the man who should have been in charge tomorrow, the man who could have freed his people. The man who was sure he would not live to see tomorrow looked back at him with the eyes of a defeated man who once was liked, respected, and even envied by other men.

"Which of your brothers did this to you?" asked Mike.

"All of them," he replied.

"Hold on," said Mike in a near whisper, as he continued to circle left.

"I'm sorry," the brother whimpered. "I'm sorry they knew. I didn't say anything—I swear that on my children."

"I know," replied Mike, looking out of the corner of his eye to see his captors back up on the pit's top. "I'm not going to kill you, but you have to do everything I say without question, or they are going to kill us both. Understand?"

"Yes, okay. I don't see that I have any choice in it."

"You do, but if we can pull this off, you will still lead this group and go home to your family. Now when I get close, hit me in the face hard," ordered Mike.

"You're not going to be mad?"

"No. No. Do it on three. One...two," as he stepped in close..."three."

The Gatelin brother hit Mike on the right cheek. Mike was shaking his head afterwards.

"Good one," Mike said, to cheers from the guards. "Now it's my turn," said Mike, pretending to punch him in the gut. "Bend down and fall to your knees," he said quietly.

"Finish him!" came the chant from above.

Mike backed away and circled slowly. "We're going to do this a few more times. Keep throwing punches but don't hit me in the nose—I hate that. After a few minutes, I'll give you the signal before I pretend to choke you. Once I do, you play dead for as long as you can. I mean, don't move at all! I've got one chance to change this back the way it should be."

"How will I know if you did it?"

"Easy. You won't die, and neither will I. Come at me again now—fast!" Mike yelled.

The brother did as he was told. Mike turned, putting him face down into the dirt with three quick but soft hits to the ribs.

"I'm going to let you up, but the next one is it," Mike told him. "Now, take my leg when I come in again."

"I don't know what you mean," said the brother.

"When I put it out in front, grab it and put me on the ground."

Mike stood up, pumping his fist in the air. Only the guards chanted.

"That's good," said Mike. "Only a few are okay with me killing you. The rest just may be on your side, after all. Now take it!" he said, stepping one leg close enough to be caught.

He took it, knocking Mike back onto the ground to cheers from the crowd.

"There they are. Those are your people... It's time," he added, circling his opponent and taking his back in a chokehold.

"Here we go," said Mike. "Do just as I say. Claw at my hands, and kick your legs... Good! Another thirty seconds and I want you to go limp, like the dead. I mean, don't move after that for anything."

"Okay, I hope this works."

"It's our only shot. Just wait for my move and you will know as soon as I do if it worked. Slow your kicks and drop your hands. Wait...wait...now. Good. Now, on my mark, no more kicks... And *now.*"

Mike slowly lowered him to the ground, holding him for another minute to complete the performance. He got up slowly, pretending to be fatigued and stumbled back up the embankment towards the top. He hoped one of the brothers would be there to talk to him, but it was two guards.

"Good fight," said the first one, with his rifle trained on him.

"Thanks. Are you Military?" asked Mike, sizing up his chances of taking the man's rifle before being cuffed again.

"Nope," said the guard. "I sold insurance a few weeks ago, and now I'm security. Hands behind your back."

"Really?" Mike replied, without complying. "How about you?" he asked the other.

"Same here. Larkin and Larkin, your insurance specialists for auto, home, boats and bikes. You may have heard our commercials."

"So, you're brothers?" asked Mike.

"Yep. Sure are. Twins, to be exact—not identical of course."

"I had one of those—a twin named Arthur. I feel like he's with me right now, you know what I mean? I would do anything for him...anything."

"Please put your hands behind your back," the command was repeated.

Mike reached into his pocket for the knife he was surprised nobody had checked him for. He unlatched the small sheath with his thumb.

"Hands behind your back now!"

"Oh, sure thing, brother," Mike replied, palming the three-inch blade. "Which Larkin are you?" he asked one of the twins.

"Oh, I'm Dave, and this here is..."

"Shut up, Dave," his brother spat and took his eyes off Mike for a split second. Mike almost smiled as he grabbed his rifle and had the blade to his throat in two seconds.

"That just might be a record, Mr. Larkin. What do you think, Dave?"

"Uh...well... What do I do, Stanley?"

"Well now, Dave and Stanley Larkin. As I said before, I'm a twin but mine is dead. Would you like to be a twin, Dave, with no brother?"

"No! No, I would not."

"Cuff Stanley's hands behind his back right after you drop the rifle."

"I'm not sure we're supposed to..."

"Do it, you idiot!" yelled Stanley.

"He's not very nice," Mike said. "Are you sure you want to save him, Dave? I've been in the pit; one more guy makes no difference at all."

"Yes, please don't hurt him. I'll do what you ask."

"Good choice. Lay your rifle at my feet, zip tie his hands tight like mine were, and then go get the man in the pit."

"But he's dead! I can't carry a dead man!"

"Is he? Tell him to meet us at his brothers' tents. Now go!"

Mike watched as the crowd around them, of mostly men and children, began to scatter.

"Now," said Mike. "Take me to the head guys—the other brothers."

* * * *

Putting his blade back in his pocket, he led the man at gunpoint to the camp center.

"Where is it? Where are they?" Mike commanded.

"There, in those three tents over there," Stanley replied with a nod, appearing a bit more cooperative than before.

"Who's the lead?"

"I guess they all are," he replied. "Everyone except the guy you were fighting."

"This one," Mike pointed to open the door as Stanley stepped inside the half-open front flap. Mike pushed his man through it, catching the first Gatelin brother off guard.

"What the hell?" he said, quickly realizing the situation.

"I got tired of the pit is all and figured I'd see what kind of man puts his brother in a dirty hole to fight a guy like me. You don't seem too busted up about it."

"No, I'm not," he said, regaining his confidence. "He was always weak, that one."

His two guards reached for their weapons, fumbling in their drunken stupor.

"Not quick enough, gentlemen," said Mike, shoving Stanley towards them and putting the same blade to the brother's neck. Mike could smell the whisky on their breath from where he stood. "Good whisky is to be sipped slowly after a win or a hard day, but it looks like you guys started a bit early today. I've got a rifle," he continued. "Two, but any sudden moves and this knife will take a life. 'Up close and personal,' as they say."

His man struggled against him in an apparent attempt at perceived defiance.

"You really should hold still," said Mike nicking his neck with the sharp blade, drawing a trickle of blood down onto his shoulder.

The two women sitting on the far bench yelled at him. "You're an animal; let him go!"

"You have no idea. Now let's go and get your coward brothers for a little chat."

"Tell your guys to drop their weapons. Rifles on the ground and magazines at my feet, and don't forget to clear the chambers, boys. Pistols too. Pant legs up, each of you, and turn all the way around."

"Do what he says!" the brother called out.

"Now, bend over real slow and pick up the magazines; you will be carrying them," said Mike to his prisoner.

* * * *

Mike led the way, walking backward towards the other tents.

"Bring the other two," called Mike to Stanley.

The other Gatelin brothers emerged from their tents, following their guards.

"Now, all weapons on the ground, magazines out, chambers cleared, including pistols!" shouted Mike. "Everyone, or he's done," he added, pushing the knife up against his neck, getting a scream out of his man.

"Here he is," called out Dave, leading the oldest brother around the tent's side.

"Back from the dead!" said Mike, getting a shocked look from his brothers.

"Round up your guys. You have five minutes."

Mike knew the odds were against him if he waited too long. *Just like going to Atlantic City back in the day*, he thought. If you win right away, you'd be smart to leave because the longer you stay, the odds go up every minute that you will go home with nothing. However, this time going home with nothing was the only goal.

He asked the small group a series of cop-type questions, just trying to kill time. He was surprised nobody made a move. Yes, their weapons were on the ground, but if only a few of them had the guts, they could get the tables turned quickly.

"What do you want?" asked the man whose neck was pressed to Mike's blade. What will it take for you to go back to your little group and hit the road?"

"What are you offering?" asked Mike. "And understand, this is a negotiation," he added, just hoping to buy more time but always interested in what a man would offer in trade for his very life.

"Okay, that's fair. I'll start then," said the brother, feeling a little cocky in his position. "You drop the knife, and we call this whole thing a draw. Maybe you get ruffed up just a bit, like a lesson to others, but you walk home and are gone by morning, to live another day."

"That sounds interesting," replied Mike, seeming to mull it over. "When you say roughed up, you just mean a few bumps and bruises, with no broken bones, right?"

"I think we can make that happen, and I'll even throw in one of the ladies up for auction. Take your pick...as long as we have a deal, of course."

"One of the ladies, you say? How many do you have to choose from?" Mike continued.

"Enough."

"Are you a fighter?" asked Mike. "I mean, do you like it?"

"This is not about me, so it really doesn't matter."

"Yes, it does matter," yelled the youngest brother, returning with fourteen men. "He's never been in a fight in his whole life."

"Really, never?" replied Mike. "What about your other two brothers?"

"Only three between both of them, and they lost two."

"Is that so?" replied Mike, motioning for him and his men to retrieve the rifles and magazines.

"These are the men?" asked Mike. "The ones you trust with your life?"

"Yes, this is the crew."

"All right, cowboy, it's your show now," said Mike, releasing his captive and shoving him to the ground. "I believe your brothers offered to rough me up just a bit before I leave. Do you think we could get the torches lit one last time tonight?"

"Now wait a minute! I wasn't talking about that, and it's not fair! You like to fight, I can tell. It wouldn't be a fair fight."

"Three on one isn't fair?" asked Mike. He was itching for a fight, like a dog might do trying to get the one spot he couldn't reach. "I didn't get to fight earlier, so what do you boys say?"

"The three of us against just you?" asked another brother.

"That's what I said," replied Mike.

"What do we get when we win?"

"*If* you win, you get to stay alive and leave this place tonight."

"I don't want any part of this," said the third brother, who had been silent until now. "We'll just leave."

"Let's take a vote on it," replied Mike.

"Okay," said the oldest brother. "All those in favor of us goin..."

"No, you don't get to vote, and neither do I," interjected Mike. "The women get the final say. Where are they?"

* * * *

"I'll take you to them," said one of the ladies who had remained silent thus far. They all walked to the other side of the camp, with Mike behind the brothers and the new security detail behind him.

She unzipped the front flap as the group moved towards the back, shielding their faces.

"It's okay," the woman said. "I have someone who wants to talk to you... Just talk, and that's all. Right, mister?"

"That's right," said Mike, holding his hands in front of him like he would carry a large bowl.

"You're okay, and I'm not here to hurt you. You have a choice. You can see the three of four Gatelin brothers leave tonight unharmed or see them fight in the pit like some of your husbands or boyfriends have done. What say you?"

It was quiet for a while, maybe a minute or two, with only one saying to leave. Nobody else spoke.

"They are all in custody," Mike added, pulling one into the tent for only a second, getting a gasp from the women as they shirked farther back into the tent.

"They can't hurt you anymore. So, what's it going to be, ladies? Leave or fight in the pit?"

"Leave," shouted one, with another yelling, "In the pit for those bastards!"

There were maybe fourteen or fifteen, by Mike's calculations, and he knew some had their men with full bellies tonight scattered across the lake. The chant started slow and built to a roaring thunder: "In the pit! In the pit!"

"I hear you, and you will all be freed before the sun rises," Mike replied.

* * * * * * *

Chapter Nine ~ Pueblo State Park ~ Pueblo, Colorado

Mike met back with the new leader for a private moment.

"They, your brothers, will meet me in the pit. Should they be victorious, you will banish them from this lake, never to return. The women will be set free tonight, and the men who traded some for freedom will be banished as well. My group will move out tomorrow regardless of tonight's outcome, and you will be left to lead. No mistakes and no second chances. Am I clear?"

"You are."

"Good. Have your men lead your brothers down to fight. No guns or any other weapons," he added, handing the new leader his pocketknife. "I want this back; my brother gave it to me."

* * * *

The torches were lit, and Mike walked the dirt trail down into the earth for the second time that night.

There were no drums this time, and only the torches showed something was off.

"Something is going on over there. Something different," I told Joy.

"I hope Mike is okay," she added.

Mike touched the new leader's swollen eye before descending.

"You remember this if they come up alive. What I'm trying to give you tonight is a gift, and in this Next-World you only get one of those."

* * * *

Mike slowly descended as the three met in confidence, like a football huddle.

"It's not the plan, fellas; it's the execution," Mike said aloud, popping his knuckles.

He paused for a moment, bowing his head. "Lord," he whispered, "watch over Sheila and Javi and those on both sides of this lake. I'm working my way towards you, zig-zagging all over, I know. These people need to not be afraid anymore. I hope you count this one as a zig...

"Shoot anyone who doesn't fight!" he yelled up to the new guards, stealing a line from his last encounter.

"Let's go, boys; I've got an early morning tomorrow," called out Mike.

They came out of the huddle with a plan of sorts. The lead brother, with the mouth, came out swinging wildly, letting haymakers fly both left and right. Mike dodged these with ease, hardly trying. He let a couple land just to feel it.

"Your shots—they hit hard but too wide," he said, driving one straight onto his chin and shaking his hand as the man fell. "Next, you fellas," he said casually. Both came at him, screaming and grabbing at his arms. He fought them off, shaking one first and then the other. "So, you guys like to traffic women, I hear?"

"It's just a business," spat the lead brother, picking himself off the ground and wobbling like most of Tyson's opponents over the years.

"This little business of yours is officially closed," said Mike, hitting him harder than he could ever remember striking another man. This time he fell straightaway and didn't make a sound.

"Oh my god! Is he...is he dead?" asked another, breathing heavy.

"That's right," said Mike. "Get mad, boys. Get your revenge!"

They came at him again, and this time he struck both at the same time, dropping them to the dirt.

"All right, I'm done," said Mike, "unless you're planning on getting up again?"

Neither man spoke through heavy breathing. Mike walked up the embankment to the waiting successor and his men.

"The rest is your choice," Mike told him, walking past. "I'll be back in the morning to talk to the group."

* * * *

He walked away, back towards camp, wondering what his new leader would choose.

"Ready...aim...fire!" he heard faintly, followed by seven, or maybe eight, shots.

"You've chosen well...that you have," said Mike aloud.

It was after one in the morning when Mike reached the camp.

"You boys aren't waiting up for me, are you?"

"It didn't seem fair to be sleeping while you were out there doing the dirty work by yourself," I said. Lonnie, Vlad and Jake nodded in agreement.

"There were a lot of shots," said Mitch.

"Yes, that's true," replied Mike. "But the good news is we can move on tomorrow after a meeting with the new leader and his group. And Mitch, you can start fishing in the morning."

"Really?" he said. "So, it's okay now...I mean, are things truly different?"

"The snakes have lost their heads," replied Mike. "The old regime has been removed from power. Now, I'm going to get some sleep. Just don't tell me I'm on guard duty tonight."

"Not tonight," I said, smiling. "I'm out too," I added, as everyone got up to leave the fire. With all of us minus Mike already completing our nightly guard duties, we headed to bed.

* * * *

Up at dawn, our camp was bustling with questions for Mike that he started to answer before announcing that any adult was welcome to join him at the meeting this morning across the lake, where he would answer all questions at once.

I took a four-wheeler, as did Vlad, and promised to get answers for Joy and everyone else staying behind. Lonnie insisted we go in fully strapped, "because you just never know," he said.

* * * *

We arrived at the camp to cheers from many who recognized Mike. He was like a hero, with men and women both shaking his hand and hugging him.

"This checks Mike's biggest fear box right there," I said quietly to Vlad. To his credit, he let them touch him and cry on his shoulder for several minutes.

"Let's get this group together for a quick meeting," said Mike to the new leader.

Men, women and children gathered around, telling each other to shush so they could hear.

"This here," started Mike, "is the last of the Gatelin brothers," putting his arm on the man's shoulder. "From what I have heard, he's also the only good one of the bunch. As most of you know, the other three are no more.

"This man is your leader now, and his security guards will keep you safe. Those men over there," pointing to the last security detail bound by both hands and feet, "will be leaving here, never to return. From this day forward, there will be no more enslavement, no more auctions, no more confiscation of weapons, and no more pit fights.

"Anyone here is free to leave right now. There is a FEMA camp in Trinidad that would be glad to have you. You won't live free there, but you will be protected. Anyone here is free to fish the lake or bathe as they see fit. I do believe Mitch over there is going to give a fishing class this afternoon for anyone needing a refresher or new to the idea. It's your best chance to eat. We have a few in our group as well that will be fishing today and would be happy to help you out. Isn't that right, Lance?"

"Well, we do need to restock. I guess so. Sure, we will all pitch in and break bread tonight. Are you okay with that, guys?" I asked Lonnie and Vlad.

"Sure," Lonnie replied. "It gives us a good early start in the morning."

"I would suggest," said Vlad, "we move our camp closer this morning to be near the activities and to be prepared to get out only what we need tonight for an early departure in the morning. The longer we stay in one place, the more stuff we drag off the trailers."

"We get a little too comfortable is what you're saying," I replied.

"Exactly," he said. "I can always count on you to see the right side of things."

"Do you mean your side?" I asked a bit sarcastically, in fun.

"Yes, that's what I said," he responded, laying on the thick accent. "Now if you will excuse me, I have a lady friend who has asked for a ride around the lake."

"There it is," I said, elbowing Lonnie lightly in the ribs. "Vlad, the ladies' man, and Mike is becoming a motivational speaker right before our eyes."

Mike smiled with us, lightening the mood for a split second, and didn't seem to mind the observation before getting serious again. He motioned for Lonnie and me to go inside the new leader's tent for a talk. It was just us and him, plus three of his apparent top security guys.

"I'll make this quick," said Mike. "I'm guessing you took care of the issue in the pit last night?"

"Yes, my guys finished it."

"Good. Then it's up to you to lead these people, at least the ones who stay, which looks like most now. They are counting on you to do the right thing, keep them protected and fed. It's harder to accomplish when you're doing the right thing, but not impossible. Can you do that?"

"Yes, I'm confident I can."

"Good. We're headed to Colorado, as you may already know, and have a good communication line. If I hear you allowing any nonsense to happen, as we had here just yesterday, I will come back here, if I have to walk, and take it from you the hard way. Are we clear?"

"Yes, we are," he replied.

"Good, let's get our camp moved and start fishing," said Mike, grinning like none of this ever happened.

* * * *

"Lance, get your boys," called out Mike, with a renewed sense of life I hadn't seen since we brought my twin son back in New Mexico. "You too, Jake; bring your boy—and Lonnie, your girl and boy. And your friends, Lance. Tell the dads to bring their kids, and we meet lakeside. Dads and kids fishing in 30!" he called out excitedly.

"What's up with him?" asked Jake, overhearing the rant. "Is he on drugs?"

"Yes, he is!" I told him, with only Vlad around. "He's on the kind that kills everyone except the taker."

"Only if they deserve it!" chimed in Vlad.

"He freed an entire village," I added, "ruled by people worse...or maybe I should say less empathetic to the common person than him. He's on a high, like last time with Nate's group, but this one is bigger. You're welcome, you know, Vlad, to join us fishing."

"Oh no, I have a thing," replied Vlad.

"You have a *thing?*" asked Jake, raising one eyebrow, not caring if he was prying.

"Yes, just a...well...just some plans for this afternoon is all."

"Bring her by the lake; we can tell her funny stories about you," I joked.

"Yes, that is precisely why I *won't*. Maybe someday we will have some little guys running around with heavy Russian accents who like to fish! Until then, I have a thing."

* * * *

We all pitched in on the pack-up. It goes quicker every time.

"Tomorrow should be a breeze," remarked Joy, "and I'm ready to move on anyway."

"Me too," I told her. "Every stop makes me want to just plant roots and not head towards the one place I'm sure we will have to help defend with blood."

"We've been doing that all along, honey—this whole time."

"You're right," I agreed, kissing her on the forehead.

"Now go and get some quality time with the boys," she told me. "Once we hit the road, it gets serious again, and I know you won't see them much."

"What about you?"

She smiled, pointing towards the women on the trailer, holding up bottles of wine.

"We will miss you boys. It's going to be so hard, in fact devastating, for a few long hours," she quipped, keeping in character with some Southern Belle from a movie seventy-five years ago. "But as God is my witness, we will never be lonely again!"

"I don't think that's the line," I pointed out, "but that's a heck of an audition. You've got the part, sweetheart!"

"Oh my," she said, with her hand over her mouth and still hamming it up. "It's everything I've ever wanted."

I shook my head, laughing.

* * * *

"Come on, boys. Let's go fishing with Uncle Mike."

"Yay, Daddy! Can Danny come?"

"Sure, Hudson. He'll be there with Javi and your friends from back home."

* * * * * * *

Chapter Ten ~ Lake Pueblo State Park ~ Pueblo, Colorado

The afternoon was good. Not expected, but safe as we could get in this Next-World. I would spend time with my boys and my wife because tomorrow was a new day—a day guaranteed by no man, only God if it is His will.

Teaching the group to fish was fun for all, and I gave up four YoYo automatic fishing reels to be used collectively by the newly named group, known as the Lake Pueblo Occupiers. Mitch, we found out, was not joking, or even slightly exaggerating, his fishing abilities as he clocked in not only the largest fish but also the biggest haul. He was officially appointed head fisherman for the new group.

"It was worth giving up my guns," he told me that afternoon while sporting a nearly new Kimber Mountain Ascent bolt action .30-06 rifle. "Check it out," he said, handing it to me.

"It's light," I replied, never having held one.

"It should be," he said. "Used to go for a couple thousand dollars before the scope. I got it from my old buddy and now new leader. It was worth the wait to get it back," he added, hugging his girlfriend.

"All I know is when you're done today, you will be bathing in this lake," she said, "and so will I... Who knows? You may even get lucky tonight," she added.

"This day just keeps getting better!" he said. "Thank you all for helping us out here. You changed all of our lives."

* * * *

I noticed a group of all men, maybe 15 or 20, off to the side of the lake.

"What's with those guys?" I asked the new Occupiers leader, as Mike glared at them.

"Those are the men who traded their wives and girlfriends over the past few weeks for a fishing pass. The women we still have here don't want them back, and I don't see as I can blame them. Even their kids won't speak to them. So, for now, at least they stay away from us and do their own thing.

"I guess I spoke too soon," he said, watching three of the men approach.

"What can I help you with?" said the leader.

They looked beyond him, and two put their hands into the air. The leader's security team had rifles trained on the men.

"Wait, hold up," he commanded to his men. "Let's see what they want... So, what do you want, gentlemen?" he asked.

"We want our women and children back, and our guns," said the only one without his hands raised.

"So, you're the leader of the misfits who cowardly trade their women to be enslaved so you can eat?" asked Mike, growing flushed.

His two friends were bumbling with some sort of apologies for even being born.

"Go back to your camp and bring the rest over here," Mike barked at the two.

They turned, whimpering like they had been smacked on the nose trying to steal food off the counter, and waved to their friends to join the conversation.

"So, you're the leader?" asked Mike again once they were all there to hear.

"Yep. Ain't nobody else got the stones to stand up for what's owed. Isn't that right, boys?"

Nobody spoke.

"Now, I want what's owed."

"Owed to who?" asked Mike, now dominating his group's side of the conversation.

"Owed to me," the man replied, smiling. "My guns and my lady... Now hand them over before things go bad for you."

"For me?" said Mike, cold and not raising his voice.

"That's what I done said, boy."

The new Occupier leader looked at Mike, surprised he was so calm. He waived for his guards to stay put, wanting to see where this exchange may end up.

"You men all want him for your new leader?" Mike called out.

"Of course they do!" said the man, feeling a bit cockier.

"I'm not asking *you*. I'm asking *them*."

"They do what I say," he said, putting a finger in Mike's face.

* * * *

Vlad and I saw the commotion from a distance. I could see clearly with binoculars, but I couldn't hear what was being said.

"I left my binos on the trailer," said Vlad. "What's happening?"

"I don't know, but it's about to worsen," I said.

Jake chimed in. "He's got his finger in Mike's face. Here, take a look. I've got an extra set," Jake added, handing them to Vlad.

We all looked and were surprised, even after all we had been through.

"Do you remember the last time someone put a finger in another man's face?" Jake asked me.

"How could I forget?" I replied. "That Lawrence guy from my office on that very first day it happened and that thug he pointed at weren't nearly as dangerous as Mike."

"I think this may end up the same," continued Jake.

"What happened on the first day?" asked Vlad.

"This guy Lawrence pointed his finger back then, and was dead in a few minutes," replied Jake.

The next moment happened fast, and the three of us would never completely agree on the gritty details. Mike stepped close, so the man's finger was touching the tip of his nose. He swung his right arm and left, clapping his palms hard onto the man's ears. This scream we could hear. Mike had him on the ground, knees on his back, with his arm stretched out.

"You just may be the first man to put his finger in my face. Which one was it?" Mike asked, squeezing each one individually. "I can't remember if it was the index or the middle one. Eeny, meeny, miny, moe, catch a tiger by the toe. If he hollers..."

The man did holler as Mike opened his buck knife with a flip.

"Please, I didn't mean anything by it. I was just horsing around is all. I'm sorry I pointed at you."

"It's not really about that anymore," said Mike, keeping a good hold on the man. "I see he's a righty," he said, now only talking to the other men up from the lake. "This means you reel your pole with your left hand."

Mike quickly let go of his right hand and grabbed his left.

Others in his group stood still, not attempting to intervene and backing away a few steps. "Every time you spin the reel, you should think of the woman you gave up to be sold. You sacrificed her; you all did," he said, lunging forward with lightning speed, catching another man's foot and pulling it out from underneath, toppling him to the ground.

"That's enough," the downed man said, slowly getting up. "We don't want any part of this—right, guys?"

"No! No! Not me!" they all agreed.

"I'm leaving tomorrow morning, either way," continued Mike, "but I always leave a memory. It's good or bad, depending on who you ask. Yours won't be good, but the rest of you will remember the lesson for a very long time."

Mike took his knife to the first two fingers, sparing the man's thumb. In a moment, they were off with a split second of crunching bone. The man screamed as he was let up, and he ran frantically back to his base.

"He'll live," said Mike to the others. "You all can forget about the women and children you left behind. You're not husbands—or fathers, for that matter. I want you all gone from this lake before morning. If I see one of you here before I leave tomorrow, hell is going to get some new recruits. Come back after that, and these boys will shoot on sight," he said, pointing to the new leader and security detail.

"You don't need those guys hanging out around here," Mike said aloud to the new leader, tossing the bloodied fingers towards him as he quickly stepped back.

* * * *

"Did he just cut that guy's fingers off?!" asked Aiden, walking up with his own monocular.

"It appears that way," I told him, "and it looks to be about the end of it. He always ties up loose ends before moving on. We'll be back on the road tomorrow."

"Can I ask him about it? I mean, what the hell?!" inquired Aiden.

"No!" we all said together.

"Don't ever bring it up unless he does," I told him. "And also, don't spread it around camp."

"It's done, like it never happened," added Vlad.

* * * *

"Here he comes," said Jake, "straight for us."

"All right, everyone. Just keep cool," I told them.

"Hey guys, what's shakin?" asked Mike, walking up.

"You okay?" I said, pointing to his blood-stained hands.

"Oh sure, just a cut is all. Let's get back to fishing," he said, rinsing his hands in the lake.

* * * *

We fished another two hours, switching poles, so everyone got a chance. In the end, we had enough for everyone to have their fill in both camps.

The new leader of the Lake Pueblo Occupiers gave a sincere apology for what happened over the last few weeks.

"As most of you saw, the threat has been eliminated, and we will start anew. We wish our new friends strength and luck as they make their way north through the mountains, and we thank them sincerely for righting the tragedies we have endured under the former rule."

The new leader vowed to have his men handle security for both groups tonight.

"No need on our behalf," said Mike. "We're always prepared."

My trust level with them, and Joy agreed, was north of 50 percent but not much over the threshold. With our main group and newer Airstream travelers, we were able to cut our security to one hour per person, and we all voted to give Mike the night off.

* * * *

The gunfire started around two in the morning, and it was all coming from the other camp. I counted at least fifteen shots from two or more AR-15s, followed by a 30-second pause, with another burst nearly the same. I had finished my shift two hours earlier and was in a dead man's sleep when it started. My leg had just started feeling better before I banged around in the dark looking for my flashlight that I always had right beside me.

I heard shouting nearby, sounding like women's voices, and those farther around the lake like men. Ringo and Mini were barking loudly.

Mike was the first one out of his tent. "So much for a night off," he said to Sheila. "Stay inside with Javi. I'll be back soon."

“What’s going on?” I asked Shane, remembering he was on duty now.

“I don’t know,” he replied. “Aiden and I heard shooting from the camp towards the other guys Mike was messing with earlier, I guess. Hard to see, even with the night goggles, but it looked like two women shooting.”

“Of course it is!” said Mike, laughing.

“What do you mean?” asked Vlad coming around on his crutches.

“They’re pissed off is what I mean. They probably started out in denial when it first happened. Each of them went through the five phases of divorce: first there’s denial, then anger, followed by bargaining, depression and acceptance. I think they just went out of order and skipped the anger part until they weren’t scared anymore. Then it’s all about revenge, and they have every right to do so. Take a couple of rifles off sleeping guards and let all hell break loose. Really, who’s going to blame them?”

* * * *

“All good?” asked Mike, sneaking right up behind the leader and giving him a jump.

“Yeah, just a couple of the women got some guns off the guards, but they weren’t trying to hurt us.”

“I know, and they will be free to go, right?”

“Yes, of course. Unless there’s more to the story.”

“There’s not, and your men dropped the ball,” pointed out Mike.

“I told you before, we’ve got security tonight.”

“No, you don’t,” replied Mike, “but you better get it in check soon or you will be sleeping every night with one eye open. I’ll be interested to see if they hit any in the dark. We will swing by in a few hours before we head out. Try to keep the noise at a respectable level,” he added, walking back towards his tent.

* * * *

“All good?” I asked Mike.

"Yep, just a little payback, long overdue. Let's get some sleep."

The dogs were back on their beds in front of our tent.

"Good dogs, staying close to camp," I said, petting them each on the head.

I slept the rest of the night like one might expect after being awakened by gunfire.

* * * *

"I want to check in on David before we head out," I told Jim and Steve.

"Sure thing," replied Jim. "I'll let you know when he's on the line."

Vlad and I took the four-wheelers. Mike rode the Indian. We checked on the scene from last night. Six men were hit at just over 100 yards out, with four dead already.

"Not bad shooting in the dark," said Mike casually, like he may be discussing a new coffee blend he just happened to find. "What are your names?" he asked the two still alive. "Let's see here. Looks like you're gut-shot," he said, pointing to one. "And you, how did she hit you in the leg and the shoulder?" he asked.

"What do you mean 'she'? I thought *you* did this."

"Nope, wasn't me. Not this time. It was your lady friends you all pimped out. Now they're armed and pissed off, as I'm sure you can imagine. Where's the rest of your group?"

"They took off and left us."

"Smart. Now, do you remember what I told you would happen if I caught you here this morning? Do you?" asked Mike.

"Yes. We want to go, but we need help. We can't just drag ourselves away, not like this."

"No, I don't suppose you can."

"Here we go," I said quietly to Vlad.

Mike pulled out his Ruger pistol, racked the slide, and took off the safety he only set with the children around.

"Who wants to be first?" he asked.

Both men begged for their lives, but Mike didn't hear it. A memory from his childhood crept in. He was alone on the playground and couldn't defend his brother, Arthur. He was helpless. It was the loneliest minutes of his life, worse than death ten times over. He holstered his pistol, clicking on the safety in the same motion without another word and rode away towards camp.

"Let's go," I told Vlad, as they yelled to us not to leave them there. "You just escaped certain death," I yelled back over the engine.

* * * *

We returned to camp and I was surprised how many children didn't even ask about the gunfire in the middle of the night. I asked mine and got blank stares as they asked, "What gunshots, Daddy?"

I felt a twinge of sadness as I realized it was familiar now, just part of their new little worlds, like when we used to watch war-torn countries on TV and kids are outside playing, with bombs exploding and gunfire in the distance. "Just another day, Daddy," I could almost hear them say.

Truth be told, I was ready to leave. My lakeside overnight campout had turned into a Freddy Krueger nightmare movie, and Mike had been the rogue cop breaking all the rules to bring the madman or -men to street justice.

"Just another episode in the upcoming Netflix series *Families First*," I said aloud.

"Season three, episode two," said Joy, playing along. "I wish that's all it was. I would be sitting in the recliner under my blanket with my cup of hot chocolate, a cozy fireplace, and kids around us whose only concern was getting to watch cartoons and eat donuts on Saturday morning."

* * * *

"Lance, we have David on the line," said Steve.

"Hey, David. Can you hear me?"

"Loud and clear, buddy. How's your trip going?"

"Slower than I thought," I replied. "We'll be headed up into the mountains today," I added, not wanting to be too specific about our location.

"Must have gotten sidetracked," said David. "I figured you would be farther along by now."

"We did get sidetracked, but we...well, mostly Mike...were able to help some people out of harm's way and back on track."

"I'm not surprised," replied David. "Probably the same as what he helped with here."

"Pretty much. Different people, same problems," I said. "But, hey, we're off again today."

"How's your mom, Tina, and the girls? Oh, and Mark?"

"Everyone is great! Veronica and Suzie made me promise to tell you they miss you, Joy and the boys, but they are having the best time here."

"That's great to hear; I knew they would be in good hands with you and Tina. They have been through more than all of us, losing their mother on the very first day."

I paused, realizing I had forgotten about his dad for a second.

"Uh, David, I'm..."

"No need, my friend. I miss him every day, but it's not the same as our girls. They still have nightmares about that day when they thought nobody would ever find them, crying out in the darkness, scared and alone. And you did—you and your friends found them and stopped to help. That is a true miracle. If that weren't enough, you then brought me a family I can love and protect. I've never seen my mom or Mark happier. I know that sounds strange, but it's true.

"Okay...moving on... We're done with the greenhouses. Worked all day on them the past couple of days. Nate and what's left of his group are sticking around, at least for a while. We planted the first seeds from James VanFleet. You remember him?"

"Sure, of course," I said. "How's he doing?"

"Mending, I guess. I haven't talked to him since the pseudo soldiers came through. They had some trouble brewing in town, I heard—some power battle between the Sheriff and the Judge guy...can't remember his name. Anyway, that's the last I've heard. Guess I'll check in on him soon. So...where was I?"

"Planting seeds, I think," I interjected.

"Oh yeah. We got one greenhouse loaded up yesterday with dirt and seeds. We threw a few worms in there that the kids found down by the lake. Probably can't hurt. Besides that, all has been quiet. It's a nice change, as I'm sure you can imagine."

"Yeah, buddy. Imagine is all I can do right now. I'm just hoping we will get a few days in a row, or even one, that's normal, relaxing and not violent. I know it's a lot to ask, but I'm praying for it. Okay, we've got to pack up. I'll reach out in a few days and see what's going on—can you dig it?"

"Yes, I can, brother. Talk to you soon."

* * * *

I got with Lonnie, Jake and Vlad to look over the map that was always in Lonnie's glove box.

"You guys see the map anywhere?" asked Lonnie.

"No, not me. Me neither," we responded.

"The ladies took it," his wife spoke up. Joy came around the front of the truck with Nancy, Lucy, Kat and her sister.

"We've got it," she told Lonnie, "and here's the path up the mountain."

Each town had a number next to it, signifying the number of miles up the road from the last one. She pointed to the light-yellow highlighted path through all the previously agreed on towns, marking off rivers, lakes, and alternate routes around each town, if it came to that.

"This is impressive," said Lonnie, studying it in earnest.

"Who would have thought an old-school map would end up one of our most prized possessions?" said Vlad, winking at Kat's sister.

* * * *

We packed up and said our goodbyes. I felt good about what we had done. It was gritty and nasty, for sure, but our group held the line and let Mike do what he does best. Yes, there was bloodshed, but there was also liberation that no man or woman can put a price on.

"Let's go! Let's go!" called out Lonnie over the radio and honking the lead truck twice. He stopped a few miles out to discuss the final route with each driver. Jake and I tagged along and promised to fill Vlad in on the specifics.

* * * * * * *

Chapter Eleven ~ Lake Pueblo State Park ~ Pueblo, Colorado

"Look! It's doggies," said Jax, pointing out the Blazer window to the east. All the children put their heads outside the window, hollering for them to come over.

"Here, puppy!" they clamored.

"They're coming over," said Hudson and Danny excitedly.

Joy was talking with the other ladies in the car when she saw it. She laid on the horn as the twenty or more dogs closed the gap from nowhere to the convoy. Some had collars, and all varied in size from small to a big Saint Bernard, like in that kid's movie, maybe called *Beethoven*.

Just one or two wouldn't have been much of a concern, but these were not house dogs. They barked, yipped and snarled, many with dried blood streaking their fur. The mangy lot closed in at full speed, with Joy scrambling to put the windows up. Ringo and Mini knew something was wrong, with Mini barking and shivering with her tail between her legs and looking down over the trailer.

"Incoming at 3 o'clock," announced Lonnie. "Everyone inside or on the trailers now!"

I jumped from the bed of his truck onto the back trailer and reached towards Ringo, standing on the trailer's side with a low growl. His collar slipped through my hand when his body launched the six feet off the trailer. He rolled at the bottom, and I was sure he had broken a leg when he popped up and ran towards the pack.

"No, Ringo!" I yelled. "Come back here!"

He couldn't hear or maybe couldn't stop, and in a moment they were on him. I could hear children's screams from inside the vehicles as the pack surrounded one of my best friends in this world. Without thinking, I jumped off the trailer with rifle in hand, only remembering to land on my good leg at the last second. It wasn't the smartest thing I had ever done, but I rolled at the bottom and kept my rifle from touching the ground.

I hobbled towards the pack, firing rounds into the air above them. Some were scared off but not even half of them left. The remaining ones were only agitated by the shots and closed in on Ringo. His barks were mixed with yelps and I felt helpless, still twenty yards away, firing into the air without a clear shot.

The *Boom!* came from over my right shoulder and another two on my left.

One of the bigger dogs let go of mine and hobbled off, limping badly. Four more shots hit their marks, dropping two more where they stood. There were still seven or eight; I couldn't be sure in the mix. One turned, running away, with no shots to be heard.

"Hold on, Ringo," is all I could think to say.

I was now five yards from the pack as they ripped at his fur with their teeth. I steadied to fire from ground level, without a clear shot, in a Hail Mary attempt to save my friend.

"On the ground, Lance. Now!" yelled a familiar voice over the megaphone. It was Lonnie, I was sure, and in a last-ditch effort to save my brave guy I went facedown to the ground. Ten shots—maybe fifteen or more—flew over my head, most with a thud and yelp to match. I looked up, expecting to try and fend off the last of them, but they were all either down or running away. Only Ringo lay on the ground, his white fur stained bright red. He tried to stand but could only get halfway up before collapsing again.

"Nancy!" I yelled. "Nancy! I need your help," I called without taking my eyes off him. "Hey, big boy. It's me," I said, approaching him. He was breathing heavily but lifted his head slowly. I put my face to his, wanting to be the last thing he saw if he died right there on the hard ground. I remembered reading an article once, written by a veterinarian, that said his biggest regret was not requiring a family member to be present when their beloved canine was put to sleep. The part I most remember him saying went something like, "The last thing they see on this earth should not be a stranger in a scary sterile room." I had had the displeasure of attending one of these events, both at home with my boys and once at the veterinary office. As hard as it was, I agreed with his theory. Nobody wants to die alone, human or animal.

"You did good, Ringo. You're a good boy, and you saved us from those dogs. Our family has been complete because of you and our boys count you as a best friend."

I looked around to make sure we wouldn't be part of a second attack and only saw people running towards us. They were calling out to each other—instructions maybe, but all I could hear was Ringo's heavy breathing. *Woosh* in and almost a sigh on the exhale. *Woosh* sigh, *woosh* sigh. Everything was moving in slow motion.

"I'm with you right now," I told him, looking into his fatigued eyes. "I'm right here, my good boy," I said, hugging him. Blood stained my clothes, but I didn't care. I looked deep into his eyes as never before and spoke to him.

"You can go right here, my friend. I am with you. Or fight and stay a while longer. I'm here for you, either way."

I put my nose to his, awaiting a response or maybe a sign of his ultimate choice. He paused, not breathing for a few seconds, closing his eyes. I put my ear to his side, and there was no *woosh* or sigh—just stillness.

"Okay, my friend," I told him, with tears running down my flushed cheeks. "We will give you a proper send-off, fit for a loyal companion."

Adults around me were still yelling, but it fell on deaf ears. I latched on to the cry "Bingy! Bingy!" The voice was getting closer. It was Hendrix. I knew without turning around. I turned to see him running full-on towards us, his little legs moving faster than the rest of him, like Fred Flintstone trying to get his Flintmobile going. He reached me, followed closely by Jake, who was apologizing for not catching him.

"Bingy, no!" he cried, hugging our friend and burying his head into Ringo's fur. "Open your eyes!" he cried. "Open them, please!"

"I'm sorry, son. He's had too much...he fought to protect us and..."

"Wait, Daddy! I hear him!" he called out, with his ear to Ringo's chest. I rested my hand on him, and it was true. In, out, in and out. He was breathing quietly.

"Did you change your mind?" I asked him, putting a hand on his head, meeting him nose-to-nose. He opened one eye...and then the other...before licking me on the nose and laying his head on my knee.

"So, we fight?" I asked. He let out a bark—less than his former self but enough to know we were in this together, and he was not ready to lay down. Then in a split second, I could hear everything. The other dogs struggling to walk or drag themselves away, or unable to move but still alive.

* * * *

I heard the yells from far away. "We're coming!" Nancy arrived first, then eight other people behind her.

"Stay back!" called Nancy. "Everyone just stay back! Lance, I need Ringo to focus on you so I can check him. If I tell you to hold him down, it's for a good reason."

"Okay," I said, stroking his head and looking into his fatigued eyes.

"It's okay, boy; she's just going to check you out." He was panting.

"Can someone get me some water?" she called out without turning around. "State your name, then go."

"Uh, Aiden. I'll be right back," he added, running back towards the truck.

Mike walked slowly around the scene, with an eye on each dog still breathing. I caught his eye.

"Don't worry, Lance. I won't do anything to scare your dog, at least not yet."

"Thank you," I said, happy that at least this time he could read my mind.

Woosh sigh, *woosh* sigh, was the only sound, with occasional yips as Nancy felt a puncture wound.

"Wait, where's Mini?" I said, not remembering seeing her.

"Vlad has her on the trailer," said Jake. "She's fine."

A full ten minutes later, Nancy whispered into my ear. "I have maybe good news and possibly bad news. The bad news first," she said, without giving me a choice I was used to, although to be fair, I always pick the bad first.

"I'm not a veterinarian, but I was a medic. He's going to need an expert, most likely. I can give him something for the pain and treat what I can see on the outside, but if there is internal bleeding, well, I just don't know. I'll get him sedated now, and we can get him on the trailer."

"Is that the good or bad news or both?" I asked, not sure.

"Oh, I'm sorry. That's the bad news. Jake and I know a country vet up the road, between Cañon City and Fairplay. Jake used to play football with his son in high school outside Boulder. They were the star quarterback and receiver. To be transparent, we haven't seen him in a few years, since before we moved out of Boulder. He was getting up in years, but he moved up here when his son went to college. He was known as the best country veterinarian in this whole area. He always traveled to his appointments, driving as far as 100 miles if the price was right."

"I'll make the price right!" I blurted out. "Let's get him on the radio and have him meet us halfway.

"I need Steve!" I said. "Somebody get Steve!" I shouted.

"Hold on. Slow down," she told me. "He's not a radio kind of guy. We can try to get through to someone up there, but I think it's a long shot."

"Will you please just give Steve his name and location?" I asked.

"Sure, I can do that. Bring the trailer around, Lonnie," she called out. "We need to lift him."

"What do you think Ringo weighs?" she asked me.

"He was 154 at his last vet appointment," I replied, without having to think about the answer.

"Okay, we're going to need a few people," she said, getting down the makeshift stretcher Vlad had used before. "Easy now... On three, roll him this way," she pointed. "Then back into the stretcher when I get it underneath."

It was clumsy, as most of us were not professionals, but his meds were kicking in and he didn't put up a struggle.

"Lift on three," she instructed. "Easy on both sides...and don't drop him. One...two...and three we go. I'll check him on the trailer so we can keep moving."

* * * *

Mini whimpered quietly and put her head on Ringo's paw. I heard the last shots before Mike returned to our outfit.

"Why did you shoot those dogs, Uncle Mike?" asked Hudson, opening his window.

"I didn't shoot dogs, Hudson. I shot animals, predators, that only used to be dogs. Now they can't hurt any other dogs or you."

"Oh, okay. I think I understand," Hudson replied, as Mike walked back towards his truck.

"Is Ringo going to be okay?" Hudson called out.

"I don't know," Mike said, without looking back.

"We have about forty-five miles to Cañon City," called out Lonnie. "We wind up Highway 96 West to 67 West, and then up to 115. Parts of this route go right through residential areas, so we'll zig and zag as needed. Everyone take their spots," he called out. "And as always, eyes open."

We were moving in the morning's coolness, back on the road I had missed the past couple of days. I was petting Ringo and Mini while Nancy glued a few of the wounds.

"Have you ever wondered what it would be like to travel the country by RV?" I asked Jake and Vlad. "Now I'm wishing we had packed up the kids and homeschooled them for a year, hitting every state."

"I'm guessing it's a lot like this, minus all of the bad guys lurking around every corner, of course," replied Jake. "How many lakes or cities have something going on like we just saw back there?"

"Not many, I hope," I replied, "or maybe a lot; it's hard to say. And the dogs, what's up with that?" I asked. "Three weeks ago, they were playing in the backyard of someone's house, and now they're...well...they're just wild!"

"We had four types of wolves in Mother Russia," said Vlad. "The Caspian Sea, Tibetan, Tundra, and Eurasian. Do you know the difference between a wolf and a dog?" he asked. "Dogs are kept," he said, not waiting for an answer.

"I see your point," I said, but can you see Ringo or Mini getting like that, no matter how hungry they get?"

"No, because they are yours," he replied. "Maybe they let them go, or they just got lost, like this one," he said, pointing to Mini. "But one thing is clear: nobody will feed them anymore."

I prayed aloud for Ringo, Mini, the lost dogs, and our family, all of us traveling together. We had only been on the road for an hour, not seeing anyone walking. Ringo seemed the same, no better or worse, and Mini never once left his side. We stopped for a ten-minute potty break thirty minutes later. Nancy said each child who wanted to see Ringo could pet him, one at a time. Our ten-minute break turned to twenty, as each child took turns petting Ringo and a still-frightened Mini.

"Nothing on the radio," said Steve, "but we will keep trying."

"Thanks," I told him. "I know you are."

"We're making good time," Lonnie announced. "Another couple of hours, if all goes good, and we'll be just below the town. Stay close; we have a few obstacles to go around. No more bathroom breaks until we get there. So, five more minutes if you need to..."

Jake and Shane got us all topped off with gasoline.

* * * * * * *

Chapter Twelve ~ Heading to Cañon City, Colorado

"Once we start up, don't stop unless I do, and if that happens, be locked and loaded," said Lonnie.

The trucks and trailers rolled again, some squeaking under the weight but each soldiering up the mountain's back in a slow climb to the next encounter. Ringo's breath seemed shallow and I asked Nancy to check him. She was still on the trailer with me, Jake and Vlad, while Joy watched over Danny.

"Sure, he's okay so far, just an effect of the meds I gave him," Nancy said. "Don't be alarmed if he falls asleep soon. He needs his rest, so don't wake him."

Although I wasn't too surprised and he was asleep in only five or ten more minutes, she was right. I resisted the urge to get face-to-face and check his breathing but kept my hand on his side, feeling the up-and-down cycle I knew was life.

Joy had accurately accused me of it more than once before with our boys. I would check their breathing every night before I slept and, honest to God, never missed a night when I was in town, which was 95% of the time. If they were sick or had a fever, I would check them multiple times each night. I wouldn't apologize for it but occasionally took some teasing from other, more relaxed parents. Ringo was breathing shallow but steady, and that's all I could hope for now.

* * * *

Lonnie and his wife navigated like true professionals with our old-school map, keeping us on track and away from most houses and abandoned businesses. The few people walking around seemed to hide from us behind abandoned cars or in the trees.

"They're lucky the Baker guy's group isn't marching through here," I said.

"I'm guessing they would be in the mountains, two miles deep by now," replied Jake, as he pointed out possible threats that never materialized.

"These are good people up here in the mountains, minus a few power-hungry ones that every small town has," said Vlad. "Same as home. The farther you get away from the city, the more people rely on each other."

"How so?" asked Nancy, overhearing the conversation.

"Well, take a city person, for example," said Vlad. "They won't know more than one or two neighbors around them unless maybe they have kids. Now, the same family in the country, in Russia or here, is the same. They know everyone around them. It doesn't mean they like them all, but they know one another. And in times of bad, they don't call the police or fire departments; they call each other and help, because next time it could be them."

"I see your point, but I knew most of my neighbors and lived in the city," I told them.

"No, no," replied Vlad. "You lived outside the city, in the suburbs. Not the best, like the wide-open countryside, but better than the city. Plus, you like people. I knew a lot who didn't. They went through the motions and spoke to those who were close family or long-time friends or those who gave them business to put food on the table. I had a lot of acquaintances over the years, owning my gun shop, but only a few friends."

"Like Lonnie, right?" asked Jake.

"Yes, like Lonnie and only a few more. I feel that I have more friends here now than at any point in my life, here or there."

"I know what you mean," realizing my radio was on, sandwiched between my leg and the trailer, with the talk button engaged. "Sorry," I said, clicking it off.

"I'm tearing up over here—really I am," said Lonnie. "But can we just focus for a little bit longer?"

"Copy," I replied, embarrassed but not feeling bad about it. "Hang on, buddy," I told Ringo, kissing him on the head.

* * * *

We slowed only minutes later, with Lonnie on the radio.

"We've got something up ahead. Be ready but don't engage. I repeat—don't engage! I'm going to use your dog, Lance, as the excuse to be here. At least it's worth a try. Make him look like its life or death, if you can."

"It is," I responded flatly. "They can take a look if they need to."

"I'll come up slow," said Jake. "I know the Vet up here—if he's still alive, of course. Let me do the talking."

"All right," said Lonnie, "but I'll back you up. Pistols only, and none visible, okay?"

"Yeah, sure," Jake agreed, hoping his man was still there.

* * * *

Lonnie and Jake walked slowly, side-by-side, up the road towards the barricade. It was a mix of vehicles, presumably not working, including an old country-style school bus with the yellow paint looking like it was out of a spray can from a not-talented graffiti artist and a VW bug that just looked out of place up here. In the middle was a purple and yellow pristine Chevrolet Corvette.

"That's a '96," said Jake—the official pace car of the Indy 500 that year and one hell of a ride.

"That's Carl's car, right?"

"Who's Carl?" whispered Lonnie.

"An old friend from high school," he whispered back.

"How do you know Carl?" came the response from behind the barricade but not revealing themselves.

"My name is Jake, and Carl and I, plus our team of course, brought the Boulder High Panthers to the state championship in '92 and won it."

"You're that quarterback, huh?"

"Yes, I was that guy."

"Hold on," came the reply.

Lonnie and Jake stood still in the middle of the road, between those they loved and swore to protect and some they had never met. Minutes dragged on, and I was getting nervous about Ringo and passing through here in general. An old truck pulled up behind the barricade fifteen long minutes later. Two more minutes and the voice was clear.

"Jake, is that you?"

"It's me, Carl! Can we talk?"

"Hang on just a minute," he said, and there were muffled voices behind the cars. "On that last pass you made to me for the championship, how many yards was it?"

"Twenty-seven, if you asked coach Riley, or twenty-four according to the refs who couldn't officiate a JV team accurately," Jake replied.

"Come on up, brother," Carl said, laughing. He added, "It's all right" to his people. "Bring your friend, but that's all for now.

"It's been a while, old friend," he said, with a handshake and quick guy hug in the neutral zone.

"This is my friend, Lonnie," Jake said.

"What brings you through here?" Carl asked.

"It's a long story, perhaps better over a glass or two of Scotch, but we have a dog, a good dog that got attacked by some others, and I was hoping your dad was around to take a look at him."

“My pops, he was a good man, but we laid him to rest a few years back.”

“I’m sorry. I know he was one of a kind, never missed a game,” replied Jake.

“Anyone around here who could take a look at the dog? We’ll pay a fair price for it.”

“No money needed, but I’ll take you up on that Scotch later.”

“Wait a minute?” asked Jake.

“I went to Ole Miss—full ride.”

“Yeah, I remember, but lost track of you after that,” replied Jake.

“I thought I might go pro until I blew a knee, and my dad helped me get through Veterinary school. I don’t drive all over the mountains like he did or get up on the bed with a lame animal, but I built a solid clinic—at least it was before...well, you know.”

“Yeah, I know.”

“Will you take a look at him? He’s a big boy, but everyone here counts on him for protection.”

“Sure. Where is he?”

“Back on the trailer.”

“Carl, it could be a trap,” came a voice from behind the barrier. “We can’t go with you; it’s protocol or some crap.”

“I’ve known this man since grade school. I’m fine; you guys just hang back until I return.”

Carl followed Jake and Lonnie back to the trailer and took a quick look at Ringo.

“Who glued him up?” Carl asked.

“That’s me,” Nancy replied, holding her hand in the air.

“Okay. All right... Great job.”

After a thorough onsite exam and questions of what happened, he pulled Nancy, Jake and me aside.

"He's got a chance for sure, with some internal bleeding maybe, but I need to get him to my clinic right now. There's room for your friends—if that's what they are, Jake—on my property."

"Yes, everyone here is a part of our group. And thank you for your hospitality."

"Ah, it's nothing. My wife—you know, the girl I was dating my senior year—is an up-and-coming chef. She had two cookbooks on Amazon and was picked to be on one of those reality cooking shows. You know the one. Anyway, she loves people and living in a town of less than 600, I'm sure she would love the company while I check on the big guy. And our little girl, Izabella, loves new friends but doesn't meet too many around here. How many pounds is your dog, anyway?"

"154," I said, ready to get past the small talk. "Can we take him to your place now?" I asked, not worrying if I was direct.

"Oh yes, sure. Right this way."

* * * *

He directed us to a side road before the barricade, where he stopped briefly to talk with the men guarding it. We drove slowly down a curved mountain dirt road, due to the steep grade, towards a lush valley below.

"Wow!" said Jake. "I've never been up here. It's beautiful country."

"Yes, that is true," said Vlad, smiling. "The kind of country where an old Russian might start over, maybe even raise a family, no?"

"Maybe so," I said, petting Ringo. "Almost there, buddy," I whispered in his ear. "Hold on."

The farm was small but efficient, sitting next to a picturesque stream where a trout would come to the surface of a pool after an insect every few minutes.

"Make yourself at home," Carl said, as we got Ringo off the truck.

He caught me watching the fish in the deeper holes.

“Yeah, there are a few big ones in there,” he said. “You all can fish it if you want while I take a look at this big guy.”

“Yes, Daddy!” said my boys. “Let’s catch a lot of fish!”

“We’ll talk about it in a minute, guys,” I told them, feeling bad I would have to break up their excitement but not wanting to miss a teaching opportunity. “Come on over, boys,” I said, once Ringo was inside. We walked to the edge of the river with them all asking to go get their poles. “Okay,” I said, getting on one knee. “Is this a big or small creek?”

“Kind of small,” replied Hudson.

“Yes, son, that’s right. And there are only so many fish in a small creek. When I was a boy of maybe 12 years old, my friends and I would start up the river and follow it down as it wound its way through several farmers’ properties. We pulled trout out of the fishing holes on their property, and in return they would shoot at us with shotguns!”

“Did you die?” asked Jax.

“Well, no. They used something called rock salt that would leave a good bruise if you got hit.”

“That wasn’t very nice of them,” added Hudson.

“Maybe so, but we were the ones on their properties, taking home fish that didn’t belong to us. It means more even now up here, because the folks living around here can’t just go to the grocery store to buy food anymore. This, what’s close by, is what they have to live on. These fish here will provide food for the people who live here—maybe tomorrow or months from now, but it will happen, I’m sure of that. We have freezers full of fish already, so we will play a fun game instead. Everyone tries to catch a grasshopper. We will have a contest when we throw them into the creek, and whoever’s grasshopper gets hit by the biggest fish wins.”

“What are you saying, Daddy?” asked Jax. “We can’t go fishing?”

“Yes, son, not here is what I’m telling you.”

"We'll just throw them back in, and they can stay alive," said Hendrix.

"That's a good plan, my little man, but not every fish returned to the water stays alive. Sometimes they get hooked wrong or just get too tired from the fight to swim again. These people here need to fish this creek, not us."

"Awe," they all said.

"Don't look," I said, pointing across to the house. "That's Izabella over there, and she could maybe use some playmates. Wait! I said don't look!"

Too late, they were full speed towards the tire swing, something no young boy can pass up.

"Y'all got lucky this time," I said in my best exaggerated Texas drawl, adding, "there's some fishermen in that bunch!"

"Talking to fish, huh?" said Mike, putting his hand on my shoulder. I probably would have jumped a week or even a few days ago, but I was getting used to him appearing out of nowhere.

"You going fishing?" I asked, seeing him with a pole and hearing Javi calling, "Wait up, Daddy!"

"Well, I was until I overheard your little speech to the boys—you're right, and now I'm not. Go play with the boys on the tire swing, Javi," he said. "I'll be over in a few."

* * * *

We both sat down, facing the river, Mike and me.

"Thanks, man, for what you did," I told him.

"Ringo is a part of the family," Mike replied. "And besides, those other things were not dogs anymore—they were killers."

"I appreciate that too, but I meant back at the lake. You took a village of people with no hope and turned them into, I don't know, a village of promise, at least. Does that make any sense?"

"Yeah, I don't know what will happen, but they are on a level playing field, at least."

"What are you going to do when we get to Saddle Ranch?" I asked.

"What do you mean?"

"Out here on the open road, there is always something to watch out for or fix. Won't you be bored there?"

Mike smiled. "I keep hearing that," he said. "The short answer, I guess, is there is always someone who could use some help, and from what I've seen so far there is no shortage of A-holes, pre- or post-apocalypse."

"That's the short answer, huh?" I asked.

"Yes, the longer one is what I came over to talk to you about."

"Ah, okay. Is there anyone else who should hear it?"

"Yes. Here she comes."

"Hey, honey. Mike has something to share with us."

"I heard," Joy replied, sitting down next to me, with Mike on my other side.

"I know you both haven't known me for too long, and what you do know is messy at best," he started. "There are a couple of reasons I'm able to do what I do without getting scared or, at the very least, too nervous about completing the task.

"First, I'm not afraid to die. I'm not sure if I'll go to the same place as my brother and sister, but it won't be so bad if I can.

"Second, I see things, or hear them maybe. I'm not sure how it works, but I know the outcome to a degree if I intervene in a situation versus if I don't. Maybe it's all in my head, or God uses me as some kind of bad angel that cleans up messes. I don't know. What I do know is none of it ever really worried me before. Even the battle we had after adding Sheila and Javi to my life didn't cause me concern. It's what lies ahead that worries me, keeps me from sleeping good—the Great Battle, the one for the Valley."

"I understand what you're saying," I said. "I still have family there and friends I grew up with. Plus, we'll all be there, and we've already faced them once."

"No, we faced a small part of them," Mike said. I see them in my dreams, I guess, but they are not just the group who headed past us, giving us a small skirmish. They are growing and his radio show or announcements..."

"More like rants," said Joy.

"Okay, rants, misguided revelations, or whatever we want to call them," continued Mike. "They're working on drawing people from all directions to Horsetooth Lake. By the time we see the Great Battle, I'm not sure even the Colonel's men can save us."

"So, what are you saying?" I asked.

"You've seen the movie *The Stand*, right?"

"By Stephen King. Of course," I replied.

"I haven't seen it," said Joy.

"What?!" we both asked, overdramatizing our concern of her missing a truly classic story.

"There are two groups after an apocalyptic event," I said. "One good and one bad. Both had dreams guiding them to either side, and this is what I'm guessing we're going to talk about with Mike. But the good group sent spies to the other side, hoping to gain valuable information before an attack. Am I close?" I asked.

"Like a shot between the eyes," Mike responded. "We are far enough up the mountain to make it to the other side, but once we do we're sitting ducks—no eyes in the air until maybe the last minute and none on the ground... I'm going in as a spy," he added, pausing for a response.

"Wait, what?" asked Joy. "Why aren't you shocked by this?" she asked me.

"I've seen the movie and read the book twice, that's why. You don't have a bicycle, Mike, and it's a long way to walk."

"But you do have *an Indian*," we both said together.

"Can't someone else go?" asked Joy, realizing she was trying to keep the guy around she nearly pushed away only days ago.

"Sure, someone else could go, but if they get wind of it or suspect anything, who else do you want to take the punishment and still not talk? Plus, I'll be riding alone all the way to their camp."

"Okay, I see your position," she agreed. "What does Sheila have to say about it?"

"Nothing yet," Mike replied, "and that brings me to my next point, Lance. If I don't make it back, I need your word you will make sure she and Javi have a safe place to call home. Always welcome, no matter what."

"Of course! I mean yes, you have my word," I added, not wanting to sound like I took the responsibility lightly.

"I'll talk to Lonnie next and then Sheila. If we are a go, I'll be gone tomorrow, and we will work out the plans tonight. I think it goes without saying to keep this under wraps until I make an announcement."

"Sure," I replied. "We always do."

* * * *

We watched him head back to the truck and briefly speak with Lonnie, pointing at us. Ten minutes later, he was back in his vehicle, and the yelling could be heard outside the closed windows, followed by sobbing, as he opened one for air.

Joy and I made our way over to outside the Vet's office, awaiting any news. We could clearly see the children playing on the swing from there. "Listen," I told Joy. "All I hear is the wind in the trees and the creek as the loudest sounds beyond their happy screams." It was peaceful, almost like home.

* * * *

A full 45 minutes went by before we saw Mike again.

"I have an announcement," is all he said, gathering every adult and not worrying about the kids overhearing. "I'll make this quick," he said, with Sheila crying softly and Joy hugging her. "I'm leaving the group for a while but hope to return when you reach Saddle Ranch. I won't go into the details of why or where, but rest assured it's for your own safety. Each of you has treated us like family, which means something to me, Sheila and Javi. They will stay on with all of you until it's safe for me to return. Any questions can be brought to Lonnie or Lance as they come up. I will head out in the morning."

"Which way will you be headed?" asked Steve.

"Towards the sun. Thanks, everyone, and enjoy your afternoon."

I was surprised not to get a litany of questions straightaway but knew they would eventually come.

"I have news," said Nancy, putting her hand on my shoulder.

"Is he going to be okay?" I asked, jumping up. Most people don't put a hand on your shoulder when they are delivering good news.

"I think so. I mean, the Doc seems to."

"Can we see him?" asked Joy.

"Just you two; no kids yet. Follow me."

* * * *

We walked back inside through the house that smelled like beef ribs and candy canes.

"I'll be out in just a minute to say hi," said a pretty middle-aged woman. "Just need to turn this roast." She looked like a cross between Jennifer Aniston and Martha Stewart, and had I seen her in New York City or L.A., I would have thought she had lived there her whole life. We all waved and smiled.

"It's a good thing you got him up here as fast as you did. Another night on the road and I don't think he would have made it," said the doctor.

"Will he be okay, Doc?" asked Joy.

"Just call me Carl—all of you, please. He lost a fair amount of blood," he started out, as he described in detail Ringo's injuries without answering the simple question.

I was interested in hearing what exactly he did to help my friend and understood the majority of it from my Chiropractic background. I knew halfway through that he would heal up with time and antibiotics, and I squeezed Joy's hand lightly, giving her an all-okay nod. It turned out mostly as we had expected. Deep puncture wounds were made by teeth that only three weeks ago housed a pink tongue used to kiss babies and chew table scraps before sleeping the rest of the day or night away. There was some concern about blood loss, but the glue Nancy applied quickly changed the diagnosis from life-threatening to concerning.

"Give him these pills, just as I wrote on the bottle. No running, chasing, or anything else strenuous for at least a week—better if it's two."

"Thank you, Carl," I said, shaking his hand. "I was worried we were going to lose him."

"This one wouldn't let us," he replied, pointing down to Mini, who laid under the operating table the entire time, not making a sound.

We all laughed, petting her, and of course Ringo.

"What do I owe you?" I asked, wanting to get it out of the way before we moved on to something else.

"All of you are our guests and are welcome for the night—unless you're planning on leaving in the dark. You will owe, but not to me."

"I don't understand," I told him.

"The boys back in town collect a 'pass tax,' they call it. Everyone pays unless you sneak around, which won't happen with those trailers you have. We have an agreement of sorts up in these parts, so your pass, once stamped, will get you through the next towns of Fairplay, Alma, and Blue River—a town, not just a river. After that, you will hit Breckenridge. They're, how should I say it, a little hoity-toity up there and have their own rules, I hear. But I do know the Mayor, so it might be worth a name drop."

"So, what's the toll?" I asked.

"Different for everybody. It is used to be $50 per vehicle or $10 per walker, but it's changed since cash money doesn't seem worth the paper it's printed on anymore. I'll help you all out with negotiations tomorrow. We'll figure it out. Now, as promised, my wife is cooking a feast for a small town. I killed a good-sized buck early this morning, so we've got fresh venison. I hope you all are meat-eaters!"

"I would say we're anything-edible eaters, at this point. We've got provisions in the freezers we can use to make up the difference if you need it," I offered.

"Nah, we're good," Carl said. "We have a nice garden down by the water and more deer than we can kill."

"I figured you would have enough city people walking up here, hoping to hunt game," I replied.

"They either don't make it this far up or don't want to pay the tax and head back down to the lake."

"That's where we came from," I noted.

"Really? Then you were lucky to get out of there alive. Some bad things are happening down there, from what we've heard."

"It's different now—under new ownership, you could say," I replied. "Thanks again for your help."

* * * * * * *

Chapter Thirteen ~ Cañon City, Colorado

I let Ringo rest and grabbed the boys to wash up for dinner. Carl and his wife filled our bellies. We returned the favor as best we could, with the ladies giving his lonely wife some girl time and a night of talking about last season's "The Bachelor" or "The Real Housewives of Beverly Hills," and of course "American Idol." Lucy stayed behind, citing a migraine she couldn't shake, and the children were playing board games inside the house. Once the wine started to flow, I overheard the ladies speaking something about "Fifty Shades of..." The men broke off with Scotch and vodka until the ladies borrowed the clear stuff. Vlad and his new lady friend, Anna, sat on the back porch talking, and a few of us went off to look at the map and talk strategy.

* * * *

Mike wanted a small group, and it was just Lonnie, Jake and me in front of Lonnie's truck. using the hood to spread the map over and a flashlight to see in the dark. Mike would head straight back from where we came, bypassing the lake altogether, and find the Baker group. We contemplated telling the Colonel, just in case he was spotted by Ronna, who would surely never forget his face from their tent encounter that seemed like years ago now. We eventually agreed to keep it between us, since he planned to bypass Ronna's group anyway.

"That's why Vlad is not here right now," said Mike. "I don't want him to have information he's kept from the Colonel."

"I'll talk to him," I offered.

"Let's get on the same page here," said Lonnie.

The story to be told by Mike was simple: "He was a bad man and didn't fit with our group. He stole—no, wait a minute; we don't want a thief going there," I pointed out. "The bike was his all along, complete with a Texas plate."

Mike would show up, looking to join the group, taking revenge for us stealing his girlfriend and his child sounded better, before we kicked him out of the group. We didn't want it any more complicated than that, hoping he could figure the rest out on the fly if he had to. He would join them, listen and run up the ranks, only reporting back when he could safely by radio or when he returned to Saddle Ranch sometime before the Battle.

"This intel, if I can get it," said Mike, "might make the end result different. If we don't do this right and wipe them out, we will never be at peace again."

"Agreed," I said, with all of us shaking our heads in agreement. "We should be there in a week or less, I'm hoping."

"We need a rendezvous spot," Mike continued. "Since I'll only be fifteen miles or so away, I could meet you—if they let me keep the bike, that is."

"I have an idea," I said. "Hold on. I'll be right back."

* * * *

I headed over to the makeshift camp.

"Lucy, it's Lance," I called out. "Are you feeling any better?"

I heard her respond with "Mmm, hmm."

"Can you tell me when we'll have the next full moon?" I asked.

There was a pause and a frightened voice from inside the tent said, "I don't know anything about the weather."

Now I paused, straining to hear the other voice whispering to her.

"Okay," I told her. "I'm just going to check on my dog, Ricky, and I'll be back later."

"Thank you," she said in a shaky voice.

I walked away, accenting my steps, and broke into a full run when I got around the trailer. I was out of breath when I reached Lonnie, Jake and Mike, only 50 yards away.

"It's..." I said, holding my side. "It's Lucy. She's in the tent, and I think someone is in there with her. I asked about a full moon, and she said she doesn't know anything about the weather."

"She's the queen of weather," said Jake, grabbing his rifle.

"Exactly. I gave her a clue back that I knew she was in trouble."

"What about the dogs?" asked Lonnie.

"They're both still in the house," I said.

"Okay, let's get this done," he replied. "I want us positioned, so we're shooting away from the house if we have to."

We quickly headed back, covering the tent from the front and one side.

"Come out of the tent now," said Lonnie in his booming cop voice.

There was the sound of a struggle inside and a low male voice accusing her of telling on him.

"You have ten seconds to come out before this goes bad," Mike said, looking flushed.

We all stayed crouched down behind the Bronco, only ten feet from the tent's front, waiting for the gunfire we knew was coming.

"Nine!" Mike started counting, moving around the truck. "Eight...seven...six..."

I would have asked for cover, but I guess he just assumed we would.

The tent door slowly unzipped from the front, with a long-haired man poking his head out.

"Do you boys know who I am?"

Mike grabbed him by his greasy hair, replying, "I don't care!"

"My dad runs things around here," the man said, maybe feeling cocky, Mike thought.

"I'm not from around here," Mike replied. "Now stop talking. Did he hurt you, Lucy?" he asked, poking his head into the tent.

"I don't know," she cried, in a fetal position, her clothes obviously torn.

"Are you going to tell my dad? You're not going to tell my dad, are you?"

"Nope," said Mike, asking me to get Joy. "Your dad won't know a thing about this; that's a promise."

* * * *

I ran to get Joy, as Mike led the man into the woods, down towards the creek. We returned no more than ten minutes later, with Joy crawling into Lucy's tent and zipping the front door closed.

"Where's Mike?" I asked Lonnie.

He put up his hands in a classic "Beats me!" gesture. Jake's old friend, our host, ran over, wanting to know every detail. We explained what we knew and his face was growing more concerned with each word.

"He's right. His dad does run things around here. Where is he now?"

"Down by the creek with Mike, last we saw," said Lonnie.

"What kind of Colorado man doesn't know how to swim?" asked Mike, emerging from the trees.

"Where is he?" asked our host. "You didn't hurt him, did you?"

"He took advantage of one of our ladies and, as I said, he couldn't swim."

"Jake, I need to talk to you," his friend Carl said, pulling him aside. "I'm not sure what happened here, and yeah that guy is trouble but he's the only son of a ruthless man who controls who goes where around here, including past the barricade. Did your guy kill him? Please tell me the answer is no."

"If I know Mike like I think I do, your guy isn't coming back, ever," Jake replied.

"Well, I'm going to need to know for sure, one way or another, and it has to be tonight."

"Mike?" asked Jake. "Is the guy still alive?"

"Nope," he replied casually, like he'd been asked if he had a lighter.

"Can you show me where he is, so my friend here can figure out what to do next?"

"Follow me," Mike said, heading to the creek.

* * * *

We all walked up the bank, next to a large pool that I would have loved to fish, to see the intruder facedown in the water, with his torso on land, as an anchor, I guessed. Our host rolled him over, shining a flashlight into his face, with no response. He checked for a pulse and found the same.

"Okay," Carl sighed. "Man... This is not good, Jake. You guys are just passing through, but we live here. Let me think for a minute. I'm guessing he came out here alone—doesn't have any friends I know of. Let's fan out by the road behind your trailers. We're looking for an old truck or four-wheeler that shouldn't be hard to spot. Mike, can you reach into his front pants pocket for a key?"

"Sure thing," he responded, pulling out two on the same ring.

* * * *

Finding his truck was the easy part. Carrying the nearly 300-pound man up to it took all four of us, minus Jake's old friend, who didn't want his prints anywhere near the man.

"Sorry, guys, about this, but I don't want his truck tracks across my property for obvious reasons."

"Hold on. I'll grab his hat," I said. "I'm so poor I can't even pay attention," it read. "Oh, that's classy," I said, reading out loud the saying written across his baseball cap.

"A real ladies' man," said Lonnie.

"Just to clarify, Mike, when they find him are they going to see any gunshot or knife wounds?" asked Carl.

"None of those, but he might be missing a tooth."

"That's all right. It happens when you end up in a river up here. The one you all crossed coming up here is the Arkansas. At least a few fishermen end up floating in it facedown every summer. Most are tourists, though, and don't know any better. This one here knows better, but he drinks his breakfast so I don't think anyone will find it impossible that he drowned chasing down a snagged line or monster trout. He's got to go in up above the gorge, though."

"You mean the Royal Gorge?" I asked. "With the bridge and like a thousand-foot drop to the river below?"

"That's the one," replied Carl, "and it just up the road."

"I went there as a kid." I added. "An incredible place"—only now wondering how I could have a casual conversation over a body, even that of a bad man.

"Okay. If you all can follow me in his truck?" asked Carl.

"You all ride with him," Mike told us. "Just in case I want to be the only one in this man's truck."

"Are you sure?" I asked. "I don't mind."

"I do," he replied flatly.

"Okay," continued Carl. "Follow us. It will be bumpy, but we have to go a ways around the barricade. Leave his pistol in the truck, too, just like it is now. His daddy never could get him to carry it. Also, don't adjust the seat, mirrors, or anything else."

* * * *

Joy was told only that we would be back soon. She didn't know any more than that and thankfully didn't ask.

The time was nearly 10 p.m. and we didn't run into anyone on the back road up.

"By the way, Lance. Looks like your dog is going to be okay."

"Thank you, Doc," I said, hearing it for the second time but feeling just as relieved.

"We get attached to them, for sure," added Carl. "Our Maggie passed on peacefully just a few weeks back at the ripe old age of 15. I haven't had the heart to get another, but nowadays it pays dividends to have a good canine at your side."

"That it does," added Jake.

"There's a small turnoff and a short trail down to the river," said Carl. "We'll have to stage it just a little but don't want to overdo it. I want to be in and out in ten minutes, guys, so everyone gets a small job."

* * * *

We parked in the empty turnoff, with Jake's friend pointing precisely where Mike should park the truck.

"Lance, take this pole," said Carl, grabbing it out of the deceased's truck bed with gloves. "Use a flashlight if you need to. Cast across the river and get the lure stuck. I mean stuck good. Then dunk the pole in the water and set it on the bank. Once I'm out, lock the reel, set the drag high and toss the pole in the river's middle. He always fished with too heavy line. Everyone knows, so it should hold the pole in the water until tomorrow, at least.

"Mike, I need the keys in the glove box and the parking brake on. Leave the doors unlocked. Don't ask me why. Then help us get this man down to the water but carried not dragged. We lay him face down in the water, and I'll get him out to the middle. Nobody else gets wet."

With the man floating, the Doc dragged him by the collar as far out as he could risk before giving him one final shove towards the middle.

"Guys, I need you to carry me back up to the truck. I don't want any muddy tracks up the embankment.

"Am I missing anything?" Carl asked, as they all piled back into his truck.

"No," each man said.

"I know one thing," I said, both nervous and looking behind us.

"What's that?" asked Carl.

The lights were coming up behind us.

"Oh no, that's not good," Jake's friend said, as the lights turned on—red after blue, red after blue. "It's Gus."

"Who's that?" I asked.

"State trooper—the ruler of this land up here now, and that guy's father. Let me do all the talking," he said, nervously rolling down his window.

The state trooper recognized the doctor's personalized plates, reading PETVET3. He approached slowly on the driver's side, tapping his flashlight on the truck's top cab.

"Window's open," said Carl.

"I know," replied Gus, shining his light through the cab of the truck. "You boys out for a Sunday drive," he said as a statement.

"No, sir. It's Saturday, and I was just showing my friends around town."

"You seen my boy?" he asked, looking at his truck. "He didn't make it home for dinner."

"No, sir. Just saw his truck parked here and thought it was kind of late for fishing, so I thought I'd check in on him."

"Have you?"

"No, sir. Not yet."

"Just been driving around, the five of you, huh?"

"That's right, sir. Just some friends up from Pueblo for the weekend."

"You're wet," he said, shining the flashlight at each of us. "It's only you, looks like. Stay here until I get back," he instructed, heading to his son's truck and quickly rifling through it. "Don't move," he called back, heading down the embankment.

"Oh no," Carl said, panicked. "Jake, what do I do?"

"Punch it," he replied, followed by tires kicking up dirt and rocks, finally catching traction on the pavement.

"What have I done?!" he yelled.

"What's the fastest way back?" I asked.

"What have I done?!" he asked again.

"What's the fastest way back?!" I said again, raising my voice.

"What...fast way back to my home?"

He hit the brakes hard and banked to the left, throwing all of us without seatbelts into dashes and doors. I felt a lump rising on my head's right side, where I hit the back-door window. He took the side dirt road at 52 miles per hour, according to the speedometer I could see with blurred vision.

"What's the plan, Carl?" asked Jake.

"I don't know, but we can't stay. She and I need to leave town. By morning he will come by with his men, and when they find his son dead I'll be locked up, or worse. You should head out, too, if you don't want trouble."

"Where will you go?" asked Jake.

"I don't know. Maybe east to Pueblo, but he'll find us there for sure, so I don't know. My wife...she's going to be devastated."

"Carl," Mike spoke up. "I'm sorry about this mess."

We all looked at him, surprised at the first time any of us heard him apologize for anything.

"Put it on me. I'll confess and take the punishment," Mike said.

"No. You protected a woman from a sick man. He tried that with my wife a few years back when I was at work, and I didn't have the guts to make him pay for it. Now he has, and I'm not throwing you under the bus for that piece of crap. That's why I pushed him into the river. I wanted to be the last one to touch him before he went straight to hell."

"You'll come with us," said Lonnie. "You, your wife and little girl will be a part of our group—an equal part."

"All agreed?" he asked, confident none of us would object.

"Agreed!" we all replied.

****

Chapter Fourteen ~ Cañon City, Colorado

Pulling into his driveway, most of our group was there. Lonnie gathered everyone, asking for a quick pack-up to leave out in an hour, while Carl spoke to his wife. Thirty minutes later, Carl announced he could add his truck and small utility trailer to the group. He pulled up with it partially packed, asking for help with food, firearms and his veterinary supplies.

We all pitched in, adding Ringo and Mini back on our vehicle, where I could keep a good eye on them. Carl asked Jake to take a quick walk with him before heading out. They walked around the main house and down by the river, flashlights lighting the way.

"We've built a life here," began Carl. "This community is what we know, and Izabella doesn't have many friends, but she has us. My dad lies in the town cemetery and our dog in the yard. I hadn't fished the creek on our property once since it happened, so I could harvest the fish when things got really bad. We're leaving everything we have built."

"I know," replied Jake. "Lance and Tina—it's a long story—but they both helped me, Nancy and Danny pack up the very first day and leave our home with only what we could carry in backpacks and wheel barrels. We have been refugees ever since. But we're headed for something. Something better, I hope, but not without sacrifice."

"It's 1:15 a.m., and we had better make it up to Breckenridge before dawn because things between here and there won't be too friendly by morning. Give me ten minutes and we'll be ready," Carl added, slipping away from the truck carrying his wife and daughter.

"Do you need any help?" asked Jake.

"No, buddy. This I have to do alone."

* * * *

He disappeared towards the barn, waving his flashlight both inside and out, and the same for the house. It wasn't even five minutes before Jake saw the first flames rise up from the barn...and only minutes later from the main house.

"What are you doing?" asked Jake when Carl returned.

"Unless you're going to kill everyone in town who's afraid of Gus, this has to be done. It's a distraction and will be put out in a matter of hours, mark my words. I won't have that SOB's father moving from his tear-down house into mine. I'll lead us up to the barricade, and we'll figure out the rest from there."

Carl led the group up the winding road, with Mike following on the Indian.

Lonnie got Carl hooked up with a radio, and he called out the possible scenarios.

"The guys in the barricade will be two or three, at the most. They are likely sleeping off a hangover. We need to bust through the barricade or surprise and overpower them. Mike, you're going the other way so you can just keep riding."

"Surprise is my middle name," Mike called over his radio. "Let me pull ahead when we're a quarter-mile out, and on my signal, everyone goes through."

"We can help with this, Mike," I called.

"I know, but I need to do this."

Mike passed us, the Indian with a full tank and 150 miles to his destination, with almost 100 fuel miles to spare over that. I'm not sure how he did it, and we would discuss it later amongst us, but twenty minutes later Mike called on the radio for us to come through. He talked to Sheila and Javi for a few minutes, and lastly Lonnie through his open window. I hopped on the truck bed to join in.

"Did you kill them, Mike?" asked Lonnie.

Not this time, boss. They just got tied up a bit is all. I even let them keep their rifles," he added, handing Lonnie two handfuls of bullets.

"Be careful, old friend," said Lonnie.

Mike handed Lonnie his radio, badge and pistol.

"Whatever happens, don't lose this," he said, handing me a thin wallet from his front pocket. "Open it," he told me, and I did, expecting it to look like mine with old credit and debit cards, a half-punched card from a smoothie place, and receipts from God knows where. I found one driver's license and three pictures—one of his mother, brother and sister.

"This is the most valuable possession I own," he said, looking straight into my eyes.

"I will guard it with my life," I told him.

"We got sidetracked with Lucy," he continued, "so I don't have an exact date but I remember the last full moon being about two weeks ago. So, in another couple of weeks, when the moon is full, I'll meet you guys at midnight on the Valley's northern border for an update. After that, I'll either stay or return to them and fight from the inside."

"You don't want your gun?" asked Lonnie.

"No, they will just take it from me anyway. Show this all the way up to Breckenridge," he added, handing Lonnie a blue ticket with the words "Paid x6" on it.

"Will do, friend, and be careful."

* * * *

With that, Mike rode east, not looking back. We headed unobstructed through the open barricade, winding up past the Gorge. I hoped we wouldn't pass a police presence on the fisherman's turnoff and relaxed just a bit as Carl called out "on your left" over the radio, without explanation. Only the four of us would ever know, and the turnoff was empty—even the truck was gone. The roads were clear, with vehicles pushed off to the sides, probably weeks ago now.

I had forgotten how peaceful it felt traveling at night. As a young man, I would go home once a year in the summer, driving from Southern California to Saddle Ranch. I would leave at four in the afternoon and always started my trip with Tom Petty's "Full Moon Fever" *cassette*. Yes, it was that long ago—not eight-track long, but long enough. Coffee was my constant companion, driving through the Colorado mountains in the middle of the night with windows down.

* * * *

We traveled the 74 miles to Fairplay in just over four hours, including a quick bathroom break and not seeing anyone on or off the road. As advertised, our little blue ticket got us through with only a few questions of how many vehicles, occupants, and if we were only passing through. The next leg was easy, heading north on SH-9, the 22 miles to Breckenridge passing quickly through the towns of Alma and Blue River.

"Break time," Lonnie called, two miles out of town. He gathered a few of us, including Carl and Jake, for a pow-wow.

"Carl, I'm guessing you have been through here before."

"Yep, we ski up here every winter and almost bought a place last year."

"I've been through here a bunch of times," said Jake, with me saying the same.

"It's a straight shot through town, up to Interstate 70. We can detour around if we have to, but not far off the main highway, not with the trailers at least," said Carl. "I know the Mayor; he used to fish with my dad nearly every-other weekend in the summer. Still, it won't guarantee us free passage, but it might help. Can I lead on this one?" he asked Lonnie.

"Sure, I'll be second in line behind you."

Steve took over Mike's driving responsibilities in the rear vehicle.

* * * * * * *

Chapter Fifteen ~ Breckenridge, Colorado

"Jake and Lance, come on up," called Carl when we hit the barricade.

"I see what you mean," I said, looking at the most impressive blockade we had seen so far, including two old WWII tanks.

"Are those T-34s?" asked Jake. "The old Russian ones?"

"Yeah," replied Carl. "Why a tourist ski town needs two tanks beats me, but they belong to the Mayor. He bought them at auction ten or so years ago, and he and my dad would race them outside of town."

"Do they still run?" I asked.

"Far as I know. They did a few years back, for sure," he replied.

"Name's Carl," he said to the guards as we walked up.

"So?"

"I need to talk to the Mayor."

"That's not going to happen," one of the guards said. "Now turn around, the lot of you, and head back down the mountain."

"I'm Doc Mason's son, and I need to speak with the Mayor."

"I don't give a rat's..."

"Hold on a minute," said another man from inside, clearly his superior.

"Did you say you're Carl Mason?"

"Yes, sir."

"You folks hold on for a few, and I'll get hold of the Mayor. Where you headed, by the way?"

"Down the other side—Fort Collins area," I interjected.

"Huh... Going the long way, aren't you?"

"Trying to stay off I-25 is all," I replied.

"Yeah, can't say as I blame you for that. All right. Hold tight."

The other guard returned. "The Mayor won't be up for a couple more hours, but I'm sure he'll want to talk with you."

We waited without a word for more than two and a half hours, and I eventually took a seat on the hood of Lonnie's trunk, taking pressure off my leg.

* * * *

"Carl Mason, how the hell are you?" came the voice of a short boisterous man of maybe three hundred pounds and round as a beach ball.

"Good morning, Mr. Mayor," Carl replied, shaking his hand.

"What brings you up my way? You headed out of town?"

"Just looking for some new opportunities is all."

"And them?" he asked, pointing over Jake and me to the caravan.

"Yes, sir. We're all a group of sorts."

“Hmm. I hear you’re headed over the pass, down to Fort Collins.”

“Yes, that’s right.”

“Do you think these trailers are going to make it down the backside of Trail Ridge Road without eating up your trannys or brakes?”

“That’s the plan. We will see, I guess,” replied Carl.

“I told your pops I would keep an eye out for you, and I’ve done a piss-poor job, son. I’m sorry about that.”

“No worries, sir. I’m a grown man.”

“Now, that lawman down in your little town, I hear he’s looking for you. I heard there was a fire a few hours back at your place, and his son has gone missing. Do you know anything about that? On second thought, don’t answer that. I never liked that poor excuse for law enforcement, and his son was no better. The boy got cross with me more than once over one of our girls in town. They didn’t want to press charges, but I made it clear that he and his daddy were not welcome here once everything changed. He won’t know you came through here, if that’s what you’re worried about.”

“Thanks, Mayor. Those tanks—I remember you racing those with my dad out in the woods.”

“Russian T-34s. Yep, they still run like they’re only twenty years old...or maybe thirty!” he said, laughing. “Kind of makes a statement to anyone coming into town, don’t you think?”

“I do,” said Carl. “I know they run, but do they shoot? I mean, can they fire?”

“Well, now,” the Mayor said, lowering his voice. “They run when you buy them, but they only fire aftermarket, if you follow me.”

“What’s the weight?” I blurted out, before even introducing myself.

“Thirty-two tons and they still do close to 40 miles per hour, Mr...?”

“Lance, sir. Good to meet you.”

I gave Jake a look, and he returned a raised eyebrow.

"Have you ever thought of selling one?" I asked, getting looks from everyone around me.

"Never would have considered it before. But I've gained a few pounds since the lights went out," he said, patting his stomach, "and it's not easy getting inside one of those things anymore."

"What would you ask for something like that?" I said, not entirely sure where I was headed with the question.

"That's a good question—at least a hundred grand before the day. Now I wouldn't take five million cash for one."

"Oh," I said. "I guess I get it."

It was a long shot, I thought, *but had to try*.

"Hell, I wouldn't take a billion dollars cash for it now," he continued. "Paper money is worthless around here, and everywhere else, from what I hear."

"Out of curiosity," I said, with a sliver of hope still, "what would you take in trade for one?"

"Guns...or maybe a thousand lobster tails—the big ones from Australia!"

We all laughed at that, with the realization we may never have another one.

"What kinds of guns and how many?" I pressed, still not sure if we really needed one, how to operate it, or if we could get it transported to Saddle Ranch.

"That's a good question and the answer I don't rightly know. I can tell you that I haven't met any man or outfit that could make a deal like that so far. Are you that sort of man, Lance?"

"I might be...we might be...but I would need to talk with our group to see if it's even a possibility."

"Why on God's earth would you ever need a tank anyway, son?"

"The Great Battle for the Valley, where I grew up," I responded with a robotic delivery. "It's coming, whether we are prepared or not."

"Well, okay then," replied the Mayor. "Make me an offer for this one here I call Bert."

I was suddenly regretting, or maybe just questioning, my motive for such a weapon of destruction. Was there some childhood need to return home a hero with a piece of machinery that may save the Valley, or something else entirely? Truth be told, I didn't ever look at the official inventory Lucy and Tina had taken of the firearms. I guessed Vlad may have a pretty good idea, but thus far our weapons had been the gateway to safe passage that had gotten us this far.

"What do you think?" I asked Jake, as we headed back to our group to talk. "Am I crazy for even asking about it?"

"You are crazy, but not about this," he joked. "I don't think they will go for it, but no, I don't think you're nuts to want something like that. Working properly, it could be a game-changer in the right scenario."

"Yeah, okay," I responded. "Let's see what they say."

* * * *

I initially thought of just getting a few people together with Lonnie, Vlad, Joy and Nancy—then figured it would be a monumental decision that all adults should vote for or against. Lucy volunteered to watch the kids run up and back down the hillside just beyond our caravan, giving the rest of us time to discuss our options. I told them what I knew of the tank, asking Carl to give his input about how rugged it was when his dad ran it through the woods.

"It's good, that one," said Vlad. "Russian-made and still running almost 75 years later—with some newer parts, of course."

I retold the story of the Great Battle we knew was coming, which was a complete surprise for Carl and his wife, as well as a few others who had blocked it out of their minds.

"The first thing to discuss," I began, "is if this option is even one worth considering. If not, we move on now. And if so, we get a relief for Lucy to agree on what we could offer in trade without depleting our inventory completely."

Kat and her sister, Anna, offered to watch the kids after a preliminary vote to see what we had to spare. Lucy gave me the inventory sheet but did not want to address the group. Joy wouldn't let me ask any questions about what happened to her, only telling me she and the other ladies would help Lucy work through it, and she would never leave her pistol inside the vehicle again.

The inventory was a wide range of makes and models, not including what we all carry on our persons. The count was roughly 170 pistols, 135 hunting rifles of varying calibers, 78 ARs, about 100 .22s, and 80 or so shotguns in 20- and 12-gauge. I was surprised by the count coming out of only one gun shop. The ones I had been to before seemed to have less than 100 total all combined.

"So, before we get too far down the road, I need a raise of hands for anyone who thinks we could use a machine like that," I said.

Roughly half of the adults present raised their hands. There was small chatter amongst the others before Steve spoke up.

"How do we know it even works?"

"It did last time I saw it," said Carl. "The Mayor and my dad used to race around the woods on them, but the last time was a few years back."

More chatter ensued.

"Does it shoot?" Steve asked.

"I think so," I said. "But it's something we need to find out for sure."

"I want to see it in action," Joy replied, standing up. She was a part of the first group in support of it, but I saw where she was headed.

"Yes, me too! Let's see it," echoed most of the rest.

"Okay, assuming it's what we hope it is and we can safely transport it across the mountains, I vote we offer 10% of our weapons, with ammo for each, in exchange for a fully functional machine, fueled and armed."

"That doesn't sound like much," said Steve, adding it up in his head. "What's the cost on that thing—dollar-wise, I mean?"

"Zero now," I replied, but about $100,000 a month ago, according to the Mayor. You can take that with a grain of salt."

"So, ten percent gets roughly a 50% value—dollars to dollars, I mean."

"Sure, that sounds about right," I agreed, "but a town like this probably doesn't need two, and I doubt there's a seller's market for these things now. There are still a lot of ifs, so I'll give everyone a few minutes to discuss before we decide on the next step."

Minutes later, most were on board to at least see what it could do without committing to an offer.

"Let me talk to him," offered Carl. "I'll be back."

* * * *

"Good news," he said, returning after a few minutes. "He's going to give us a preview. He wants us to all drive across the barricade to the inside first. He said he could have his mechanic demonstrate for any three. Any takers?" I wanted to go but was willing to give someone else the opportunity of a lifetime. "No, takers?" asked Carl. "Going once...going twice..."

"I'll go," said Joy, squeezing my hand.

"Second that," I called out.

"Me too," said Jake—unless you want to?" he asked his wife. "No?"

"Okay," said Carl. "Then you three follow me."

I felt like a kid getting his first boat ride—or maybe bumper cars was more like it.

"My mechanic will take you for a ride, and only if you like it will we talk," said the Mayor. "Sound fair?"

"Yes, sir, Mr. Mayor," I said for all of us. "But, you're not coming along?"

"As I said, the past few weeks have caught up to my midsection; I'm not sure I could get in or out of one. We won't get ahead of ourselves, so my guy will just show you the basics of operation for now."

* * * *

"What year is this?" I asked, as we walked up to the front side.

"1940—look here," the mechanic said. "Every one of these has a code. The first two numbers are the year made, the next two the month, followed by the date, and finally which number produced out of the factory."

"Is that last number per week, month, or ever?" I asked.

"I'm not sure about that. It's a good question, though."

Inside wasn't what I was expecting, feeling more like a cramped submarine hull than the H1 Hummer feel I had imagined.

"Is this cool or what?" said Jake, once inside. "I bet this thing burns a lot of fuel."

"Sure does," said the mechanic, sliding inside. "Five hundred horsepower and goes maybe 200 kilometers on a tank. But it's a game-changer, even when you don't use the big gun—if you get in a bad scrape, that is. You folks planning on one of those?"

"Yes, unfortunately we are," I said, not caring to sugarcoat or avoid the question. It was the truth, and not talking about it didn't change anything.

"Well, unless you're an army, one is all you need; that's why I'm keeping one here, either way," said the Mayor, climbing back down a ladder put on the side of Bert.

"For that reason alone," he said, pointing to the men outside the security barrier that we couldn't see. "That man and his goons run Carl's...well, his old town now, I guess. And

I'm sure they have questions about his son gone missing. Maybe even found him by now, floating in the river."

The men were not politely told to hold on until the Mayor was ready to speak to them.

"So, you all aren't that friendly, I hear," I said, gauging myself.

"I'm okay with most towns north of us, and even west, but those on the south never had anything good come out of them except for Carl's family. His beautiful wife used to be a resident right here, went to our high school. Her mother still has those same good looks to this very day, if you can believe that. And his dad, of course, who taught me truly how to fish. Her momma, working breakfast at the diner, makes a man want to get up early and get his fill, and I do. Anyway, you all get going before I have a mortar round put into that state trooper's front grill—the one who just showed up over there."

"Fine by me," I said, with Joy and Jake remaining uncharacteristically quiet.

* * * *

Working our way down from the top of the turret, we got seated and ready for instructions. The ride was bumpy and the tracks mechanical, but it was honestly one of the best experiences I had ever had. Our boys were going to give us grief for going without them, that was a fact. We were taken on a dirt road in the woods and through a shallow stream before ending up back at the inside barrier.

Heading back to the barricade, the Mayor could be seen arguing with the trooper and not giving up an inch. We pulled up to the front, as he was pointing his finger and shouting, motioning to his tank operator to swivel the turret to face the trooper's car and made a loud gesture of counting down from ten.

"Nine...eight...seven..."

"Now, wait a minute. I'm just here to talk with Carl is all."

"Not in my town," the Mayor replied. "Where was I? Seven...six...five..."

"All right," said the trooper, now standing away from his vehicle. That's quite enough. Just give me Carl, and we'll leave peacefully."

"His daddy and I were good friends, as you no doubt have heard, and I'm not sending him out. You keep interrupting me," said the Mayor. "I should already be at one, but I'll start back at five! Five...four...three..."

"All right...I...all right," said the trooper. "But if we find my boy anything but alive and well, I'll be back. That there is a promise," he spat, gesturing to his men to turn around.

"That there is why it's good to have a Bert," the Mayor said aloud.

"He will be back," said Jake, "at least that is what he said. What then?"

"Well, we either have two tanks, or one and all of the firearms we got in trade from you folks, to help them make a better choice. Don't matter much either way to me. Make sense?"

"Yes, sir," replied Jake.

"How would we trailer one of these?" I asked.

"Not on one of yours," he replied. "But if we strike a fair deal, I'll throw one in that will carry the weight."

"Why the name 'Bert'?" I asked.

"That's a good question. All I know is the guy who sold it to me said the soldiers named this one Bert. Even carved the name into the big gun. I figured if it was good enough for them, by God, who was I to go changing it?"

"That makes sense to me. Hello, Bert," I said, patting the big guy on the track.

Lonnie, Jake, Joy and I made the final deal we were hoping for, with both sides deeming they got the best deal they could have made.

The Mayor scouted out a trailer to carry the metal monster down the mountain and threw in an old hulk of a truck he named "The Beast." He cautioned that it might not make it much past the destination. "It's strictly a get-to-where-you're-going truck," he added, "and nothing more."

* * * *

Vlad and Sheila spent the rest of the day learning the mechanics and basic maintenance of the machine.

“The key with these things,” said the mechanic, “is not to put too many miles on them.”

“I think we’re good on that,” replied Vlad. “I’m guessing it will be an effective deterrent or close-quarter fighting machine.”

“So, no joy rides?” asked the Mayor.

“Unfortunately not,” replied Vlad, laughing. “Well, maybe one or two for the kiddos.”

“Can you imagine the day we roll up to Saddle Ranch with this tank?!” I said to Joy, not even trying to hide my excitement. “I was worried about bringing everyone with us and showing up without a big contribution. Now we have weapons and what some might call an ‘attitude corrector.’”

We spent the night inside the protected town in typical fashion. Vlad and Sheila had a few final questions for the mechanic, and we planned to move on by noon the following day.

* * * *

With Shane driving the truck and Airstream trailer, Aiden volunteered to command The Beast. Saying our good-byes, we headed north towards Silverthorne. There weren’t more free passes from here, as far as the Mayor knew. “Just lead with the tank at each crossing, and I’ll bet you will sail right through,” he suggested. We all thought that was good advice, agreeing it would be unlikely to be overpowered, at least before reaching Saddle Ranch.

It felt good to be on the road again. I never imagined it would take this long to travel what used to take us 16 hours on a family trip. I, and most of us, took that for granted—not only the speed of travel but the level of safety we had all become accustomed to in this country. Sure, there were wars going on every year. Still, they were “over there” somewhere...anywhere but here. Yes, there was famine. Still, it was somewhere else; of course, there were people afraid to walk down their own street in the daylight, but that was “over there” somewhere...anywhere but here. I had lived in rough parts of town as a young adult, but no matter how bad it seemed, there were no rockets exploding near my apartment or soldiers looking to take me away to God knows where. Now there was all that, and my children, everyone’s children, would bear witness.

"They, the children, are going to age more in one year than we have in a lifetime," I told Jake and Vlad, as we pulled out for another stint on the road.

"I think they already have," replied Jake. "Our only hope is to hide them away in a protected place to grow up, maybe not like before but without the daily fear of what's next, like we have now."

"Obviously, I don't have any children yet," said Vlad, with a who-knows hand gesture and nod to his new, maybe girlfriend in the Airstream trailer. "But if, or when, I do I will give them the best life to be had. Mark my words, comrades. Their best life was not before the day; it is yet to come. A simple life with family and friends at the forefront, not just weekends and a week or two each year for a vacation that costs too much and ends up too short. Tell me I'm wrong about your children now, Lance. It's okay. Tell me."

"I'm not sure what you're asking?"

"Tell me you don't know them better now over the past few weeks, even though you spend most of your time up on this trailer with Jake and me. Tell me you knew them better before than for all the days they were here."

"I guess I can't," I said. "I know them better now, but it's raw, primal—even getting down to the core through physical and emotional pain and triumphs a gladiator could be proud of. It's a full circle. We're coming full circle, and it stings, it bites. It is heavenly and exciting all at once."

"Ah, yes, that's it! We are alive! Feel it, taste it, bleed it, live it! We are alive!" Vlad called out, bouncing off the mountaintops. "We are alive!"

****

Chapter Sixteen ~ Headed to Silverthorne, Colorado

"Silverthorne is about 15 miles up," said Lonnie over the radio. "We got a late start today, and there is a lake just southeast of town, called Dillon Reservoir. Hopefully, we can catch some fish and filter water, plus wash up a bit if all are agreed."

"Good for us on the trailer," I called out, with both Jake and Vlad nodding in agreement.

Others called the same over the radio, and in only one hour we were at the south end of the lake. Lonnie called for a quick meeting at a bluff overlooking the beautiful mountain lake.

"The town of Silverthorne shares this body of water with Dillon to the east and Frisco to the southwest. There is an inlet to the east that appears to be our best bet for some privacy—right down there for those who can see it," he said.

Those of us on the trailer scanned the inlet, with only a few small campsites to be seen. "They look harmless to me," I said aloud, counting six clustered near each other.

"I'm sure they will mind their own business," I added fifteen minutes later as we pulled slowly past them.

"I would say you're right; they look spooked," pointed out Vlad as men and women ran around, scooping up their children and supplies. Most stumbled, nearly tripping over each other to gather their belongings and move down the road.

"That's not what I was expecting..." said Jake, trailing off when I pointed to the children.

"It's The Beast they are pointing to—I mean Bert," I said. "Hold up, Lonnie. I want to talk to these folks for a minute."

"Are you sure?" he replied. "Bad things tend to happen when we stop."

"Yeah, just a minute. I'll be quick."

We slowed to a stop, and all could hear the squeaking brakes of the old truck in the back.

"Excuse me," I called out to a woman gathering her children in a panic. "Excuse me, ma'am. Can I talk to you for a minute?"

"We've got this," said Joy over the radio, opening the door of their vehicle and stepping out with Nancy and Lucy.

I couldn't hear what they told the woman, but minutes later she seemed no longer frightened, and the small groups returned to reset their camps.

* * * *

The men got together, deciding to give the ladies a break for the day. Not just a "we-will-watch-the-kids day but a full-on Next-World pampered afternoon." We guys got a plan together and presented it to them at 2 p.m.

"In appreciation of all that you do for us and the kids," I announced, "we offer you all an afternoon of leisure. I'm guessing, but certainly not suggesting, most of you would be interested in bathing first? We will be serving mimosas in about an hour, thanks to Mel's donation— chilled, of course—paired with Tang. It's not quite old school, I know, but it's close. There will be a wine bar set up on the trailer over there, with various whites and reds available from Mel and Tammy's private collection. Vlad has offered to tend bar—no tips necessary but a good joke is appreciated, if you have one."

"Woo hoo!" was the general response, with a few women whispering amongst themselves, giving Kat's sister Anna a tease.

"We have the kiddos and a very special dinner, compliments of Carl's friend, the Mayor," I continued. "And before anyone asks, it's not fish—maybe for breakfast, though, if we catch some. So, please enjoy your afternoon and let us know if you need anything."

* * * *

We put the fishing lines out half-heartedly, as our freezers were full, and we had promised something else for dinner.

"We'll set up a smoker," said Steve and Jim, "for the fish, if we catch any. Never hurts to have some jerky on the road."

"I'll coordinate the fishing for the kiddos," said Carl, with Jake offering to help.

Lonnie sat up on the trailer for the two-hour security shift we would all pitch in on. The women finished bathing, with only a few casual looks from other campers, before being scolded by their wives. I helped serve the mimosas, glancing over at Lonnie, who was talking to a man and a child.

"All good?" I called out.

"Yep, no worries," Lonnie called back.

* * * *

The first round of the fizzy Tang went straightaway, and Vlad was quickly taking wine orders, like a real bartender.

"You've got fast hands," said Kate's sister, Anna, joking.

"You didn't think I only knew about guns, did you?" he fired back.

"No, I guess not," she replied, asking for a glass of Chardonnay.

"You should have seen me tend bar with two legs!" Vlad added, getting a smile but no words from Anna.

"Hey, Lance," called out Lonnie. "Bring Hudson up here when you get a chance."

I found him fishing and nearly had to drag him away from his pole. The fish were biting, and the kids were enjoying the casual afternoon.

"Yes, sir, Mr. Lonnie. I heard you asked for me," said Hudson.

"Yes, I did," he replied. "Hold on a second."

Lonnie whispered his intentions to me, asking if I minded my son getting a gift of sorts.

"Sure," I said aloud. "He would love it!"

"Hudson," started Lonnie. "Do you remember what I told you I would keep an eye out for?"

"A red motorcycle?"

"You sure have a good memory. You see that man walking away over there?"

"Yes, sir," replied Hudson.

"He and I just made a deal. How about you get down and look under the tarp over there." Lonnie pointed under the trailer. "It's not red, but it's the real deal," he whispered to me.

Hudson carefully pulled the tarp back.

"It's okay, son," I told him. "It's not a puppy. You can pull hard."

Hudson's face lit up, eyeing the blue Yamaha PW-50 that he had a picture of on his wall since he was two.

"What did this run you?" I asked Lonnie.

"My watch."

"It didn't even run," I said.

"I know. The guy swore he could fix it when the power came back on."

"That could be a while," I replied.

"That's what I told him, but he swore he was getting the better end of the deal."

"Okay then. What do you say, Hudson?"

"Thank you, Mr. Lonnie!"

"It runs too. The man started it right up and it comes with a kid's helmet—not sure of the size, though."

"What do you think, Hud?" I asked him. "Should we let all the kids use it?"

I knew the answer before asking the question. No kid I had ever met shared their toys more than him.

"Sure, Daddy-o! I love to share."

The children all gathered around for basic instructions. As many would argue, the beginner bike was the best and easy to operate, once they had their balance.

There is no gear shifter or clutch—just the throttle, front and back brakes, and a kickstart facing backward that an adult, and most kids over age seven, could kick. A few low-speed crashes later, they were all racing around inside the circle.

Lonnie insisted on grilling tonight. It would have to be propane, not as classic as charcoal or a wood smoker, but it was still a formidable fine dining machine in the right hands.

"We have steak on the menu—the very best fillets!" he announced to everyone.

"Is that deer meat?" asked one of the kids.

"No. It's all cow, and the best-tasting part of it. We're also grilling vegetables and have a fresh killer salad, so there should be something for everyone's taste," he added.

I took my guard shift, watching the lake party from atop Bert.

Jax sat with me, just for some Dad time, I guess, or maybe it was just cool for a young boy to sit on top of a tank. Either way, it was moments like this I would always cherish. He wanted to ask Lonnie a question but was too embarrassed.

"Hey, Lonnie," I called out, not giving him a chance to back out. "Jax here has a question for you."

"Sure, little man. I'll be over in a few minutes. I don't want to overcook these fine steaks."

Minutes later, he had them pulled off the grill.

"I've got to rest these cuts," he said. "How do you like your steak, Jax?"

"Medium-rare, with a shake of salt and nothing else," he called back.

"Really? Is he joking?" Lonnie asked me.

"Nope, that's how he likes it, and it's his favorite thing to eat," I replied.

"It's my favorite supper ever!" Jax added, barely containing his excitement.

"That boy knows his meat," he said, walking over.

"Uh, Mr. Lonnie...I was just...if we had any extras could we maybe give a little to those people over there?" he said, pointing across the shoreline to the group of maybe twenty we saw coming in.

"Maybe," he replied. "We do have extra, I know. But I'm not sure how much."

"I understand, but I would like to give them mine at least, if it's okay. It's not much, but it might help a little bit."

I put my hand on Jax's shoulder. "You're a generous boy. I'll give up mine too," I called out to Lonnie. Besides, I swallowed a big June bug when we were driving—I'm not really hungry," I joked. "But seriously, me too."

"All right. All right. Don't go getting crazy on me," replied Lonnie. "There's enough to feed them also, I suppose—just don't ask me for steak and eggs for breakfast."

"I won't," I told him, laughing.

"Can I go tell them, Daddy?" asked Jax.

"I think I should be the one. My shift is over in fifteen minutes, and then I will go."

"Please, Daddy. Can I be the one to go?"

"They seem harmless," said Jake, walking up. "I'll tag along if you're okay with it, Lance."

"Yeah, okay. Let's go at shift change. You'll do the talking," I told Jax.

"Yes, sir. I'll try," he replied.

* * * *

Shane took over on shift, and Jake and I walked over with Jax to the campers.

"Do you have to bring your rifle, Daddy?"

"Yes, son, I do...always now. Right, Jake?"

"That's how it works, Jax," he replied. "We hope everyone is good, but if they are bad we're going to be okay. Look at Shane up on the tank," he added. A hardly visible Shane could be seen covering us, watching every move through his scope.

"Hello," I said as disarmingly as I could to the group huddled around a fire, with no food to be seen. "This is Jax, and he has a question for you all. Okay?"

"Yes, okay. Sure," several replied.

He started: "Mr. Lonnie is cooking some meat steaks, and I wondered if you would like some?"

"It does smell awful good. If it's not too much trouble," said one man with blonde hair and a three-week beard. "We haven't eaten much lately."

"Are you fishing?" I asked. "This lake should be full of them."

"No," responded a woman, who I assumed was his wife. "We came up from Pueblo but didn't think to bring any fishing tackle...or whatever you call it."

"So, what do you eat?" I asked. "Surely, there is some game around here to shoot."

"We gave up our guns down at the lake. Or one gun, I should say. But once we saw what was happening there, we just took off up here. We couldn't go back to the city, so I guess we're stuck," she added.

"How did you get through the barricades?" asked Jake.

"It's not so hard," said the man, "when we don't have trailers like you. We just go around them at night and get back on the road. We didn't think it through is all."

"Can I borrow two of your guys?" I asked the woman. "Only for maybe 30 minutes."

"I don't know," she said. "It's hard to know who to trust nowadays."

"I understand that," I replied. "If I told you those in our group liberated the lake camp and took out the three brothers who ran it, giving it back to the people, would that help?"

"You did that? I mean, they were selling the women and making the men fight!"

"Not anymore," I answered. "They are all free to come and go as they please—no more pit fights or auctions."

"My sister, she has blonde hair and sparkling blue eyes. Did you see her?"

"I'm sorry. The man in our group who would have maybe done so is no longer with us."

"I can tell you the ones who were there only a few days ago have been set free."

"Thank you," she replied, with tears in her eyes.

* * * *

"Shhh," said Jake, pointing up to the tree line at 100 yards out.

"Can anyone here skin a buck?" he whispered, sighting his rifle in.

"I can," said one man, holding his hand up.

"Cover your ears, kids," said Jake just before squeezing the trigger.

"Ah," he said after the shot. "He is hit but he's running."

A few of the men jumped up, looking to run down the animal.

"No, let him go," said Jake. "He's gut-shot and won't go far if we let him be. We'll pick him up when we get back, and he won't be far if we're lucky. While we're gone, get some good coals going in this fire. You will need to smoke the meat to preserve it, and you'll need a new pit over here," he said, pointing a few feet away from their small fire. "Make it long—about five feet and three feet wide. Dig a foot down and fill it with coals. At least a few of you will be up all night slow-smoking the meat, but it should feed you all for a while. You and you," he pointed to a man and woman, "gather fifteen sticks. Make sure they are green or still alive and bring them back here. I'll bring some rope back, and we can make a smoking rack. Any questions?"

One man raised his hand.

"You," he said, pointing to him.

"Some here in our group don't like deer meat."

"That's First-World thinking," I said. "We are Third-World, or maybe Fourth-World now. I'm guessing a lot of folks in this country are now eating things much farther down the food chain than venison. It's what's for dinner and lunch right now. We have some powdered milk to add in that will take the gamey taste out for now. We're all having fish for breakfast, so we have to make due," I added. "Any other questions?"

None held their hand up or responded.

"Thank you, Jax, and you men!" they all replied. Their smiles reflected their gratefulness.

* * * *

We returned a half-hour later with the two volunteers, who surprisingly never asked if they all could join our group. I guess a caravan traveling with weapons and a tank is not all that appealing to folks looking to lay low and stay out of a fight. We found the buck—a six-pointer—75 yards from where he was shot. He bled out, and we dragged him with one of the four-wheelers back to their camp.

Jake and I gave a how-to short class on smoking meat while they nearly devoured the steaks and sides Lonnie fixed up. We made sure the fire pit was ready and tied the green sticks with rope for the racks as three men skinned and processed the venison. Lucy, feeling about back to normal, if that was even possible, volunteered to show them how to cook the meat. We tried to convince her to return with us for the night, but she refused. She would stay, according to the deal, and help them process the meat that would nourish the group for weeks to come.

"We will be back to get you tomorrow," I said. "And I'm counting on all you ladies to watch out for her until morning," I added.

* * * *

Dinner was nothing short of spectacular. The kind of meal one might expect after a two-week jaunt in the woods camping. I remembered going on such a trip, hiking the Collegiate Peaks in Colorado as a teenager with a group of 15. We hiked the two or more days to get to the base of the peaks, needing to be up and down by noon to avoid dangerous weather.

Not even a week in, we would all talk about our first meals back, like McDonald's or Arby's, Wendy's and Burger King. Nobody was eager to get back to a garden salad or anything resembling healthier food.

* * * *

Lonnie wasn't joking. We had fish for breakfast with some kind of rice. Jake and I went back to check the progress of the group and fetch Lucy.

"We've smoked most of the meat already," said Lucy, sitting close—too close—to a man about her age, not getting up to leave with us.

I gave Jake a look but didn't speak about it yet.

"Does anyone here have a rifle?" I asked, already knowing the answer straightaway.

Nobody raised their hand.

"Okay. Who can shoot?"

A few raised their hands, both men and women. I handed the rifle to the man sitting closer to Lucy than I had ever seen someone do.

"It's a 30.06 with 100 rounds of ammo," I said, holding the box out as well. "Shoot straight and no targets; you will have a steady supply of meat for quite a while."

Jake handed them two fishing poles and some light tackle. "Take care of these, and you will feed a lot of people from this lake," he said. Everyone in the group expressed their thanks for this provision that could in fact save their lives.

"We're packing up, Lucy," I told her.

"I'll miss you all," she replied, looking to the man next to her.

"Are you sure?" I asked, pulling her aside for confirmation.

"I am," she replied. "I belong here; I feel like it's been my home forever. I do want to say goodbye, though."

* * * *

I didn't want her to leave, and I was still reeling from her past trauma, but she was an adult and single, so I guess I got it. Joy was none too happy about it, giving her own speech to get Lucy to stay.

"We are so close to a life of safety in a protected Valley," Joy offered. "We have come so far, and spilled blood to get here. Why would you want to leave now?"

"I appreciate everything you have done for me; we were neighbors for many years back in McKinney. But I'm a loner with no family—just a tagalong in the caravan across the country. You are close to the Valley you call the final destination, but it's not safety. It's going to be a battleground and everyone knows it. There is a man here in this other group that all of the women swear is gentle and God-fearing. He thinks I'm pretty and says nice things to me. That's enough for now. Here, I'm somebody who knows things and can help the group. This is my bird-in-the-hand moment and I want to take it."

Joy nearly commanded me to give them a year's supply of alfalfa sprout seeds with four precious mason jars and planting seeds.

"We'll miss you," we all told Lucy.

"If you ever change your mind, you know where to find us," added Joy.

* * * *

Our caravan packed up quickly and headed around the lake to new adventures, only dreamed about by most.

“That was a good thing we did back there, everyone. It surely was,” called out Lonnie over the radio. “And it was all thanks to Jax!”

* * * * * * *

Chapter Seventeen ~ Mike ~ Heading East, Colorado

Mike left the group, the only true friends he had known outside of his family and former girlfriend, Kelly. He rode unafraid towards the man he knew would take away his new family and friends that he trusted without a second thought.

"I'm coming for you, Baker!" he yelled aloud.

He had forgotten the freedom of the road. Just a man and a bike, cruising winding roads with a bandana-wrapped head and sunglasses. Mike missed the open road, remembering the smell of the earth and the wind in his face when he rode the back roads of upstate New York, and sometimes as far as Maine, cutting through the center of Connecticut before hugging the coastline just north of Boston and straight up.

Before entering the police academy, he flew to Miami. He purchased a used 2001 Harley Davidson Heritage, "a truly classic machine," he would tell his girlfriend, for the 2,369-mile solo trip to Fort Kent, Maine, at the Canadian border on U.S. Highway 1. The route was the longest north-south highway in the United States, he remembered, when mapping it out.

The girlfriend of the month, like they all were before Kelly, had asked to go but he wouldn't invite her. If he were pressed, he would have told her he needed to clear his head after his brother's and sister's deaths.

The trip could have been complete in a week, but Mike took five weeks—grieving, sightseeing, and looking for ways to calm his vengeful mind. More than a few men fit the bill...from seedy bars to dirty motels, and even a few at a random gas station or rest stop that would disappear, only to be found later once Mike was far up the road. The connections to him would never be made by law enforcement, as the route touched fifteen states from bottom to top. Sure, there were rumors and rumblings, especially after the news of the church janitor killed by Mike and his partner, and the nickname "Cereal Mike" was floated around Brooklyn and New York City. Mike wondered what the record was for justified extermination—not that he was trying to break one, but was only curious.

* * * *

He rode the Indian back the way our group had come, up the mountain, meaning to bypass the lake and continue due south towards his new life, if only temporarily. He could have kept going but couldn't resist checking in on his newly appointed leader at the lake, making a surprise visit they would surely not expect this soon. The more than six-hour detour would have turned most around, but Mike didn't sleep much; he never had. He could travel day or night, and couldn't say which he preferred. He rolled in early, just after lunch, and saw Mitch and his girlfriend teaching a fishing class to many of the now full-time residents.

"All good here?" Mike asked. "As I left it?"

"Yes, sir. There are no more fights or auctions, only people helping people, as it should have always been. Are you looking for the new leader?" he asked.

"Nah. Just tell him I stopped in to check on him. I'll do so in the future when I can."

With that, Mike rode out, not concerned about the time loss and considering it a win.

* * * *

The new route took him on roads he had never traveled. He knew the direction of Interstate 25 and the Baker group's general location, so he didn't worry too much about the roads with the nimble bike, as long as he was headed in the right direction. He rode north and was lost in the euphoria every rider feels riding across open land. He was aware of his surroundings in a general sense and was not going to run off the road or hit an abandoned car. But he felt also a calm, at peace, like a car driver may feel arriving at work as a safe driver but spacing out on the trip to get there, thinking of a honey-do list...or maybe a new love interest.

Mike rode peacefully into just another part of the landscape when he heard it. The shots echoed in his head—*Pop! Pop!*—followed by five or six more before he felt the sting in his right side. The heavy bike skidded left, then right, as he pulled his right hand on the front brake and his foot on the back. He didn't want to stop, but the pain was intense, like nothing he had ever felt, and his head was spinning, dizzy and disoriented. The Indian motorcycle came to rest on her side, throwing him ten feet farther, landing with a thud. He lay on the side of the dusty road, hearing his breath in and out, like listening to another man dying.

"No, this can't be it," he whispered. "Not now. They need help; my friends need help."

He lay on the road, turning onto his back, and without a weapon could only wait for the next shot, the final nail. He smiled as they came towards him.

"Is that all you've got?" he laughed, spitting on the ground.

"You're done this time," said the man he could see maneuvering the bolt action on his hunting rifle. "'An eye for an eye.' Isn't that what they say, or is it a life for a finger? Yes, I think that is what they were trying to say. Don't worry; it will be quick."

"It's you!" Mike said defiantly, "'The eight-finger man!' How's your fishing been?" He was not concerned with showing fear. He had none. "You better hurry if you want revenge. I think I'm going to pass out soon. Come on, let's get this done," he enticed.

"Or what?"

"Or you let me go so I can get my message to Colonel Baker."

There was a pause as the men talked amongst themselves.

"What do you know about Colonel Baker?" another guy asked.

Mike couldn't be sure and thought it was a long shot, but he assumed they had some form of communication and had heard the man's sermons, or whatever they were passing for nowadays.

"I can fix him, maybe," said one man coming up from behind the group with a bag in hand. "I mean, if that's what you want."

"The Medic to the rescue again," said the sarcastic eight-fingered man.

"I took good care of your fingers, didn't I?"

"They are still missing, aren't they?" he snarled, holding up his hand. "Now we're talking about the man who cut them off. Why would I let you help him?"

"What's the message?" asked another, clearly the leader in Mike's eyes. "And it better be good, or I'll end this right here."

"Tell Baker I have news about the Great Battle for the Valley."

"Take a look at him," he commanded the Medic, "and let me know if he can be saved. Let's get on the radio and see if his story checks out."

Mike had a plan formulating in his mind when the morning turned to dark in a split second. He came to hours later, sweating and still in pain. This pain he embraced, using it as a drug thinking about Arthur and his sister, Lily. He always thought if he could endure enough pain, it would lessen what he felt with each passing day since their loss. *This is my test*, he thought. *I'm still alive and have a chance at saving my family and friends.*

"The Colonel wants to speak to you," said the man who had saved him from the second shot.

"Where?" asked Mike?

"No, *when* is the question—when he is back on the line. So, stay awake for me; your life depends on it."

Mike did stay awake, playing mind games to keep his eyes open and focused on something...anything. He felt that he could go to sleep, drift off, and be done with it. He wasn't afraid to die and hadn't been for a long time, but he thought about Sheila and Javi. He thought about his new friends heading towards almost certain annihilation, only to be killed or enslaved.

Fighting to sit up, he took stock of his injury and didn't remember much about what happened. *Did I lose focus, or was it just unavoidable?* he thought, not entertaining the what-ifs, had he skipped the lake check and headed straight for his destination. Did he spot me? He answered his own question, eyeing the eight-fingered man looking across the desolate valley through the largest set of binoculars he had ever seen. *It doesn't really matter*, he thought.

"That looks more like a telescope," Mike called out. "Overkill, don't you think?"

"It made the difference between me seeing your face instead of just letting some random guy pass by on a motorcycle."

"I see your point," Mike agreed. "Lucky you, and one hell of a coincidence."

Minutes turned to hours, and the bandage was replaced by the Medic, kneeling down.

"Sorry about this, man," he said to Mike. "It's going to hurt."

"You don't look familiar," said Mike, remembering he had seen nearly everyone's face at the lake.

"That's because I haven't seen you before," said the Medic.

"So, you weren't at the lake with those other guys who sold their better halves for food?"

"What? I mean no, sir. I'm not sure what you mean. I'm Max," he offered.

"Mike," he replied, shaking his hand with nobody else noticing, as his captors passed around a liquor bottle between them. "I heard you cut that one guy's fingers off for no good reason," he whispered.

"Do you believe that?"

"No. Something is off with all of these guys," he added. "I just can't put my finger on it—no pun intended."

"Really?" asked Mike, smiling.

"Well, maybe just a little. Anyway, I was headed for the lake and ran into them. They told me that all of the men have to fight in a hole."

"Not all of them," said Mike. "Not any of these guys at least. You can go there now if you want. I was there right before this happened and everything is fine. They are free, all of them now."

"Thanks, mister...I mean Mike. I'm not with these guys, but I'm going to stick with them until they reach that bastard Bak... Um, well, I've said too much. As long as this doesn't get infected, you will live," he mumbled, gathering his medical bag and walking back to join the group.

Hmm, Mike thought. *Not sure if the Max guy was sincere or trying to play me.* He observed for another hour, as the Medic steered clear of the others, minding his own business and not participating in the drinking.

* * * *

"He's on!" one man shouted. "Shhh! Shhh! It's Colonel Baker on the radio!"

Three men helped Mike hobble over to the radio. There was some background noise and talking on both ends before he came on.

"They call you Mike. Is that right?"

"That is correct, sir. And you are Colonel Baker?"

There was a pause without a response...long enough for Mike's captors to think they had lost the signal.

"What do you know about the Great Battle for the Valley?" Baker asked.

Mike had planned for this question all day—at least his conscious hours. He played up the pain, in case he said something wrong.

"I know people who are headed there, a group who clashed with some of your people not long ago."

"We have *clashes*, as you say, every day. They don't last more than a few minutes."

“How many have dynamite, fireworks, fire, and the Military involved?” Mike asked.

“Raton Pass—are you part of the militia group up there?”

“No. My old group just passed through.”

“And you spilled our blood. Is that right?”

“Sir, I am a soldier, like you,” Mike replied. He held his tongue, knowing full well the man on the other end of the line was not a Colonel or a soldier but a zealous fanatic, preaching his distorted religion to the most vulnerable.

“I am a soldier, like you,” he repeated. “I fight for the side I am on.”

“Where is your group now?” Baker asked.

“Deep in the mountains, I guess. When they kicked me out, they took my guns and my boy.”

“Your guns and your boy, huh? But not your bike?”

“It’s mine, and I took it back is all. They didn’t chase me down, if that’s what you’re asking.”

“So, how can you help me, Mike?”

“I know their plans and I want revenge, plus my boy back.”

Mike decided to leave Sheila out altogether, knowing how the Baker guy felt about women anyway.

“Just a man and his boy wanting revenge—all that’s missing is the pet dog.” There was another long pause.

“I hear that you fought three men at once in a pit and won. Is that true?”

“Yes, sir, you have heard right.”

“I could use a man like you on my team, but how do I know I can trust you?”

“You don’t!”

Baker laughed, saying something inaudible to those around him.

"Mike, you may just be the first honest man I've met. Tell me what you know about the Valley."

"Yes, sir. I can do that, but only in person."

Those around Mike looked at him like he had defied a commandment from God Himself.

"I'm not sure you know who you're speaking with here," said Baker.

"I understand completely," replied Mike, not wanting to come off rude but realizing a meeting with him was the only way to get close.

"Should we kill him, Colonel?" asked the guy with less fingers now.

"I didn't save him just to have him killed," said Max, joining in the conversation.

"Who's that?" asked Baker.

"His name is Maximillian, or something like that, and he says he is a medical something or other."

"You kept Mike alive?" Baker asked Max.

"Yes, I did, and I won't stand by and see him killed on my watch."

"You two—Mike and Max, Max and Mike. I like you. Can you ride, Mike?"

"Sure...I mean, probably."

"That's a no," said Max. "Not for a while, at least."

"How long?" asked Baker.

"A week or two, maybe three."

"Hold on," said Baker, as he shouted orders to his men. "We have your location. Our helicopters are not ready yet, so we will send a truck. Expect them in a day or two."

"A truck for all of us?" asked one of the men.

Baker didn't answer, only adding, "If any harm comes to either of those two, you all will deal with me. Understood?"

"Yes, sir," they all mumbled.

"I said *Understood?!"* he screamed.

"Yes, Colonel!" they all said loudly.

The call was disconnected on Baker's end, and soon after, the negotiations began.

****

Chapter Eighteen ~ Mike North of Lake Pueblo, Colorado

Mike and Max were wooed over the next few hours by most of the other men in camp, asking for a good word so they too could catch a ride on the "Salvation Truck," as they now called it. Max stayed close to Mike, talking about their backgrounds as much as either one would share with someone they had just met. Mike told him about these men and what they had done, knowing it was common knowledge now, and he did feel a sense of immunity waiting for transport.

"This Baker guy... You like him?" asked Max. "Maybe you trust him or are looking to protect him from harm?"

"I have a sense about people," said Mike, without directly answering the question. "I've fine-tuned it over the years, and it's pretty spot-on. So, I'll ask you the same. Do you like him? Do you trust him? Do you want to protect him?"

Max paused, taking a deep breath before telling a melted-down story of the last month in his life.

"I was a medic in the Navy. Served four years and saved more than a few guys. Later, I worked as a paramedic and saved a few more. It's what I do. I help people. I've even delivered two babies—a boy on a ship and a girl right on a city bus. My pops worked three jobs to put my siblings and me through school. He worked construction, did some landscaping, and was a part-time bookkeeper for several small businesses. He used his hands and his head.

"When Baker and his group came through our town, they took everything they saw: men, women and children. The dogs ran free or were shot for sport by his men, ours included. I was at the hospital when my father was killed trying to save our dog from some pointless game they called mutt cuts. They cut them down and took bets on how far out the shot was. They shot my dog and my dad, like rats in the street. I saw it, coming home. My father told me everything and died right in my arms."

"You didn't do anything?" asked Mike.

"No. There were dozens of men with guns, plus the Baker guy. I don't even think he's a real Colonel, but he was watching the massacre from atop his Military-style SUV and I think he paid the man who took my father's life. My mom passed on several years back, thank God, but I did nothing. They shot twice from a distance while I was holding my father. Both shots barely missed me, and I laid down, playing dead on the side of the road until they left. I'm a coward through and through."

"You came upon a scene and evaluated it accurately, it sounds like," replied Mike. "You can't take them all on," he added. "If you did, we would not be talking now, and I would surely be dead. Revenge is slow-cooked, like a European meal with all seven courses. So, you now have courage?"

"I don't know, but I have nothing to lose. Maybe that's the same thing."

"It's close, that's for sure, Max. So, what's your plan?" Mike continued, knowing he may have taken the questions too far.

"My plans are to ki... What are yours?" he said, stopping himself from saying too much.

"My plans are complicated," said Mike, holding back for now. "Do you have a weapon, Max?"

"No. I did, but these guys took it when I got here."

"Okay. Bring your things over and sleep by me. If they try anything, I'll get up the strength to do something, I'm sure of it. I don't think they are that stupid, though, to mess with us now."

Mike awoke in the middle of the night to Max's yells. "Don't hurt him, you bastards! Don't hurt my father!" And another time, later on: "I'll kill you if it's the last thing..."

Only Mike heard this—only him and the eight-fingered man.

* * * *

Both men were left alone during the night. The next morning, they were offered only water.

"I hope they come to get us," said Max, "or we will starve for sure."

"They are keeping us alive as instructed," replied Mike—"no more and no less. Tell me more about your plans."

"Okay, but I need to know I can trust you. How do I do that?"

"Have you ever looked a man in the eye and knew his word was true, whatever he said next?" Mike asked.

"Yes, I guess I know what you're saying. I saw it in my father and grandfather, and I see it in you, but somehow it's different," replied Max.

"How so?" asked Mike, feeling he was getting somewhere with his questions.

"Well, they were peaceful men—hunters and fishermen—but never violent towards another person. You are different. I can see it in your eyes. I heard you defeated three men in a pit fight to the death, and you don't even bring it up. I think you have a much more sordid past than that, and I'm hoping you will remember I saved your life out here in this outlaw of a camp."

Mike laughed, holding his side but not showing pain on his face.

"I do, and I know what you need."

"You do?"

"Yes. You need revenge for your father. You need to kill the man who authorized the murder. Am I right?"

Max paused, still not sure how to proceed... "You may be close... How many people, do you think?"

"How many people what?" asked Mike, having an idea of where this was heading.

"How many men and women have you killed?"

"I never have and never will take the life of a woman or a child, before you ask," replied Mike.

"As far as men go, well the three in the pit, I guess?" asked Max.

"Nope, only one of those," replied Mike.

"Maybe two or three more?"

"I don't know; I lost count. How many girlfriends have you had in your life?"

"Three. Just three," replied Max.

"Are you sure you're telling me the truth?"

"Yes, I am."

"I know. I can see it in your eyes. Now look in mine. I have had many. Most didn't last more than a month or two, and I only cared about two—Kelly and Sheila. Do you believe me?"

"Yeah, Mike. I do."

"Baker is a bad guy, and together we can take him out," said Mike.

"Okay," said Max, breathing heavily. "But nobody else can know about this."

"My family and friends' very lives depend on it," Mike replied. "I'm glad you were in the Military," he added, "because I think they will interrogate us both."

With as much trust as each man could come up with, they made a plan of sorts. Both agreed that going into a group that large would likely see them separated from the start. Max came clean about his plan to take out Baker but didn't have any plans after that, assuming he could survive the response. Mike told him of his group and thought Saddle Ranch might be happy to add a Medic, if it came to that.

"I mean, who would want another medical professional," Mike told him as a statement. "But?"

"But what?"

"They don't call it the 'Great Battle' for nothing. Did you hear him say the helicopters aren't ready yet?" asked Mike. "How long until they are—weeks or maybe days? You may want to steer clear of Saddle Ranch, if you make it that long."

"If I have a chance at peace when this deed is done, I'll fight for it without regret. Besides, like I said before, I've got nothing to lose now."

With the hot sun fully overhead, they were thrown scraps of bread and a gallon of water to split.

"Are we going to try and get these guys a ride?" asked Max.

"Nope," replied Mike. "They are probably the exact lot Baker would look to add into the group, but I'm not interested in spending any more time with them."

* * * *

Their ride showed up just before dark. Four men and a pickup truck, the kind with an extended bed, drove into camp and took over. Mike and Max were moved into the tent of the eight-fingered man, and he was moved out.

"You guys get some dinner?" asked a tall, clean-cut man with a freshly healing scar over his right eye. It was clear to everyone he alone was now in charge.

"We fed them," said Mike's foe.

"I didn't ask you. It appears that you men had some stew," he said, looking at the near-empty pot by the fire. "Mike, Max, did you get enough?"

"Just some bread scraps at lunch," said Mike, winking at the man in charge.

"Let's have a chat," the new leader said, grabbing the man by his finger nubs, getting a stifled scream out of him. "Just so we're on the same page here, the Colonel told you to take care of these two men, and you guys ate without them?"

"Well, it's not exactly like that. They said they weren't hungry."

The man in charge chuckled but didn't laugh. Max wondered what may happen next, but not Mike. He saw it in the man's eyes, the very same look he had seen in the mirror every day since he was 14.

The shot was quick under the eight-fingered man's chin, dropping him straight away.

"Who's next?" called out the shooter.

Everyone stood still, not answering.

"How about you get some food going for these two and us," he said, motioning to his men who brought over a bag of canned foods. "Since you guys have already eaten, it would be a bad idea to take some for yourselves. Now, who can cook?"

They all raised their hands, and he chose the two most confident for the task.

"What's your best dish?"

"Chicken cacciatore," said one, with the other adding in "porterhouse rare."

"Well then, boys. This should be easy tonight. Max," he called out, "take a look at my cut."

"Sure thing, sir," he replied, making an extra effort to be respectful to a man he felt could get him close to Colonel Baker.

"Knife wound?" asked Max.

"How did you know?"

"I've been in this line of work, sir, for a while. I guess I've seen a little bit of everything. I'll need to clean this up if that's okay? Have you had anything done to it?"

"No, I haven't had any medical care. Just too busy, I guess. And yes, you can take a look."

"Okay, but it's going to hurt. I can put some cooling spray on it, though, and give you something for the pain."

"I don't need any of that; just fix it!"

Max was concerned about inflicting pain on this man who had the power to take his life or get him close to the man who ordered his father's death.

Mike knew better. A killer, regardless of his morals, never minded enduring pain.

* * * *

Thirty minutes passed. Max was done and still alive, sitting down to the best canned meal he could remember. "Chili con carne with beans and a kick" was advertised on the can. Mike still didn't have much of an appetite but ate for the strength he would need soon. Surrounded by men they didn't trust, both Mike and Max slept surprisingly well.

* * * *

"Up and at 'em boys," came the leader's call. "These two fine cooks have volunteered to make breakfast."

They ate and got packed up. It took three men to get Mike in the back of the truck.

"I see you grabbed my bike," Mike said.

"Belongs to the Colonel now," said another man. "There are no possessions kept where we're going."

"Let's head out," called the lead.

Mike shared the truck bed with Max and the two new chefs. The others looked on as the truck pulled out but didn't say a word. The old truck had lost its shocks, guaranteed if Mike were asked, with every bump causing a sharp pain in his side.

The leader of the four-man transport team occasionally rode in the back, talking to one of his men quietly, so as not to be overheard.

"You take the pain well, Mike," he said. "It hardly shows on your face."

"We have something in common," said Mike, pointing to the man's forehead.

"How many, Mike?"

"How many what, sir."

"How many lives have you taken?"

Mike paused, knowing anything could be a test, and a careless lie could get him and his new friend killed on the spot.

The man continued before Mike could answer.

"It's in your eyes—cold—the thousand-mile stare. Same as mine. So how many?"

"I don't really know," replied Mike.

This got a whoop out of the leader, followed by a bang on top of the truck's cab.

"He doesn't really know!" he shouted. "I believe you! I do!"

"How many for you, sir?" Mike asked before he could take it back.

"Fifty-six, before it went dark, and thirteen—no, make that fourteen with your guy back there—in this Next-World."

"How do you know?" asked Mike, now curious.

"This here notebook," he said, pulling a small pocket-sized navy-blue spiral notebook from his backpack. "Every kill has a name, or at least something about it, to jog my memory."

Max sat quietly between the two killers and wondered if his father's name was in the notebook. He hadn't seen his father's executioner, only the man who ordered it. Was he sitting next to the man directly responsible? He couldn't be sure but thought it possible, at least.

* * * *

The drive took a little over eight hours, with two small skirmishes that were over in seconds. Mike mostly kept to himself on the ride over, not wanting to appear too close with Max. They got him out of the truck once to pee, but even that took two men holding him up. He had a rendezvous at Saddle Ranch that simply could not be missed as long as he was breathing, so he focused on healing fast.

Mike thought about his favorite movie ever, called *Tombstone*. There is a scene when Doc Holliday, played by Val Kilmer, pretends to be sicker than he is and shows up at the last minute to help Wyatt Earp defeat a man called Johnny Ringo. It was a masterpiece and his favorite part of the movie. *Would it work now*, he thought? *It would have to.*

He was pretty sure he would get regular visits with Max, since they both heard the group was short on medical practitioners. Hopefully, they could finalize the plan a little at a time, only carving out a rough idea ahead of time. Mike needed to be careful about balancing his injury while still being productive and moving quickly up the ranks. No outfit needs a sick man hanging around for too long, he remembered hearing in a movie, or was it a TV show?

They pulled in late, after dark, with an announcement. "We're here. Everyone sits tight, and nobody leaves the truck."

****

Chapter Nineteen ~ Mike ~ Camp ~ Colorado

Mike, with Max's help, rose to a seated position. He saw a slew of small campfires, with men, women and children milling about and a few laughing out loud.

"This isn't what I expected," Mike whispered to Max. "I thought the women were all locked up. It doesn't make sense."

"Over here," said the pickup truck leader, still without a name, who could be Mike's twin both in looks and behavior. "We'll stay the night and move on at first light," he added.

Mike was confused, and that didn't happen very often.

"Move on tomorrow—to where?" he asked Max.

* * * *

He would have his answer in only another minute as he stared into the eyes of a Military man.

"Ronna, is that you?" Mike asked, already knowing the answer.

"The last time we met, you were pointing a pistol at me and threatening my leadership, I remember," he replied.

"I was just trying to make a fair deal for my people," Mike replied. "I didn't realize who you were," he added, careful not to say too much in front of his fellow travelers.

"And who might I be?" Ronna asked.

"All I know is we have a mutual friend who travels by helicopter most places," said Mike, wondering where this was headed.

"Bring him inside for a chat," Ronna said, walking away.

"Okay, Mike. Let's go," said the two men who had helped lift him before.

Mike tried hard to use his legs and got some traction, at least more than before, he thought. He was brought to a tent much bigger than the last time they had met and with ten times the security.

"I see you have grown your little group," said Mike, waving his hand in a half-circle.

"I have," he replied. "Not bad for a former coffee barista, don't you think?"

"So why am I here?" Mike asked, cutting the small talk. "I was expecting to see Colonel Baker."

"He's no Colonel—just some crazy guy who has, successfully I will admit, amassed a large army of cult followers willing to die for him," said Ronna.

"Join or be killed is what I heard," said Mike.

"You're not far off… This man," Ronna said, pointing to Mike's doppelgänger, "is Sergio. He is a spy and has worked with me for many years, before all of this. He has a special set of talents that I hear you share."

"What's that?" asked Mike.

"He cleans things up, gets rid of loose ends, and is loyal to his government. Now, he has infiltrated Baker's group and gained his trust. It's what you intend to do, isn't that right?"

Mike didn't answer, and it didn't matter.

"Let's see if I have this right," said Ronna. "You have a wife, or a girlfriend, now and a new boy you took from them. Your group with Lance, the other cop (Lennie, I think), and the rest are headed for Saddle Ranch in the Valley. Am I warm?"

He continued, "You know about the Great Battle for the Valley, and you have an ally with a real Colonel who is my commander, and he has intervened on your behalf at least once that I know of. Is that correct?"

"Yes, that's right," replied Mike. "It was right after he intervened on your behalf, when Baker took you prisoner."

"You do know your history," replied Ronna.

"I pay attention is all," replied Mike.

"You will return to Baker's group, you and Sergio, alone at first light and mention nothing of this stop. Your truck was attacked at dark with only the two of you escaping. You reclaimed the vehicle, camping for the night somewhere down the road," added Ronna.

"And the other men we rode here with—what about them?" asked Mike.

"Collateral damage. You should know that."

"I want Max," said Mike, as if he were in a bargaining position.

"The Medic? Why?"

"He's not a part of this, and I want him alive. We need him at Saddle Ranch. Call the Colonel."

Ronna laughed. "I don't care about it either way, and my commanding officer likes you for some reason—maybe the boxing—so you can keep him. But I need you to help me with Baker. I assume you have some plan cooked up already to help your friends when they get to the Valley. But mark my words, I will be the one to take him down and everyone who willingly works for him. You will report only to Sergio, who will treat you badly in front of Baker. Your friend, the Max guy, will need to toe the line and keep quiet about this stop here tonight. If he doesn't, Sergio will quiet him his own way. Understand?"

"Yes," replied Mike, "but what about the other five guys on the truck?"

"On the next stop, keep Max in the truck and put your heads down. This business is messy at times, but a soldier like you doesn't mind, do you? Don't answer. Just keep an eye on your friend."

* * * *

Everyone slept next to the truck and headed out at first light, as planned. Sergio kept the radio with him and brushed off questions from the other men working for Baker. "We'll sort it out when we arrive," Sergio told them.

"When we stop, stay in the truck, no matter what," Mike whispered to Max as he checked his wound. "Don't ask why. Just do what I'm telling you. No bathroom break or anything else, okay?"

"Yeah, okay. What's going to happen?"

"Nothing you will want any part of, trust me," replied Mike.

* * * *

They had to go around most towns and stayed off the freeway entirely, adding a few more hours to their destination. An hour and a half into the trip, Sergio ordered the driver to stop at a state-sponsored picnic area—the kind of rest stop a traveler who had to use the bathroom was tricked into pulling over at, with the blue sign they hoped said "Rest Area."

Who needs to stop here without a bathroom? Mike thought.

Apparently, now it was a thing, as many tables were filled with trash and the cans overflowed long ago, never to be emptied. A few people wandered about but kept their distance.

"We'll get breakfast going here. By the time we pull into camp, we'll miss it, and I'm hungry," announced Sergio. He wasn't sure how this would go over with Baker's guys, but no man wants to miss breakfast. He has used this little trick more than once before, and successfully every time.

"Breakfast sounds good," said one. Another added, "Plus we have two cooks, and I don't want to wait until lunch to eat."

Sergio got the two self-proclaimed chefs of sorts to start a fire and heat the water for three pouches of Mountain House scrambled eggs with bacon. Mike could smell it from the truck and felt like he hadn't eaten a thing in weeks.

"Everyone gather around the fire," called out Sergio, when breakfast was done cooking.

"I'll be right there," hollered Max at Mike's instructions. "Just changing his bandage."

"Put the food up on the picnic table," ordered Sergio.

"Stay low," Mike told Max. "It's about to get loud."

Mike peeked over the side of the truck bed after hearing the first shot. He watched as Sergio took out Baker's three men before even one could fire back. And the two cooks? Well, they had cooked their last breakfast.

Max jumped when the truck tailgate was opened two minutes later.

"Hold on," said Sergio, returning promptly with a small package of tortillas and a jar of hot sauce. "These meals make one hell of a burrito, and now there's plenty for everyone." He made one for himself before saying, "Dig in, fellas.

"Twenty or more men ambushed us, and the truck took fire," he said, standing back and unloading nine rounds into the truck's side, missing Mike and Max as well as the vital parts of the vehicle. "Like I was saying, we took fire and gave it back. The three of us barely made it out alive and couldn't even save our friends' weapons. That's the story, and no more."

He made a sweeping motion with his hand towards several people looking to pick over the downed men and recover what they could. "Have at it, folks. Today is your lucky day!" Sergio said, with a mouthful of egg.

"Okay, Max. You're driving. Mike, holler if you need anything," he added, climbing into the passenger's seat."

****

Chapter Twenty ~ Heading to Baker's Camp, Colorado

"Okay, Max. What's your story?" asked Sergio.

"I'm not sure what you mean, sir."

"What I mean is, where are you from? How did you end up with those idiots where I found you, and what do you want?"

Max was tongue-tied for more than a few seconds, wanting to ask the only question he had but afraid of the answer. He answered Sergio's questions as well as could be expected, carefully picking his way around the obvious.

"That's interesting," Sergio replied. "If I told you I was from a small tribe in central South America that rarely saw any outsiders, would you believe me?"

"Well, that sounds unlikely is all, sir," said Max. "So, no disrespect but you don't look like a South American tribesman, I guess."

"But I am—adopted by the tribe when my father was killed on an expedition of some kind. It was just him and me far back in the jungle. I was only six years old... I found my father's killer from another tribe downriver at age 13 and killed him dead in his sleep—with no remorse. I had to leave my tribe, my family, after that for fear of reprisal."

"That's amazing!" said Max. "But why are you telling me all this?"

"Because you lost someone close to *you*, and you seek revenge."

"How would you know that?" asked Max.

"I have instinct, and I've been trained. I see it in your eyes. Who was it—a parent or sibling, maybe?"

Max paused.

"You're only telling me part of the truth. I can't have that where we're going," continued Sergio. "So, what's it going to be?"

"My...father... They killed my father!" Max blurted out.

"And?"

"And I want to know if his name is in your notebook."

Max felt a weight off his chest and was scared to death at the same time.

"Stop the truck!" ordered Sergio.

"Right here?"

"Right here!" he commanded.

"Meet me around back," Sergio said, with Max wondering if this was the end.

He didn't see a weapon visible but thought it didn't make much difference in the long run. *Maybe he will beat me to death with his bare hands or choke me out, like those MMA guys do in the ring*, he thought, getting more nervous by the second.

Sergio half expected Max to run and was prepared to tie up loose ends right here, but he didn't.

They met at the back of the truck, with Mike asking what was going on.

"We need to get some things straight, and I wanted to talk to you guys anyway about what happens next," said Sergio.

"Are you going to kill me?" asked Max.

"I don't think so, but it's good you didn't try to run. You know too much to be running around here by yourself now... Who killed your father?"

"I don't know, but I saw Baker order it."

"Was he shooting at us when he died?" asked Sergio.

"No. He was unarmed and pleading with them not to kill our dog."

"Are you sure he didn't shoot?"

"Yes—100 percent. He doesn't...didn't, I mean, even own a gun."

"He's not in my book!"

"How do you know? His name was Alphonz..."

"I know because I have only killed men who are shooting in my direction. I don't know who did, and that game they play with the dogs is enough to make me want to kill them all," replied Sergio.

With that, he pulled out his notebook and tossed it to a nervous Max.

"Go ahead. See if he's in there."

Max turned the notebook face-up with trembling hands and lifted the cover halfway before closing it, and tossing it back.

"I believe you, sir," said Max, "and you can trust me too."

With the truck's solid back window, Mike had missed the cab conversation but got the basic idea.

"I showed you both my cards when we were at Ronna's camp. Now it's time to show me yours. You first, Max."

"Okay. What have I got to lose? I aim to kill Baker and the man who killed my father."

"You have a plan?" asked Sergio.

"Not really, but I thought maybe I could get close to him if he needed any medical attention at some point."

"How about you, Mike?"

Mike paused and would never have revealed his plans if he hadn't seen Ronna with his own eyes.

"My plan is to protect the Valley by any means necessary," Mike replied. "What's yours, Sergio?"

"Fair enough. I can't tell you everything. I don't even know it all yet, but I take orders from Ronna, who takes orders from the Colonel, who saved your asses back on Raton Pass."

"I thought we put up a great fight," said Mike.

"I'll give you that. You should have seen how pissed off Baker was. I've never seen him like that before or since. I am in as good as can be expected with Baker's group and the number four guy from the top. I don't think anyone suspects me to be a spy, but who knows. When I come back with only you two, he's going to be suspicious. We need to make his first impression solid."

"How do we do that?" asked Max.

"With pain," he replied, brandishing his concealed pistol and pointing it at Max.

"Left, or right?"

"What? Wait a minute... I thought we were..."

"Left it is," Sergio said, firing a single shot through the upper part of Max's shoulder.

Max fell onto the ground, holding his arm through the burning pain. The shocked look on his face amplified when Sergio said, "I'll take right," using his left hand to fire a bullet through his own right arm, just inside the elbow.

"Through and through on both accounts," remarked Mike, not at all surprised with the happenings. "What about me?"

"You're good," said Sergio through grit teeth. "I forgot how much it burns," he admitted, laughing.

"Are you going to be okay, Max?" asked Mike.

"Yeah, I wasn't expecting that...but it's better than dying."

"It's like ripping off a Band-Aid," added in Mike. "You have to get it done before you think too much about what's coming. Will they buy it?"

"I think so. Ronna or the real Colonel would never buy two flesh wounds to extremities only, but that ragtag crew Baker's got won't know the difference. So, Max, stand up for me and get us cleaned up a bit."

He did as he was told, breathing heavily. "Did you really have to do that?"

"Yes, he did," chimed in Mike.

They spent 25 minutes on the side of the road, with only temporary dressings applied.

Sergio discussed what he could about his orders, refusing to answer a few questions from Max and Mike about what was going on with the country.

Sergio finally commented. "The whole thing is a chess match, and there are a lot of high-stakes players, with most running other countries."

"Why would another country want to do harm to ours?" asked Max.

"Land. But not just any land—usable land, with resources in farming, forestry, minerals and petroleum," replied Sergio.

"Don't they have enough land already?" asked Max, as he wrapped Sergio's arm.

"There's never enough. Have you seen how many people live in China and India?"

"I have one question you probably won't answer," said Mike.

"Shoot!"

"I met with the Colonel several times and saw an old friend from my younger days setting up boxing rings across the country in FEMA camps."

"Okay," replied Sergio. "Is that the question?"

"No. The question is why were they hired, paid, and everything a full two weeks before the EMP hit?"

Sergio smiled. "You're right, Mike. That one I won't be answering today. Let's keep this focus on the Valley for now. As you know already, the Colonel has a good friend and mentor named Samuel there that he will bring hell from the skies if he has to in order to protect him.

"Follow my lead when we get to camp. Don't talk to anyone else about this, and Max, reign it in. If you kill Baker or anyone else before I give the word, you will be a liability and no longer an asset. The Great Battle for the Valley is only the beginning of their plans, not the end."

* * * *

They pulled in to the compound early in the afternoon.

Mike had a guesstimate of how many people might be here, but he only calculated those marching with Baker across Raton Pass. He would come to learn quickly that the daily radio broadcasts Baker had done from the beginning, never missing a day, were working like gangbusters.

Throngs of people came from all four directions, packing in like cattle waiting for the slaughter. *No wonder the President said only twenty-something percent of people had reported to the FEMA camps so far*, Mike thought.

Tents filled the wide-open camp, with ponds scattered haphazardly throughout the area. At first look, it appeared to be a random shuffle of people, like Times Square at noon on a Monday, but over the next few minutes a pattern formed. Not as choreographed as the FEMA camps but a pattern, just the same. Walk-in checks were all done from the east side, and vehicle check-ins—or forfeitures, as they should be called—were recorded on the north end of the camp.

Any citizen entering the camp relinquished everything but their clothing. Weapons, including rifles, pistols, crossbows, bows, knives, baseball bats, tire irons, pepper spray, and even bear and wasp spray were all confiscated and logged, not for an eventual return to its rightful owner but for bargaining tools, and they were now the sole property of just one man.

Pets were not allowed, with no exceptions. The deranged mutt cuts game commenced each night after dark, with most new residents only hearing the gunfire, and included shooting at any living thing someone could care enough to bring along.

Sergio pulled through the north gate ahead of a line of old cars, trucks, trailers and motorcycles on two, three and four wheels. He made a point to end up behind a few to give Mike and Max some final instructions.

"A few more things, gentlemen. Don't even look at the women, single or not. They are all processed and evaluated on check-in. The first picks go to Baker and the next to his higher-ups."

"Like you?" asked Mike.

"No, I don't participate in that, and so far, Baker has never asked why. Next, always address him as 'Colonel' and 'sir' if it's a long conversation. I don't know where he came up with it, but he will have you killed if you forget it. Last for now—no fighting, no matter what. They don't have a fighting pit here, but they do have a large hole dug a half-mile up the road for the bodies of all participants of disorderly conduct."

"I thought the point was to get the most people they could in the group," said Max. "Dominate with numbers, right?"

"Not exactly," replied Sergio. "They have to feed everybody, so to him it's about adding the right people. The ones who toe the line and don't question anything—at least not out loud—are the ones who stay."

"What if someone wants to leave on their own?" asked Max.

"Just like that song 'Hotel California'—the one by the Eagles where he says something like Check-out time is whenever you want; you just can't go anywhere. The only ones walking out of here are the ones who never came in."

“What about the kids?” asked Mike. “Are they abusing them?”

“Not that I’ve seen, but it’s a big camp and I can’t be sure. They are going to frisk you first and take your bike,” he whispered to Mike. “Once inside, I’ll give you this,” he added, jingling the key to the Indian before stuffing it back into his pocket. “Actually, better put this in my boot in case I have to talk to Baker today. You will need it later, and I topped it off with gas at Ronna’s camp. Okay—here we go, fellas. Stick to the story, no matter what, and wait until I find you in the next few days before we talk. Last thing, I’m going to be not so nice to you in just a few minutes; trust me, it’s part of the plan. Game faces! Let’s go!” he said, as he drove through the gate.

“Hey, Serg,” said the gate guard. “Where’s the rest of them?”

Two other guests walked around to look in the truck.

“We got ambushed—outnumbered five to one,” replied Sergio. “The guy, Mike in the back, wasn’t worth a crap, but I guess he’s got the worst of the injuries. And this guy,” he said, pointing to Max, hid under the truck and let the rest of us take fire. Good thing he’s competent at patching things up ’cause he can’t fight for crap,” he added, dragging him out of the truck with his good arm and pushing him to the ground.

* * * * * * *

Chapter Twenty-one ~ Baker's Camp ~ St. Vrain State Park, Colorado

"They're here," said a guard on his walkie-talkie. "Colonel Baker wants to see you, all of you," he clarified.

He turned around, talking into his radio for several more minutes. Two men were called over to help Mike off the truck, where he and Max were patted down, revealing no weapons.

"Open your bag," they told Max, referring to his medical bag. "You have any needles in there or anything sharp?"

"Yes, it's a medical kit. Of course, I have needles and scissors—even a scalpel."

"All right. I'll take it for now," said a guard, adding to another guard, "Follow behind them."

Sergio held on to Mike's key, knowing full well they would be frisked again before talking with Baker.

* * * *

The leader's main canvas tent, with three more attached, amassed a footprint of nearly 2,000 square feet in the center of the camp, complete with a top-of-the-line portable toilet and rain-fed shower. Armed guards and middle-level guys surrounded it on all sides, facing outwards and doing their best to hold still like Buckingham Palace guards.

Mike and Max were frisked again, even removing their footwear and socks while Sergio got a quick pat-down fully clothed.

"Welcome, gentlemen, to my little piece of the country," came a booming voice from the other side of what could have passed for a nice house in any town before the day. Living room furniture matched perfectly with area rugs. Ceiling fans throughout the tops of each room kept an even, cool temperature.

Baker walked out in a long red robe, like the eccentric Hugh Hefner was famous for wearing. His stature was plump, one might say, standing no more than 5'3", or maybe 5'4", Mike thought. This wasn't the man Mike was expecting to see after hearing all the stories; but to be honest, he had never really thought about it.

Max clenched his fists at the sight of this man so close he could touch him. Would he ever get this close again?

"You look like you've seen a ghost," Baker said. "You must be Max, 'cause you're not gut shot."

"Yes, Colonel. It's good to meet you," he heard himself say, instinctively reaching out his hand.

"We don't do that here," said Sergio.

"Oh...sorry," said Max, now resigned to take his time and not do something stupid on his first day here.

"It's fine. One can never be too careful," said Baker. "Can I get you two something to drink?"

"A beer would be great, Colonel," said Mike, half joking.

"Well now, that's the problem with cutting the line," Baker replied. "You missed the sign out front with the rules of conduct. Let's get them in front of it when we're done here," he said to a guard.

"We don't drink here; nobody does. How about some lemonade?"

"Yes, sir! Thank you, Colonel," said Max, with Mike agreeing.

"I hear you ran into some trouble on your way here. Is that right?"

"Yes, Colonel, we were headed..."

"Not you, Sergio. I want to hear from them," Baker replied.

"We were ambushed," said Mike, speaking up. "Some got hit, and some got killed on both sides."

"Is that so? Lucky, Sergio, that you and Max here didn't get shot in the gut like Mike, or in the face. Just arms, I see, but not the same side."

Max was getting nervous and was not expecting this much scrutiny.

"And Max, I hear you hid under the truck during the what-did-you-call-it, Mike? Oh yes...ambush. Is that right?"

"Well, sir, I am a medic and we are trained to lay low. We can't help someone else if we're dead."

Baker paused.

"Colonel, it's time for your bath," came the voices of females from the back.

"I guess the good Lord was watching out for all of you today. He knows we have much more work to be done in His name. Sergio?"

"Yes, Colonel?"

"Try to be nice to Max, will you?"

"Yes, sir. I will try."

"I know you will because I'm putting him under your supervision," said the Colonel. "Mike also for now, but only until he heals up. I have other plans he can help me with.

Show Max around and get him introduced to the other medical staff and get Mike settled into the infirmary.

"I'll call for you in the next few days, Mike, to go over your pledged information."

"Any questions, Sergio?"

"No, sir. I can do that."

* * * *

Mike had his own room, or tent suite, at least for now, and Sergio appointed Max as his primary caretaker.

"I see what you did," Max told Sergio. "You had to make it look like you didn't like me so he would tell you to watch me."

"I don't like you. Never have," Sergio replied with a straight face, "and Mike's the same."

"Wait a minute. I thought... I mean, have I ever done any..."

"He's messing with you," said Mike, laughing.

"Wait, are you?"

"Am I?" Sergio replied.

Max looked confused.

"Yeah, I'm just messing with you, as Mike said. Now," he added in a whisper only they could hear, "don't trust anyone—and Max, that includes all the medical staff too. They may not be okay with everything, but they will rat you out in a cool second to save their own skin. Got it?"

"Yeah, but what about Mike?"

"He's been around the block a few times and needs no such instructions. Here," he said, tossing the Indian key to Mike. "It smells like sweaty boots but starts... One hell of a machine!"

Mike pretended to take a big whiff, holding the keys to his nose.

"I smell bacon," he joked.

"Ooh," said Max. "That's just not right."

* * * *

Mike and Max spent the next few days quietly observing their surroundings. Mike didn't get around much—only twice a day to sit in the sun for a couple of hours each stint. He didn't mind; it was enough to see the pace of the camp. Who came, who went, and the interactions between the guards, the citizens (if you could call them that) and the hardware. Keeping an eye out for the helicopters Baker had talked about, he saw none, and heard even less.

He talked to a few people casually, asking when they were moving on again. It was clear they didn't know or care as long as they were fed, showered, protected, and preached to daily at 10 a.m. sharp. Mike wondered about the men who lost their wives and girlfriends to Baker and most of his higher-ups. So far, he hadn't heard any rumblings about it. And after what he had witnessed at the lake, it didn't seem too out of the ordinary, at least for these times.

"Spineless converts," he said out loud to no one. "I should start my own community. You can keep your wives and girlfriends, keep your kids and your dog," he continued.

"Yeah, but you can't preach for crap," said Max, tapping him on the shoulder and getting a rare twitch out of him.

"That doesn't happen often," Mike admitted, "but you're probably right. I wouldn't want to talk for an hour every day to a group of strangers."

* * * *

It had only been a few days, but Mike was eating regularly and getting his strength back. Today he walked unassisted outside the infirmary tents to his usual perch on the outside of the bustling main drag through camp.

"Mike, we have to go," said Sergio. "Baker wants to talk. I'll get some guys to help."

"No, I'm good. Just walk with me, and I'll get there on my own."

"Okay, but you know what this meeting is, right?" continued Sergio.

"Yep. It's the one I've been waiting for since I left my real group."

"One misstep is all it takes," said Sergio.

"I know. Trust me, I have a lot more to lose than you."

"Don't be so sure," Sergio replied. "I know everything you do and a lot more that would scare the hell out of most men."

"I'm not most men," replied Mike.

"I know. That's why you're here. We make our move in one week."

* * * *

"Mike," said Baker on introduction. "Are you clean?"

"He is," said one of his guards, after patting him down.

"Good to hear. Situational awareness is half the battle; I'm convinced of that. Anyway, have you been enjoying the sermons?"

"Yes, Colonel," Mike replied. "I haven't heard that pitch before."

"It's no pitch, Mike."

"I'm sorry. I didn't mean that as it sounded. I mean, I haven't heard..." that angle, he almost said, catching himself mid-sentence and changing to "I haven't heard the Word spoken in such a way before."

"So, you like it?"

"Yes, it's refreshing, and it makes me wonder why any other man of God would keep that to himself."

Mike paused, certain he was laying the story on, two layers over the top.

Baker paused as well, rubbing his chin.

"They are selfish," he finally spoke..."all that have come before me. But God spoke to me on the very day the lights went out, telling me to give my knowledge to the suffering, the sick, and weak-spirited. Give to the poor, the starving, and to the women who have not known a godly relationship their entire lives. I am the Chosen One; there is no other. I am to settle in a lush valley four miles long and a mile wide with my people, vanquishing all opposition in the name of my Father, who sent me down from heaven to gather the sheep for the final reckoning. Tell me what you know."

Mike weaved a tale with some truths he felt authenticated the story, without giving up something not already glaringly obvious.

"I was hoping you had better information," said Baker. "But you are a fighter, and I need more of those. Plus, you're out for revenge, and that can't be underestimated. Don't disappoint me."

"Can I ask you one question, Colonel?"

"Maybe. What is it?"

"I already heard you were headed for Fort Collins, but you held up here in between. Why is that?"

"That's what you heard?"

"Yes, from your lead guys up on Raton Pass."

"It figures. They were idiots, not worthy of information, but I will grant you an answer just this time. Our compound in Fort Collins is not ready yet. It seems there has been a small setback, a minor inconvenience, really. It is to be our last stop before the valley and seems to be common knowledge now. We likely leave in a week or less, but that can change either way. I hold in my hand," he continued, reaching down to a locked box he opened with a key on a chain around his neck. "I hold in my hand," he said again, holding up a leather-bound notebook, "the plans for our future. Every detail mapped out, every victory foreshadowed, every soul to be redeemed in the name of my God."

"Thank you, Colonel," is all Mike said, having to remind himself why he shouldn't just grab him by the throat and be done with it.

Half his mind said he could have grabbed the book and made a regime change in an hour and saved the Valley, and the other half—the more rational half maybe—kept him from doing so. He walked back to the medical tent, refusing help of any kind, and was resolved to at least be able to ride the bike and meet Lance at the rendezvous spot—if it killed him.

* * * *

Sirens woke Mike up after midnight, sounding like the tornado sirens at the FEMA camp but somehow different.

"Everybody out that can walk unassisted," came the call throughout the infirmary.

Mike was up and out, followed by Max, who bunked in the back next to a pretty young doctor named Sally.

Max vaguely remembered Sergio's instructions about not talking to any woman, but in fairness, he thought, *She talked to me first.*

"You are in my world now," she told him the very first day, like any new medical staff man or woman, so I will call you New Max."

"Okay, but can I ask you something?" he finally got up the courage to say.

"One thing," she replied.

"How does a pretty woman such as yourself bypass the Colonel and his men? I mean, don't they take the pretty ones for themselves?"

"You're asking a question, New Max, that you shouldn't be concerned with. But I will give you an answer, true to my word. My name is Sally. 'Dr. Baker' to non-medical residents. My mother is/was his daughter and I never knew my father, so the maiden name stuck. Does that answer your question?"

"Uh, yes, ma'am...I mean 'Dr. Baker.' Sorry to ask, I guess."

* * * *

"Steer right clear of that one," said Sergio to him later. "She sure is something to look at, but she's a fast track to your demise—I guarantee it."

"Has anyone tried to get close to her?"

"A couple of guys that I know of, and they're not around to tell you the tragic story. Don't be number three."

The sirens were a warning, Mike learned. A test of bad things that may come. The one thing he saw that maybe nobody else in camp did was that the Colonel and his men were outside amongst the others for a full five minutes before the sirens stopped.

"How often do these things go off?" Mike asked Sergio.

"Twice a week, like clockwork, only it's a different day and time with each one."

"And he always comes out?"

"That may be his downfall, but I've never seen him miss one," replied Sergio.

Mike's purpose changed that night, and he focused solely on getting hold of the book. After all, it could change the entire playing field.

* * * * * * *

Chapter Twenty-two ~ Saddle Ranch Loveland, Colorado

Sarah called out instructions to the other doctors.

"We have an 18-year-old male with two gunshot wounds—left elbow and right upper thigh, as well as a posterior head contusion. He's semi-conscious, so all hands on deck."

Mac and Cory arrived at the West Hospital, only to be turned away by one of the new doctors.

"I'm not even sure why we come down here anymore, at least not at the start," said Mac. "It was like that before too. Unless it was a cut or broken bone—something simple like that—they would make everyone wait outside in the lobby."

"This is our lobby, only outside," replied Cory.

"Doc," said Mac, before one of the other doctors disappeared back inside. "Just tell Sar...I mean, Dr. Melton, and Drake when he wakes up, that Cory and I...we're here."

"Sure. Will do. Now I need to get back to work."

* * * *

Mac got the call late in the afternoon from Sarah that he was hoping to receive, or maybe dreading. It felt like every call from the hospital was bad news. This one was good news, at least so far.

"He's conscious and talking, and the swelling on his head has reduced significantly. He's not out of the woods, though, like I always tell you, Mac."

"I know," he replied, "I won't be counting any chickens until he's up and around for at least a week, just in case. I'm sorry you had to miss the funeral, honey."

"Me too, and the other doctors here, as well. We didn't think it should be postponed on our account. Our new mother needs to concentrate on her daughter now. How was it?"

"I don't know," Mac replied. "Okay, I guess. I'd never been to one before...for a child, I mean. It's different for sure from a 90-year-old who lived their whole life and got to experience everything. Little Alex didn't even get a single day. It sucks."

"I know, and I've been to my fair share of both over the years," Sarah replied. "All I can tell you is that God has a way of bringing little guys like Alex back up quickly. I don't know why, but He must have other plans for him. As hard as it is, I trust that He does."

"Yeah, I see your point. It still sucks, though. John said some nice words, so that helped... Hey, can we meet for dinner tonight?"

"Not tonight, Mac. I'm pulling an overnight shift to keep an eye on Drake. You could bring me dinner here to the hospital, though, if it's not too much trouble."

"No trouble at all," he said excitedly, like every other time he got to see her. "Plus, I can check on Drake."

"We'll see how he's doing then," she replied.

"Okay. See you at 6:30 sharp. Oh, wait...have you told Samuel about our little?..."

"Yes, and I'll tell you about it later."

"Is he upset?"

"No, Mac. He's fine, so tell your people and let's be done with it. Now, can I get back to work?"

"Ah...sure, honey."

"Love you, Mac."

"Love you."

* * * *

Mac spent the last hour of the afternoon talking with the MacDonalds and Whitney, telling them Drake was improving.

"We'll have you back home in a day or two," said Mac. "My guys are getting your home cleaned up, and the window should already be replaced."

"How can we thank you?" asked Mrs. MacDonald.

"None needed. It's what good neighbors do."

"Come up and check on us every now and then, will you?" asked Willie.

Mac smiled as Whitney blushed.

"You may be seeing more of some of us than you bargained for," he replied. "But yes, I'll personally check on you, probably a few times a month."

* * * *

Mac shuffled over to the Pavilion at 5 p.m. and found Chef Rico observing his crew, with the occasional hand gesture and every once in a while his hand over his face.

"Hey, Rico. Can I talk to you for a minute in private?"

"Sure, Mac. I always have a minute for you. Follow me," he said, leading Mac into a private office.

"Oh, hello Patty," said Mac. "I didn't know you were up here tonight."

"Yes, it's my day off, and I brought Joshua up to learn some skills from a famous chef," she said, elbowing Rico lightly in the ribs. "He's quite famous, I'll have you know."

"Oh, I've heard!" Mac replied.

"I'll let you two talk," she said, turning to leave.

"Oh no, Patty. Please stay. I want you to hear this as well. I'm only telling a few people, including you two, John, Sharon, Bill and Cory about it... Sarah is pregnant!"

It sounded strange coming from his own mouth, but he couldn't hide the smile that accompanied the statement.

Chef Rico only smiled.

"Is something wrong?" asked Mac.

"No, no. I was just thinking is all. Everything is just perfect. Congratulations to you both, and I guess no more wine pairing for a while!"

"I'm taking her dinner tonight," said Mac. "What's on the menu?"

"Excuse me, Mac, for just a minute. I have an idea," said Rico, pulling Patty aside.

"Will you trust us with the menu for you and Sarah?" asked Patty.

"Sure! I always do, but I did tell her I would have it to her by 6:30. She's at the hospital with Drake."

"Meet us back here in one hour," said Rico.

"Okay. Sounds good."

* * * *

Mac spent the next hour telling the rest the good news. He knew John would need to tell the Council, and that would just save him time.

Everyone was told, and John and Bill already knew anyway when Sarah got sick talking with them. Cory was happy to be included, not having known Mac all that long.

An hour later, Mac was back in the kitchen, being handed a covered tray by a giggly Patty and Rico.

“If I didn’t know you two better, I would be worried you messed with the food.”

“One should never mess, as you say, with food,” said Rico. “Don’t look until you get to the hospital, and read the card to her first. Promise?”

“Yeah, okay. I promise. Thank you both.”

* * * *

Mac headed down the road with a surprise in the truck’s passenger seat, being careful not to spill the large tray of food.

He always had a knack for guessing a meal his mom would cook just as soon as he walked in the front door. It got to be a game of sorts, and she would try to trick him, she would say. But really, she just wanted him to come home for dinner!

This night Mac rattled off a litany of smells, starting with Pasta Alfredo and jumping over to what would be Patty’s “almost famous” smothered burritos he had only heard about from John.

Curry filled his nostrils and sweet meat. *Wait a minute...one more second. Yes, something Indian maybe—curry chicken and Korean barbecue beef.* “They better be South Korean is all I’m saying,” he said aloud.

He smiled as he smelled what could only be some of his fish, no doubt saved from the other day, and something sour he couldn’t put his finger on.

Sarah greeted him at the door, hearing his truck pull up.

“How’s Drake?” he asked straightaway.

“Good—better than good so far. Oh, I didn’t see you there,” said Sarah, looking past Mac. “Please come in.”

“Can I see him?” she asked.

“Sure, let me just check first... Of course, you can come back,” she said a moment later.

"Whitney!" said an upbeat Drake. "You came to see me."

"Of course, silly. You had me sick with worry all day."

"Guess I'm not as good of a tree climber as I thought, huh?"

"The way I see it," Whitney replied, "is you got shot twice before you fell. That's pretty hard to beat."

"At least I broke my fall," Drake said, putting his good arm over his head.

"That just means you have a thick skull, like all men," said Mac, coming in behind Dr. Melton.

"What's that smell?" asked Drake.

"That's the question of the hour," said Whitney. "The chefs whipped it up for Mac and Dr. Melton. And he's been guessing the whole ride down here."

"We'll leave you two alone for a few," Mac told the kids.

* * * *

"What's for dinner?" Sarah asked Mac. "I'm starved!"

"A bunch of different things, I think. I'm supposed to read you a note from Rico and Patty first—who say 'Congratulations,' by the way."

Mac and Sarah,

Congratulations on your growing family. We appreciate your friendship more than you can know.

All our best, Rico and Patty

"There's more," said Mac, turning the note over.

Please enjoy a sampling of our collective work, just in case you are having cravings already.

Dishes include Patty's famous Smothered Burritos, the best cut of Mac's last trout...

"Check and check," said Mac, working his way down his list.

South Korean Barbecue...

"Wait, it says that?" asked Sarah.

"Okay, it just says 'Korean,'" he joked. "Anyway...and that's another check, by the way. Three so far."

"Continuing," Sarah interjected, acting playfully annoyed.

Curried Beef... "Okay, I was close. Got the curry right, though."

"Will you just finish already?" she said, trying to grab the note.

"Too slow!" he said, holding it in the air. "But seriously, the last ones are:

Pasta with White Truffle Sauce, Vinegar Vegetable Medley, and Strawberry Ice Cream.

"Why do they always make us so much food?" she asked. "Not that I'm complaining!"

"They're chefs. It's what they do."

"Drake and Whitney, I hope you're hungry," she called out.

They pulled up chairs around Drake's bed and set up TV dinner trays.

"Will I be home tomorrow, Dr. Melton? My dogs are okay tonight, but they'll be out of food by this time tomorrow."

"I think so," she replied. "If not, I'll have Mac check on them. All right?"

"Yes, ma'am. I'd be happy to," replied Mac.

"Don't forget these," she said, pulling out two airplane-sized bottles off Dewar's Scotch with "Mac" written on them in black Sharpie. "Look, they even put a glass with ice in there."

"Oh no, that wouldn't be fair to you. Thanks, though."

“I don’t even like Scotch,” she said, smiling.

“You know what I mean,” he told her.

“What I do know,” she responded, “is if you were the one pregnant,” she whispered, while the kids talked amongst themselves, “I would totally be having a glass of Chardonnay.”

She made his drink, not giving him a choice in the matter.

“What did I ever do to deserve you?” he asked.

“Everything,” she replied.

* * * *

Mac dropped Whitney off at her grandparents’ temporary apartment before 9 p.m. and headed home. He made a quick stop at the kitchen, finding Rico’s young chefs cleaning up the last of dinner.

“Are they here, Rico and Patty?”

“No, he’s gone for the night,” said one young man, adding in a lower voice, “he’s spending the night down the road.”

“Oh, I see. Better keep that to yourself, though,” replied Mac.

“Just tell him I stopped by to thank them when you see them.”

* * * *

Mac walked out of the Pavilion at nearly full dark when he heard it—a rumbling coming from the south end of the Valley, heading north.

“What in the world is that?” asked one of the cooks, stepping outside behind Mac.

“I don’t know,” he replied, “but you may want to stay inside for a bit.”

Mac was at a full run across the Ranch, not having to knock on Cory’s door.

“Is that what I think it is?” asked Cory, still not seeing anything in the dark sky.

They walked out onto the lawn, straining their eyes to see something matching the sound. *Whoosh!* came the first helicopter over the reservoir, followed closely by another, and one more after that, with lights illuminating the Valley walls.

They flew low, fanning the Valley from east to west.

"Those are Blackhawks, right?" asked Cory.

"Yep," replied Mac. "I haven't seen one since it went dark, but they were kind of a regular thing before that, chasing around the silver discs."

"Do you mean UFOs?"

"All I know is I don't know what they are, but they're fast and quiet as a Prius. So, unidentified and flying? Absolutely."

The three passed overhead in succession, hovering less than a minute later over the West's property.

"The only problem with the helicopters is I've never seen one land," said Mac.

Two helicopters hovered over the West's property, with one lowering to the ground, as best they could guess.

"What are they doing here?" asked Mac aloud, running now with Cory towards his truck.

"Easy now, Mac. We don't know if they're friend or foe yet; and either way, we need to be careful. One wrong move, and that's a wrap."

"Yeah, I know. But Sarah is there, and I need to get a message to Samuel."

"Unless he's dead asleep, I think he already knows," Cory replied.

Ranch citizens popped out of their homes, one after another, talking amongst themselves.

****

Chapter Twenty-three ~ Saddle Ranch Loveland, Colorado

Mac drove the truck on the back canal road, with lights off. He could have done it in his sleep, but the moon and clear skies helped visibility to at least 20 feet ahead to the west end of the property. His night-vision goggles gave him a basic idea of the situation.

"Stay here, Cory, and radio me if you see anything."

"Wait a minute! Where are you going?"

"To check on Sarah. She's at the hospital tonight."

Mac crept towards the backside of the hospital, climbing through the middle of the barbed wire fence, staying clear of the light beams shone down by the two hovering choppers. Sarah peered out the window at a figure coming from the direction of Samuel's house. The figure looked like him, but she couldn't be sure. Three soldiers exited the landed helicopter that shut off its propeller.

"What's going on?" asked Mac, sneaking up on Sarah through the back door, scaring the daylights out of her.

"Please don't ever do that again!" she said.

"You should really lock the back door," he replied.

“I think I know what this is,” Sarah said. “I’ve seen it before, but it’s been a while.”

“What’s that? Wait! Is that Samuel?” he asked.

“Yes, I’m pretty sure, and one of those men is the Colonel.”

“The one Lance and his group were talking about?”

“Yes, that’s the one. My father had been something of a mentor to him in earlier days. Here they come. Mac, please don’t do anything that could get you hurt. Stand behind me.”

Sarah opened the front door, with a reluctant Mac behind her and Drake sleeping right through it.

“Sarah, how are you?”

“Couldn’t be better, Colonel,” she said, hugging him.

“How’s Bradley, right?”

“He’s passed on, sir. This is my boyfriend, Mac,” she answered, trying to avoid the obvious next question.

“Well, I’m sorry to hear that about Bradley. Good to meet you, Mac,” he said, shaking his hand.

“Likewise, Colonel.”

“Do you know why I’m here, Samuel?”

“Yes, I’m guessing it’s about the Battle for the Valley business. Am I right?”

“That you are. Sorry for the late-night arrival, but we travel better after dark.”

“I understand. It’s no problem,” said Samuel.

“Are there some people you trust, those in a decision-making role you could get together in, let’s say, 30 minutes?”

“Sure, of course!” Samuel replied. “Mac, where’s your truck?”

"Just around the corner, sir."

"Great, can you get John, Bill, Cory, and any of the Council who want to hear this firsthand? I'll get mine together, and we'll meet at my house in 30 or so."

"I'm on it," said Mac, nearly sprinting towards the back door.

"Hold on there," said the Colonel. "Let's call it 45 minutes. My guys out there," he said, pointing up towards the ceiling, don't play nice with people running on the ground. Walk slow and drive slow. We'll be here if it takes a little longer."

"Sure thing. And thank you, sir," Mac replied, taking a deep breath and forcing himself to a walking pace.

"Just out for a night stroll," he said to himself. "Nothing to see here."

* * * *

Cory was standing outside the truck when he arrived.

"Nice and slow," said Mac. "They're friendly but not too. We need to pick up John and Bill and any of the Council if they want to come down here."

Cory radioed Bill, who had always been the easiest to reach. They picked him up, waiting outside his house, and John the same. Only one Council member was ready to leave their home at this hour, and she wanted to hear the information firsthand. They returned to the West's property, pulling up to Samuel's place under the *Womp! Womp!* of the two helicopters overhead.

"Are they going to stay up there the whole time?" the Council woman asked.

"You can count on it," replied Bill. "They have their commander down here."

* * * *

Samuel caught up with his old friend while waiting for the others. They hadn't seen each other for quite a while but reunited like a father and son. He introduced the Colonel around once the group had arrived and made night coffee for everyone, with most accepting.

"We have many things at play here," said the Colonel, taking center stage, "and I'll tell you what I can. Even now, some things are still highly confidential and won't be discussed here. So, I'll tell you the why, the what, where, and when. Try to wait until the end before asking any questions. I'm told we have about an hour.

"I am here tonight because this man, Samuel, helped me become a man and mentored me at an early age, with my father not being around. I have always vowed to pay him back in some way, and now may be that time.

"The what and where is an idea by a self-proclaimed fanatic leader and 'Colonel,' as he refers to himself, named Baker. Their idea they call the Great Battle for the Valley. This is that valley, just as you have it blocked with the northern and southern barricades. Baker wants it all, both this West property and Saddle Ranch, and they are not looking to share it with any of you.

"Why here? It's protected, fertile with more than one water source, and can hold an army-sized base for their future agendas. I don't know how they found this Valley, and the timeline is not confirmed at this point, but my best guess is that in three to six weeks from now they will be at your door. Questions?"

"Are you the same Colonel who spoke with my son Lance?" asked Bill.

"Yes, several times in the past month. I'm not sure how much he's told you over the radio, but he has a group of maybe 20 to 25 men, women and children. They teamed up with a Russian former gun shop owner—funny guy, that Vlad. Anyway, they are headed here through the mountains and should be up near Steamboat about now. I'm guessing they will be here in a few days. They have a fair number of weapons and ammo that I know, Samuel, your group will not pick up, but the rest of you should seriously consider it.

"Yes, John. You have a question?"

"Colonel, if you know there is a bad group heading our way, and you are close with Samuel, why not just persuade them to end up somewhere else?"

"That's a fair question. I don't have that jurisdiction at the moment. There are other things at play here on a much larger scale, and others who share my rank have different agendas. I do have a group, although smaller than theirs, running a day behind them. This one I run, and it gives me a general idea of what they are up to."

"Where are they now?" asked Bill—"I mean Baker's group."

"They are held up on I-25, south of Loveland, at a place called St. Vrain State Park. The place off the highway with all of the ponds."

"I know it," said Bill.

"Me too," added John, "but what do you mean 'held up'?"

"Their first base of operations was to be in Fort Collins—Horsetooth Lake, exactly—and it's possible there was an accident at their camp, delaying the arrival of such a large group. It's both good and bad for you, as it delays them long enough for Lance and his group to arrive first, but it also might just drive the whole Baker camp straight here, bypassing Horsetooth Lake altogether... I have to head out in a few minutes," said the Colonel, checking his watch, "but the bottom line is you will need to fight to keep the Valley. And as Lance can tell you, we will support you in your defense. My men can't just take them out before they get here, for reasons already discussed, but we can assist in your defense as long as they attack first."

"Sir," said Mac. "It's off-topic, I know, but your choppers out there look like the same ones I've seen chasing the metal discs around here for years."

"Is that so?" he replied. "Do you think ETs are real, Mac?"

"Yes. Yes, I do."

"They are," replied the Colonel. "Ask Samuel about the ones we know of."

"How do we keep in touch?" asked John.

"I'll get hold of you, so keep radio channels monitored at all times, if you don't already. I talk with my friend Vlad on a semi-regular basis, and rest assured when Baker's group is on the move again, you will hear from me!"

The Colonel spent a few more minutes talking with Samuel in another room before flying out.

"Are you going to tell me the truth?" asked Samuel, once they were alone.

"You and only you," he replied.

"The short of it is that North Korea dropped the EMP on us officially but not off of a satellite, as reported. It was launched from a tanker ship off the coast of southwest Louisiana, sold to them by China only weeks before the day. China runs them and many others in the region, besides South Korea and a few select more that are helping us behind the scenes."

"The Baker guy is not a plant, but he is somehow in direct communication with Beijing. The working theory is they are using him, and others like him, to amass large groups of people who will eventually farm this great land of ours. China has a population problem, and has for a long time. This ensures more food for their citizens, and according to my intel they will be dropping ten thousand workers a day in our ports to work the land that Baker's group has already left vacant. Think of it as a soft takeover, where Chinese farmers face no conflicts, only virgin land for plowing. And the kicker is, all the equipment to farm is still on-site; it just needs some electrical work, and they have teams for that also. They aren't pouring seasoned combat troops inside our borders looking for a fight, but instead families—men, women and children only striving for a new and better life, as we once did moving here from England. We can't just wipe them out."

"You're right," replied Samuel. "They should have a chance to work the jobs and become families known in the community, to prosper for years to come. And at the same time, they have been planted by a tyrannical government whose only desire is to take down our great country and pillage it from within. I can see how your hands are tied. It's good that you have Ronna, a man you can trust, following just behind the Baker fellow."

Once the Colonel left, Samuel rejoined the rest of the group. "I propose we all sleep on this and discuss it at length tomorrow, to include your Council, of course, John. Let's say noon at your Pavilion for lunch? I can send Patty up to help Rico prepare."

"Sure, that's fine by me. Noon tomorrow it is," said John.

Sarah hung back, asking her father if everything would turn out okay.

"We have God and the United States Military, led by a man I trust unconditionally. So yes, my dear, we will be okay in the end," answered Samuel.

* * * *

Mac woke early, wanting to bring Sarah breakfast. Drake would be released this afternoon but would be on modified duty for a few weeks.

"You can go home today, but take it easy," Dr. Melton told him.

"Long as I can ride my four-wheeler and feed my dogs. I just hope I can keep my job," he said, as Mac walked in carrying breakfast for them both.

"What did I miss?" Mac asked.

"Drake will be discharged this afternoon, and I think you should modify his four-wheeler so he can ride it up to his house. I don't want him using that right arm yet."

"Sure thing, I'll figure something out."

"I also want him on light duty for two to three weeks, and I told him his job was safe," Sarah added.

"Of course. You did good up there, Drake—real good. You are becoming a trusted part of the team. Now, I brought breakfast for you both, and it is getting cold. I'll check back on you later," said Mac, kissing Sarah on the forehead.

* * * *

The meeting was held at noon, as planned, in the Pavilion basement. Rico and Patty would not disappoint today, serving a charcuterie board with various meats, cheeses, pickles, crackers, fruits and jams, all originating in the Valley. Besides one council member calling in sick, all showed for the most important meeting of their careers. John led off with the best-case scenario, asking Bill to give its opposite.

"We will pray daily for His guidance and know He is steering us in the direction that is His will," said John. "The best-case scenario could take many forms, including but not limited to the group having a change of heart. Maybe they will decide they like where they are at now, at the ponds. It's not easy to move a large group over and over. Maybe something or someone steers them in a different direction, heading to the East Coast or back to the Midwest, where they started. Without direct involvement of the Colonel and his team before they reach us, I can't think of any other scenario that is at least reasonable to consider. Over to you, Bill."

"Thank you, John. As the Colonel said, Lance and his group will be here in a few days, God willing. I think he and that Vlad fellow the Colonel mentioned will have a better idea, having come up against Baker's group just a week or two ago. With that being said, I stayed up late last night thinking about this very question. We have a man going by the name of Baker, apparently posing as a Colonel to his people. We have had thousands of guests here over the years. He may have been one of them or just heard about it from someone who has been here. Either way, we should assume 100% that they will be at our door in three—I should say two—but between two and six weeks. With the Ralph situation hopefully at an end, we have the resources and personnel to start preparing as soon as tomorrow. Mac, I think you and Cory should take the lead, if that's okay with everyone?"

Most agreed, with no one disagreeing out loud, at least.

Bill continued: "We need likely entry points, preparedness for firepower we can't be sure of yet, and a safe place for anyone not on the front lines. As far as I'm concerned, there is nothing more important, starting tomorrow, than preparing for this assault on everything we have worked so hard to build for more than seventy-five years. In the off chance that they are dissuaded or make other plans, we will be that much more prepared moving forward, and that's never a bad thing."

"That sounds like a plan," said Samuel, with John agreeing.

"I have some ideas I'll jot down." Bill continued. "Mac, do you think you, Cory and your team could give us some defense options by breakfast tomorrow?"

"Absolutely," he replied. "We will have three plans, and the Council can choose."

"That sounds perfect," said Bill, getting an approving nod from all in the room.

****

Chapter Twenty-four ~ Saddle Ranch Loveland, Colorado

Mac and Cory spent the afternoon brainstorming—from the most likely scenario to the most far-out ones they could come up with. The word from the MacDonalds' place was no new sightings of anybody, and the upstairs window was replaced.

"Let's start with likely weapons to unlikely," said Mac. "Deer rifles, maybe a few ARs or AKs. Hopefully nothing automatic, unless their contact in the Military supplies them."

"They are a large group, we hear—hundreds strong, at least, with some type of Military backing," said Cory. "We can't completely rule out the possibility of Military vehicles, tanks, and some type of air support. We just don't know, so we need to plan for everything."

"Agreed," said Mac, always feeling better overanalyzing a situation and grateful to have someone like Cory to remind him of that. "I love it when a plan comes together!" he said, borrowing a line from one of his favorite TV shows growing up.

"I pity the fool who messes with this Valley!" replied Cory, getting a laugh out of Mac.

* * * *

Mac wasn't sure which plan the Council would be most comfortable with. He met with Cory again at the end of the afternoon.

"Okay," said Mac. "Here's what we do. We have been asked to submit three plans.

"Our bottom option, let's say Plan 1, should be what we really want and nothing less.

"The next tier, Plan 2, should be Plan 1 plus something more, but not over the top.

"Plan 3 includes Plan 2, plus something crazy enough to make them feel comfortable with Plan 2 or 1. Make sense?"

"Sure," said Cory. "If the lowest plan has what we want, we can't lose."

"Exactly. That's what I love about the three-plan deal, especially when there are no rules ahead of time.

"Okay, Plan 1," said Mac. "We beef up our guard presence from both groups on the north and south borders. The only likely way besides that is over the Rimrock, somewhere in the middle. They have a large group, making it easy to spot with a couple of forward observers, but that also means more people trying to take what we have fought for, more than once already. Right now, we have time—at least two weeks or more—and manpower. We don't have to officially add to the security team, but we do need to pull some people off of other less-essential projects to help fortify the property."

"What are you thinking?" asked Cory.

"For starters, we see who here can run the backhoes and tractors. We have some barriers to move and trenches to be dug. I want one all the way across the north end, just the other side of our current barrier, ten-feet deep and twenty wide. It doesn't need to be pretty, just effective. I think one or two full-time operators can get it done in a week. The south end is quite a bit wider, and it can't be done, at least not in the timeframe we have. On that end, we need enough old cars from the North Forty, and anything else we have, to funnel them into the middle. It's a big project, but our current barrier isn't good enough for a group like that. And last, the Rimrock cliffs create a natural barrier partway across, with only one road coming over the top. A pit dug on our side across the road should be sufficient. Of course, Lance and his group should have more info, having already faced them once, but I don't want to wait until they arrive to start working."

"Plan 2 is all that plus pulling any nonessential workers from tasks that are less than vital to life right now, like housekeeping and construction. I'll talk to Rico about a delivery food service to bring food out to our workers who can't make it up here for a meal."

"What about Plan 3?" asked Cory.

"That's Plan 1 and 2, plus we add frontline jobs for the Council. Most are up in age and won't want to be involved physically, so they will likely settle on Plan 2. Anything I'm missing?" asked Mac.

"Just a daily checkup at the MacDonalds' place—for a few weeks at least—so we don't have a repeat of before," said Cory. "I hope that Ralph guy is gone for good, but who knows? I want to make sure we are concentrating on only one hostile group at a time. Oh, and a shelter for anyone not participating, once it gets real."

"That's the easy part," said Mac, realizing he had never shown Cory the wine and beer cellar. "The best part is, you can see it from your house, but I bet you had no idea it was there."

"No way! Maybe out a side window or something?" asked Cory.

"Nope. Straight out the front living room window. You see it every day. Come on; I'll show you."

Mac took Cory back to his and Cameron's place. "Hey, Cameron, come on out," his dad called.

"Sure, Pops. What's up?"

"Mac said there is an underground shelter we can see clearly from our front window. Have you ever seen anything?"

"Uh...well, I mean..."

"Spit it out, son."

"Some of the teenagers showed me a few nights ago."

"The wine and beer place?" Cory asked.

"Yes, Dad," he replied sheepishly.

"What do they do in there?" he asked, not having to be a cop but only a dad to figure it out. "Okay, we will talk later about this. I guarantee it!"

"That settles it," Cory said to Mac. "It seems I'm the only one who hasn't seen it."

"It's over there," said Mac, pointing to the faded red wooden door, looking more like a part of a retaining wall than anything else. They walked over to see it. "We can fit everyone in here, but it will be tight," he continued, opening the door and walking down the cement stairway.

Cory observed the inside, walking around impressive wine- and beer-brewing setups that looked as though they were monitored daily.

"I've never seen the door open," remarked Cory, "so there is another way in, right?"

"Two ways actually," replied Mac. It was built as a storm shelter, or maybe a bomb shelter, in the 1940s. It's as solid as you can get without having a container sunk twenty feet underground."

"Hmm," said Cory, thinking out loud and finally answering. "I like it—three ways out and hard to spot. I don't want us to end up like the Branch Davidians in Waco. Most of them were trapped when it happened and couldn't get out if they wanted to. So why would Lance and his group fight all that way to get here, knowing the minute they do they will face a group much larger than the one that nearly took them out?"

"I've asked myself the same question and even spoke to Bill and Sharon about it. Their answer made a lot of sense. He's promised those traveling with him a safe place their kids can grow up in and will not starve trying to do so. They already have a good taste of what's out there on the road, and they are willing to fight for freedom. There's no getting around that now, wherever somebody ends up. The only alternative is the FEMA camps, and there is certainly no freedom there."

"That makes sense," said Cory. "The same reason I brought Cameron out here. What do you think our chances are?"

"Without the Colonel's help, not good, I'm afraid. Let's pray he shows on game day and fight like heck if he doesn't."

* * * *

Mac and Cory were up early the next morning, reviewing the plans one more time before meeting with John, Bill, Samuel, and the Council at 9 a.m.

Patty's smothered burritos killed this morning, and Rico didn't mind taking a back seat.

Mac and Cory pitched Plans 1, 2, and 3. The Council started with Plan number 3, voting it down, as Mac knew would be the case. There's a reason the Military has an age limit on new recruits.

Plan 2 got the most votes, with Council members seeing the need to divert nonessential jobs to security temporarily.

"Everyone wants clean clothes and a jammed front door unstuck by maintenance," said Mac, "but we only need them for a few weeks at most. It is a small sacrifice for a shot at saving our Valley."

John took a final vote and officially declared Plan 2 a go. Mac, in true fashion, didn't stick around to hear a change of heart.

"Let's go. Let's go," he said to Cory after thanking Rico and Patty for an awesome breakfast.

* * * *

They garnered the old crew and reached out to new recruits. They were not at liberty to tell everything of what they knew was coming—only a watered-down version, citing a need for increased security over the next few weeks.

Every tractor, backhoe and shovel was accounted for and moved into precise locations for imminent work. Mac personally marked each trench to be dug and entrance to be blocked. He spent the night at Sarah's, telling both her and his dog Bo that he may be heavily occupied for a week or two, maybe more if it came down to it.

"Be careful," Sarah told him, with one hand on her stomach. "I know we can't just sit back and wait to be run over by some crazy dictator, but we also need you back with us. You can't raise a family if you're lying in a ditch somewhere," she added.

"I will do what needs to be done to keep you, our baby, and those in this Valley safe—nothing more, nothing less. It is all one and the same now: all for one and one for all. I will be the sacrifice if it comes down to it, but I'm praying it won't."

"Me too, Mac. I...we, I mean, pray every day: 'Protect these people, all of us, every last person in this Valley.'"

* * * *

Mac dug the Rimrock trench himself. They were short on heavy-equipment operators, and it brought him back to easy days in his mind. He learned to use this equipment as a teenager and skipped more than a few school days to earn extra money—paying for his car, insurance, gas, an occasional date, and mostly helping his mother out with monthly expenses. She never knew he skipped school and would have had his hide for it, but she was grateful for the extra help and it meant more to him than she would ever know. Minutes blurred into hours, and half days slipped away from him.

* * * * * * *

Chapter Twenty-five ~ Saddle Ranch Loveland, Colorado

Sharon and Karl made their way to Mabel's house with homemade mint tea. Sharon knocked on the front door, not seeing her on the front porch, like always.

"Mabel," she called. "Are you in there? We have mint tea. It's not Starbucks but Karl thinks it tastes like it."

With no answer, Karl tried the front porch door, finding it opened a crack, and pointed to a half-covered meal on the front-porch table, ravaged by one or more critters.

"Mabel, I'm here with Karl. I'll have him wait out here. I'm coming in."

Sharon reached the door of the back bedroom, past the open bathroom, with no sign of her friend.

"Mabel," she said, knocking on the bedroom door. "It's me—Sharon. I'm coming in."

She slowly turned the handle, hearing a faint voice from inside.

"Oh, Mabel," Sharon said, seeing her under heavy covers, sweating and frail. "Mabel, how long have you been in here like this?"

"A day...maybe two. It's hard to tell," Mabel replied.

"Someone is supposed to check on you when they deliver each meal. It looks like you never even touched anything."

"Oh, sweetie, I feed half my dinners to the animals anyway. Everybody is always checking on me, but you're the only one who brings me mint tea.... I'm dying, you know—headed up to the Pearly Gates," she said, with a deep cough.

"I'm sure we can get one of the doctors from the West to come take a look at you. You will be feeling better in no time. I'll be back in just a few with one of them."

"Wait," said Mabel, with a firm grip on Sharon's arm. "I have dreams," she said softly but clear as day, "but not in the night."

"Daydreams?" asked Sharon.

"Yes, I suppose so...or visions maybe. But they are straight from on high—that, I know."

"Let me just get the doctor up here," said Sharon, "and we can finish this talk later. Or I can get Karl to go."

"This is no talk, sweetie; this is a confession. I won't be here when you get back. My body will, but my Spirit is headed up, and sooner than you think. So, sit with me and listen closely to what I have to tell you. I told you before that I have a deal of sorts with God, always have. He was going to take me yesterday right out on my front porch, but I wouldn't go without talking to you first. Stubborn as all get out, I suppose," she added, laughing—the slow deep kind that ends up in a coughing fit.

"Now listen, child, and hear every word. You have taken care of my earthly body and been a better friend to me than anybody I can remember," she added, not taking her hand off Sharon's wrist.

"They're coming..."

"Who's coming, Mabel?"

"Those who don't believe in our God. There is a man who goes by the name of Baker. I see him clear as day. He wants what you have."

"You mean what *we* have?"

"No, sweetie. He and his bad men want what you all have here in this beautiful Valley. The women and children are just along on the ride but will flood the Valley like locusts on a farmer's last crop. He aims to put an air strip—like used to be here many years ago—right out in the fields. They are not coming as you think—through one of the borders already guarded."

Mabel paused, coughing hoarsely.

"You can take a minute," offered Sharon, "or we can discuss this later."

"There is no later for this," said Mabel, looking her in the eyes.

"They will pour over the Rimrock like locusts, from one end to the other—in vehicles, helicopters, horses and on foot. A thousand or more zombies of sorts looking to devour the land and everything on it."

"When will they come?" asked Sharon, knowing Mabel couldn't know about the man called Baker.

"At first light, when the birds stop singing. When the deer are agitated and the rabbit runs for its hole. It starts with a rumble, like a thunderstorm echoing across the Valley. Lightning will fill a cloudless sky until you aren't even able to hear your own thoughts."

Sharon sat speechless, not questioning what she was hearing but simply frozen, unable to process a response.

"Don't be afraid, for God is with you. He will tell you when it's time and send others to help. This is His Valley, and He will make sure it stays that way."

"How do we protect it? How do we defeat them?" asked Sharon.

"Burn it!"

Mabel took one shallow breath, closed her eyes, and her hand fell from Sharon's, resting gently on the bed.

"Mabel, Mabel...are you still with me?" asked Sharon, watching a faint glow rise towards the ceiling and beyond.

"Mom, is everything okay?" asked Karl, standing just inside the front door.

"Yes, Karl. Mabel has passed."

Dr. Melton personally checked her an hour later, making the official time of death 3 p.m. The following day, a service would be held for the oldest resident to be laid to rest in the Valley cemetery.

Sharon spoke with Bill about her conversation with one of the best friends she had ever known.

"I'm sad to see her go, but I was there with her and that's what matters most."

"We need to gather tomorrow morning for another meeting," said Bill.

* * * *

They had the usual crew assembled for the news Mabel had shared only yesterday. Sharon told the story exactly as she remembered, ending with the ominous command.

"Burn what?" asked one of the Council to the others.

"Why would we burn our homes?" asked another. Most held up their arms in a questioning stance.

Bill whispered something to John and Samuel before addressing the group.

"Mac," he asked. "Do you have any questions for Sharon or any of us here about what we have heard?"

"No, sir, but I would like a few minutes to speak with Cory and then use the easel board, if that's okay."

Everyone in the room shook their heads yes, with Mac and Cory disappearing outside for ten minutes. There would be no breakfast served to the small group this morning. It wasn't that kind of meeting, Bill told Rico when he asked about it last night. Mac and Cory were on the same page with security defense. Mac took to the board, drawing a few landmarks, including the Pavilion with the "You're Here" designation you might see at a mall kiosk or National Park trail. The dome Chapel, Green Mountain, and the Rimrock also were marked.

"Our current borders are here, to the north, and here, to the south," Cory pointed out.

"Mabel left us a message that can be interpreted in several ways, I suppose," continued Mac. "I'm not sure how she could have known Baker's name, but she did. What she said makes sense about them coming over the Rimrock, from one side to the other. Why bring a thousand people through one chokehold, or barrier in our case, when you can fan out and hop from one valley on the other side of the Rimrock to another here, where we stand?"

"Why don't they just take the valley on the other side?" asked a Council member.

"It's too big to defend," said Cory. "It runs nine miles from Big Thompson Elementary School up to Masonville, and then splits two ways. There is a small river running through it, but damming it upstream is not hard to do. The long valley also lacks much of a barrier on the Loveland-facing side, and therefore is open to multiple points of attack. Plus, even if they did settle there, we would never have another day's peace in our Valley, being so close to them."

"That's what we believe she meant by her statement 'Burn it,'" added in Mac. "She wasn't referring to Saddle Ranch or the West community's homesteads or fields, but to the Rimrock itself. We have had our share of forest fires over the years here, with most up on Green Mountain. The keys are controlling the spread and hoping the wind is in our favor. It may be a long shot, but it could be the only option."

"What exactly are you saying?" asked John.

"We are suggesting a controlled burn across the Rimrock, away from this Valley. There are enough bushes up there to keep a flame, but not enough trees to make an inferno, like on Green Mountain. We use the tractors to build a fire road across the entire Rimrock, like they do fighting forest fires. Timing is everything, though. Too fast, and they come over when it cools—not fast enough, and they will already be on our side. If anyone has a better idea than Mabel, please let me know," Mac said.

* * * * * * *

Chapter Twenty-six ~ Raton Pass, New Mexico

David settled in with his new family, as if they had always been together.

Nate and his group, not yet part of the Raton Pass Militia officially, fit in as well as anyone else, David supposed. Everyone worked hard since Lance and his group had left, erecting all of the greenhouses, preparing the soil and planting seeds.

David and Mel gathered the groups at Beatrice's house after a well-deserved one-day break from all but the basics of work.

"Thank you all for coming here for supper tonight," said David. "Our Chef extraordinaire, Beatrice, has whipped up a meal fit for the hard work you all put into the greenhouses. Once the food cycle gets going, we will consistently replace what we consume. There will be challenges, but paired with proteins of fish and game, it is sustainable for the long haul.

"The key point moving forward is to not fall into the trap of comfort and laziness. For anyone who has never wintered up here, like Tina, our spring and summer can be deceiving. The more work we do over the next few months, the easier the winter cold and snow will be on all of us.

"Our houses aren't bad right now without air conditioning; in fact, most don't even have it installed. Houses like my mother's here," he said, "have both a wood-burning fireplace and stove in case of a power outage. Some of the other houses, like where my family and I are staying currently, do not have a usable heat source. They were only occupied in the summer months and didn't need to be kept warm in the winter. There is a hole in the wall with fake wood we used to call a California fireplace, more for looks than heating of any kind. Why would anyone install one of those in a Colorado home? I don't know, but the bottom line is we need to covert or build a wood-burning fireplace into each home. For those never having done this, it means firewood, lots of it, and all split. Nate and some of his group have assimilated easily into ours, and I always believe an extra hand is worth more than an extra mouth to feed. Enjoy your dinner, and we will meet for breakfast and new work assignments in the morning."

"Dad! Dad!" called Mark, waiting until David had finished his speech.

"What is it, son?"

"We have James VanFleet on the radio!"

"Is everything okay?" asked David.

"I don't know—just said he needed to talk to you and that it was important."

"Sure. Tell him I'll be right there," he said, whispering something to Tina.

* * * *

"Hello, James. To what do I owe the pleasure?" asked an upbeat David.

"Hey, David. How you all doing up there? Get those greenhouses up?" asked James.

"We finished yesterday and even planted the seeds. I do have some questions, though, about crop rotation."

"Sure thing, old friend. I'll show you firsthand."

"Great! Are you headed up this way?" asked David.

"Not exactly. I'm not in a position to make it up there now, but we need to meet."

"You want me to come down the mountain?"

"Yep, I have some news you will need to hear from me off the radio," replied James. "I reckon I need about two or three hours of your time. Can you make it?"

"Yeah, I guess I could do that. How's the road down to your place?"

"Oh, I don't know. Can't be as bad as when Janice and I rode down it."

James looked at Jason, getting a smile out of him. Both never expected to be able to joke about how they met, but somehow they could.

"When should I come?"

"Tomorrow works," said James.

"That quick, huh?"

"Yeah, that quick," replied James.

"Okay, hold on for a few and let me talk to Tina and Mel. They're right here, so it should just be a minute or two."

David was back on the line in five minutes.

"Not everyone is happy about it, but I'll be there, and I'm bringing Mark with me on the four-wheelers. I have a quick group meeting at breakfast, but we can head down right after. We'll need to head back up here by three or so. I want plenty of time before it gets dark."

"I don't blame you," said James. "Lunch is on us tomorrow, so tell Mark to bring his appetite."

"He always does," said David, laughing.

"You remember how to get here?" asked James.

"That I do. We should be there by 9 a.m."

"Okay then. We'll be watching for you, and Jason will come up and unlock the front gate."

"I hope I'm not up all night wondering what the news is," added David.

"Well, I'll tell you this much now. It's not the kind of shocking news, like a missing kid or injured adult, that might make you worry. However, it is the kind of news that one way or another will impact you, whether you stay home or not."

"Kind of like beachfront living with a hurricane you can't see heading straight for you, right?" asked David.

"Let's just call it a tropical storm," said James. "Nothing to lose sleep over yet."

David believed his old friend but had a restless night's sleep anyway. Mark only knew he was taking a day trip with his dad and was happy for the change of scenery. *Maybe I will get lucky and meet a girl my age*, he thought, realizing it was unlikely.

* * * *

Mel helped David with the breakfast meeting, not handing out jobs but asking for volunteers. Breakfast was delayed by an hour after a strong summer storm dumped on the Pass most of the night. David would remain head of security and Mel in charge of supplies, but teamed up for the last two-man job on the list that nobody volunteered for.

"It looks like we're on latrine cleanout duty," said Mel.

"I think we should get started on it right away, like after breakfast," David replied with a straight face.

"Nice try and not a chance in this world!" said Mel, breaking David's stone face into an "it was worth a try" grin.

"I'll pitch in cutting wood while you're gone today and save you the pleasure of working with me tomorrow, elbow-deep!"

"Okay, okay. That's what I figured," David replied, still grinning.

David and Mark said their good-byes, getting a late start. Both Tina and Beatrice were concerned, with only Tina showing it on her face.

"Would you be a dear?" Beatrice asked Tina, "and help me prep some food for the coming week? We should be finished about the time these men come back. Bring the girls, and let's invite Katie to help."

* * * *

David and Mark headed down the mountain, with Mark's father leading in front. The winding mountain road sucked Mark into its world, navigating ruts and spots washed out by recent rains. The road was masterful at clearing his mind of recent tragedies that he could not seem to escape for more than a few minutes at a time throughout the day. He steadied his breath, with warm wind careening off his helmet and the occasional bump of a flying bug flattened on his visor. Mark let his dad get a little ahead and would gun it until he caught up with him, hitting the breaks hard and fishtailing the quad, only to fall back and try it again. The center of the old fire road was in decent shape, as those roads went, but the shoulders loosened up more than expected during last night's rain.

David started to slow to say something a dad would about being careful and watching out for one's surroundings when he saw it up ahead on the corner.

She walked with her cub down the center of the narrow mountain road.

David stopped quickly, applying both brakes hard, hoping Mark didn't run into him. He waived an arm up in a stop position as Mark careened past him and halfway around the corner before applying his own brakes, just as quickly. His momentum was too much for the corner, too sharp maybe. The back of his machine slid around, hitting the soft bank and throwing Mark off towards the tree-line when it started to roll. It all happened in a split second, David would recall later. When the scene cleared, his only son lay motionless at the base of a large pine tree.

David jumped off his four-wheeler and had taken ten steps toward the accident scene when he remembered why he stopped in the first place.

The roar from his left side snapped him back into focus. The large female black bear would likely have minded her own business, but Mark's wreck had her scared and agitated.

"Listen to me," said David out loud, not taking off his helmet. "I'm not going to hurt your baby, but I need to check on my son."

In his haste, he hadn't grabbed his rifle strapped to his machine. Another glance towards Mark and one back to his bike had him conflicted. He started to go for his rifle when Mark groaned.

"Mark, Mark," he called out and was headed his direction without a conscious decision.

He ran to him with a flash of an elementary school class in New Mexico. People may be taught about hurricane preparedness in Florida or tornado survival in the Midwest, but in this part of New Mexico it was bears, and the first rule is *Don't run!*

David could see that Mark was moving more, even at a full run, and he tried to get to a sitting position before falling down again with a scream of pain piercing the mountain valley. David's mom had always let him ride bikes as a boy but insisted he wear protective boots, pants, a jacket, and always a helmet. Mark had the same. Of course, they were not meant to lessen a tree impact.

David ran towards his son with only a ringing sound in his head, like one might experience being close to a loud explosion. His heavy breath and heartbeat filled his ears but somehow on the inside.

"I'm coming, Mark," he yelled, "Mark, I'm comi..."

The hit from behind felt like a Mac truck rolled over his back, pinning him facedown in the muddy ditch, only twenty feet from Mark. Large teeth clanked loudly on his helmet, scratching the outside, sliding down like fingernails on a chalkboard, with the first jolt pushing his face visor into the soft mud. David instinctively, or maybe he learned this in school also, pulled his shoulders up to the helmet to protect the back and used his hands to protect the front of his neck.

The bear gnawed at his jacket, shredding his backpack. David had never been this close to a bear and thought the sounds were a mix between a growling dog and a cow in heat. He waited for the first bite or flesh tear from a large claw, looking towards Mark, who was still again. *Play dead*, David heard in his mind. *Play dead!* It went against everything he would have thought up on his own, but now it was worth a shot. He lay motionless, face into the ground. The weight on his neck was tremendous, forcing him to take shorter, quicker breaths—not on purpose but it was all he could suck in.

"Oh God, don't let me die—not here," he may have said out loud or only thought. "My son needs help."

His head was foggy, disoriented, and the grunts and snarls seemed far off now, but he couldn't breathe. The face shield of his helmet cracked under pressure, driving his face into the mud. The first and only other time this happened was in a local rugby match his senior year of high school. Thirty minutes into the second half, he was driven face-first into the mud by an opposing player. The beast of a boy nicknamed "Piledriver," and a transfer student from England, of all places, landed on him before several more players piled on top. It was scary, even with referees only taking a minute to pull the bodies off. Now there were no referees, no time-outs or forfeits.

He felt the snap of the first rib on his left backside. The second one took his breath and, on the inhale after, filled his lungs with mud and leaves. He tried to cough and exhale the grit, but it wouldn't come. David looked at his son on the ground, as his father had been. He didn't get to tell Dean good-bye, and now he wouldn't get his chance with Mark. He felt sleepy, and his lungs no longer hurt. A sort of peace came over him and a calm voice was telling him, "It's okay. You can come Home."

"I'm sorry, my son. I'm so sorry..." He managed to choke the words out loud enough for Mark to hear.

****

Chapter Twenty-seven ~ Raton Pass, New Mexico

Boom! Boom! The shots seemed miles away, but the pressure on his back was gone—only the sharp pain of snapped ribs remained. He turned his head to see a man with a rifle walking up the road, firing two more shots into the air. *Boom! Boom!*

David lifted his head, drawing his first breath in over a minute, immediately coughing up thick brown chunks as leaf stems scratched his throat, and yelling out in pain. He had never broken a rib before but had heard the worst part was a sneeze or coughing fit before they fully healed. He was a believer now as he crawled towards Mark, every pull making his ribs scream with a knife-like stabbing pain. He ignored the bear, not seeing where she went and the shooter who he would have no chance of defending against anyway, and reached his goal.

"Mark," he said lightly, shaking him. "Are you okay?"

"I'm alive, Dad," he replied, not moving anything but his lips. "Is the bear gone?"

"Yes, I think so...maybe," he replied, before looking around and seeing it walking back up the road with her cub in tow.

"I'm so sorry, Dad," Mark said. "I was messing around, and all this happened."

"Where are you hurt?" asked David.

"My chest hit the tree, I think. It hurts—hurts real bad. Am I going to die?"

"No, son. I'm not going to let that happen."

"I feel a crunching when I breathe, and I can't move my leg."

"Your legs? Both of them?" asked David, hearing it wrong and worrying about a spinal injury.

"No, only my left one," said Mark, yelling as he turned over.

It didn't take a surgeon to realize his left leg was snapped above the knee. *It's not a compound fracture*, thought David, as he couldn't see bone or blood, but the angle was all wrong. Anyone could see that.

"Son, did you hit your head?"

Mark took a deep breath before answering. "It just hurts so bad," he said quietly. "I don't think I hit my head on the tree...only in the dirt."

David glanced again up the road, seeing both mama and cub disappear around the next bend. He almost forgot about the man with the gun who would surely take his four-wheeler and weapon, leaving him and Mark to fend for themselves. He could see him talking on a radio, still 50 yards out.

"Okay, Mark. I want you to hold tight. Where is your rifle?"

"I don't know, Dad. Maybe on the machine or somewhere on the road. I never saw it."

"When I say three," said David, working what was left of his pack off his back. "I'm going to make a run for my machine and grab my rifle before he gets it. Lie still as you can until I get back."

"No! Wait, Dad. What if he shoots you?"

"I won't shoot first is all I can tell you, but he's on a radio now and I don't want us to be here when his men come. It's our only chance."

"Wait, Dad. Where's your walkie-talkie? It might still work. We're only 20 miles away."

"Probably won't work here, but maybe if we got to the top of the mountain… That's as unlikely now as us walking out of here. But I'll try to grab it too, just in case."

Once more, he glanced at the man who was looking in a different direction and still talking.

"Three," said David springing up and turning before he lost his nerve. One step, two, and his tattered backpack strap caught his foot, face-planting him down on the ground.

He scrambled to get up, fighting the pain and stumbling forward. *Boom!* he heard, seeing the man with his gun pointed in the air and walking towards him.

"You don't need to do that, David," he called out, not slowing his pace.

"How do you know my name?"

"Name's Jason Davis and I met our mutual friend, James VanFleet, right here on this very road. We live with him and Janice, my whole family does, helping out on the ranch. He saved my life, and now I'm going to save yours. That must be Mark over there?"

"Yes, that's my son, and you already know my name. How did you know to come up here?"

"You're late. We were expecting you more than an hour ago. So, James sent me up to check on you. He is still healing up, but Janice should be up in just a few with the truck."

"She's coming up by herself?" asked David.

"Yep, I just rode up, so I know it's clear, plus we're only a few miles from Second Chances Ranch and my radio still works. Let's see if we can get your boy over to the road."

"Are you taking us home?" asked David, as they slowly helped a one-good-legged young man with severe chest pain.

"There's a bear up there—went right up the road."

"Yeah, the one who nearly killed me!" replied David.

"Unless you have a good medical team up there, I suggest we bypass mama bear and let a doctor take a look at your boy. Janice has medical training—fixed me right up with a gunshot wound to the hip. Let's see what she thinks. Besides, James may never forgive me if I just drop you off back at home and something happens to one of you."

"How are you feeling, Mark?" asked Jason.

"Not good, sir. Something isn't right—inside, I mean. Dad, I don't want to go home yet; I want someone to look at me. I'm scared. I really messed up this time. How is it when something really bad happens, I'm always involved?"

"No, Mark. It's not like that at all. If the bear hadn't been on the road, we could have raced down the mountain and had a good time. Bad things happen to everyone, even the good guys like you. It's a tough part of life, and now it's amplified a thousandfold. Jason, you don't know what it means to have your help. I'm glad you were here, for both our sakes."

"Oh, I think I do," Jason replied. "Like I said, it was James expecting you an hour earlier and asking me to check on you is all. Plus, he has a sense of things other people don't. I wasn't expecting this, though, if I'm being honest."

"Neither were we," said David. "All right, we'll have Janice take a look before making a decision."

Mark laid on his back in the road, with the truck showing up fifteen minutes later. Janice took him first, examining him where he lay. She made him as comfortable as possible but inflicting more pain than she had wanted to.

"He needs a doctor," she told David. "Not a medic but a surgeon. Do you understand?"

"Yes, ma'am," said David, grateful for the honest opinion. "I don't know any," he added, lowering his head.

"Well, it's a good thing then that I do. A couple of good ones used to work in Trinidad. Jason and I will get your four-wheeler on the truck and leave that pile of junk here," she said, pointing to Mark's machine.

"Wait," called out David. "I need his rifle."

"I'll get it," replied Jason, as they loaded the bike into the truck.

"Three guesses," he said upon his return.

"Guesses of what?" asked David, not aware of the retrieval process.

"Where the rifle was. Three guesses. First, it was on the totaled bike; second, in the ditch; or third, right in the middle of a tree, just hanging on a branch."

Mark, still semi-coherent, guesses the bike. David reluctantly participated, saying the ditch.

"I kid you not," said Jason. "It was in the friggin' tree, just hanging on a branch partway up, like the good Lord Himself put it there for safekeeping."

"Saddle up; we're headed out," said Janice, as she inched the truck forward. "No more guessing contests, Jason. I want Mark to stay quiet and calm on the way to town."

"Sure thing. Sorry about that," replied Jason.

****

Chapter Twenty-eight ~ Weston, Colorado

It was strange, Janice thought, driving right past her property and waving to her husband sitting on the front porch. They were in contact by radio with James, agreeing to have them bypass the ranch for now and get the best medical help in the area. He even called ahead, flexing his Mayor muscle to get a recently overworked and underpaid Dr. Walters to wait for the new arrival.

Dr. Walters and two others, one less competent and one probably more if an official vote were ever taken, helped Mark out of the truck and onto a gurney. They whisked him inside after getting the mechanism of injury from Jason.

"He crashed his four-wheeler to avoid hitting a mama bear and her cub is the extent of it," he said.

Before the day, the explanation would surely be followed up with ten or more questions. After all, doctors needed a good and thorough daily note on each patient and an initial exam of easily 4-7 pages. Now it was different, and every doctor knew it. "What happened and where does it hurt?" were the introductory questions, followed by an immediate treatment plan and execution of it.

****

"Mark has a fracture of the sternum," Dr. Walters said an hour later. "It's not a major concern, but the pain is going to be tough at times. We've had our surgeon in for a second opinion, and she thinks the sternum is nonsurgical for now. His left femur will require surgery, and the sooner the better."

"How soon?" asked David.

"Tonight! He also has two broken ribs on his right anterior—I mean the front side—and a concussion."

"He told me he didn't hit his head," David spoke up.

"Where's his helmet?" the doctor asked.

"Here. Right her... " David paused, looking at the crack on the front right side. "This is a good helmet, best in the industry!"

"I know," replied Dr. Walters. "My son used to race in one of these. He's right next door—just jumped the courthouse yester..." He looked at a shocked Jason and back-tracked as gracefully as one could, trying to cover a truth, or scandal maybe, in the small town of Weston.

"It's going to be a double shift, everyone!" he called out to his staff.

"That why we get paid the big bucks!" one nurse joked.

The medical team's compensation was a bit of a sore spot lately, with most patients having nothing to pay with beyond old-school bargaining items. The usual suspects lately were eggs, chickens, vegetables, and items that didn't work anymore, like watches and electronics. Jason promised to bring it up to the Sheriff when he returned from fishing.

Jason stepped out to radio James. "Is he going to be okay?" James asked.

"David has a couple of broken ribs in the back. Mark has a fractured sternum, the Doc says, and two broke ribs on the front, as well as a concussion. He needs surgery on his left leg tonight, and not everyone is happy to work overtime here. Oh, and Doc Walters let it slip that he is Ken's father and quickly changed the subject. Maybe nothing...just seemed weird is all."

"I had no idea; it never came up. Everything is weird right now," said James. "Do me a favor and check on the folks from the bleacher incident."

"Will do," replied Jason, heading back inside.

"We need to keep your son overnight, at least, and probably longer," said Dr. Walters. "Do you have somewhere you can stay tonight?"

"I'm staying right here as long as my son is inside," replied David.

"Please, sir. We are at capacity around here, as you can see. We simply have no room for family members to wait. So, I ask again, do you have somewhere to stay tonight?"

"Yes, he does," said Jason quickly. "I'll take him out to the ranch and bring him back in the morning."

"All right," said the doctor. "David, you keep that rib belt we gave you on, and we'll check it again tomorrow. You already know what coughing does for rib pain, and if you don't have to sneeze, don't do it."

"Thanks, Doc. You going to be okay, Mark?" he asked, catching him looking at a young blonde-haired blue- eyed girl about his age heading into his room.

"Oh, yeah, Dad. I think I'll be just fine; the meds are kicking in. Kelly here, I mean Calie," he said, trying to pronounce her name tag written in cursive, "is taking good care of me."

"That's right, and it's Calleigh," she said, writing it on a napkin.

"How old are you, Calleigh?" asked David.

"Almost seventeen," she replied, not taking her eyes off Mark.

"How old do you think I am?" Mark asked, smiling from ear to ear.

"Hmm, I would say sixteen in about a month."

"How did you? Ohhh...it's in the chart," he conceded as she held it up.

"They let you work here at your age?" he asked curiously. "No, disrespect," he quickly added, as she paused.

"My daddy kind of runs the place," she whispered. "Should I ask to help take care of you while you're here?" she added quietly.

"Yes!" Mark blurted out. "I mean...that would be the best... Sure, that's fine," he added, putting an end to the bumbling. It wasn't like he didn't know girls. He had a few girlfriends before everything changed. None of them were too serious or as pretty as her and there were exactly none even close to his age at camp.

"So, you'll be okay, Mark?" asked his father again.

"Oh, sorry, Dad. I just...well, you know. I'll be fine. See you tomorrow."

* * * *

"One minute they're wrapped around a pine tree, and the next they can't wait to ditch Dad," David said to Jason as they walked out of the hospital.

"Yeah, I don't know that feeling yet, but my girls are still young."

"Girls—all of them?"

"Yep. We have three beauties."

"Well, you'll be busy fighting off those country boys eventually, like Al Bundy in the TV show *Married... With Children* used to do," said David.

"That's what everyone says," Jason replied. "It's why I carry a small voice but a big stick," he added.

"Who's that girl's daddy?" asked David. "She said he ran the place."

"That would be Doc Walters, who apparently has a son I didn't know about, but that's a conversation for another time," said Jason. "Let's head back to James' and Janice's place. I'm sure you want to get word to your group about you and Mark staying the night."

"Oh man, with everything that's happened, I forgot we wouldn't be home tonight! They are going to be expecting us pretty soon," said David.

They reached Second Chances Ranch without incident, which was common practice recently.

"The Sheriff has a hold on the town, and most around it," said Jason after commenting on how safe the roads were recently.

"I thought he shared the responsibility with the town Judge. I forget his name, though," replied David.

"Not anymore, but I'll let James get you up to speed on that story. It's really why he asked you to make the trip down."

"I wondered what could be so important that it couldn't wait, but any trip down the mountain before winter is always better," replied David.

* * * *

James, Janice, Lauren, Billy, and the girls were all on the front porch when they arrived.

"David, how are you?" asked James, reaching his hand out.

"Good to see you, old friend."

"Mark, it sounds like he's going to be okay?"

"That's what the doctor is saying. It was a scary day, to say the least."

"And you were attacked by a bear? What's that about?"

"It was more of a wrestling match really. Wrong place at the wrong time. Just a mama bear protecting her young. She almost suffocated me, though. That's something you don't expect from a bear encounter. How about you and the family?"

"Oh, we're doing just fine. A lot has happened here since we talked last, and I was hoping you could come down for an easy lunch and conversation."

"Nothing is that easy," said David. "Not anymore."

* * * * * * *

Chapter Twenty-nine ~ Weston, Colorado

"You up for a talk?" asked James.

"Sure, I still have the meds kicking in, so my rib pain is down to a dull roar. I need to get a message to Tina and my mother, though. They are expecting us back already."

"I'll work on that while you talk," said Jason.

"Thanks. Mark's friend should be on right now," replied David.

"We're a mess, you and me both," said James, laughing. "It only took a month to put me in this chair after being shot by some random thugs and have you cheat death more than once."

"Yeah, makes me miss the boring office days sometimes, where the biggest concern we had was choosing barbecue or a sandwich for lunch."

"Those days are long gone, my friend. And like it or not, things are changing around here," James added.

James told David about the fiasco with the Sheriff and Judge, the exhibitions, and the bleacher accident.

"That's all interesting, for sure," replied David. "But I don't see how it affects my group and me."

"David," called Jason. "I have your wife and mother on the line, and a man called Mel, I think."

"Excuse me," said David, slowly rising, holding his ribs. "I'm not looking forward to the ride back up the mountain," he told James, as he hobbled to the next room.

Tina and Beatrice were worried about Mark and weren't happy about them not returning today. They wanted to know what was so important that they had to make the trip in the first place.

"I don't have that information yet, but I will soon," he told them. "I can only assume it was necessary to talk face-to-face. Keep an eye out on security, will you, Mel?"

"Sure thing, David. Don't worry about a thing."

* * * *

"All good?" asked James when David returned.

"So far, so good."

"All right. Then I won't keep you waiting any longer about why I asked you down here. Everything I've told you so far is about to have an effect on you and everyone in your group."

"How's that? We're not even in the same state."

"There are no states, my friend—not anymore. Only cities, towns and territories. The town, this town of Weston, is becoming just that—a territory. Judge Lowry declared a ways back that they would be expanding the town limits by twenty miles in all directions. This made my family and our property a part of Weston overnight. We didn't have a choice in it unless we dug in and prepared for a fight we couldn't win. So, I accepted a high position, giving me the freedom to sway most town decisions and matters in favor of the citizens. I have done that thus far, but some things are beyond my control.

"You, David, and the Raton Pass Militia are about to be incorporated into the town of Weston by Sheriff Johnson, who aims to add another 20 miles in all directions, with the exception of straight east and the city of Trinidad. You sit approximately 34 miles from the town square, placing you and yours in this town. Sheriff Johnson doesn't care about state lines, or even county lines, anymore."

"Why would he want to add more people he's responsible for?" asked David.

"The political response would be something like there is safety in numbers, and an expanded territory protects more people... The friend's response is, he wants more taxes collected."

"Wait a minute! You pay taxes?"

"Not property taxes, like before, but a sales tax, yes. We have a market of sorts every Saturday, and the town takes five percent of collections or that much in goods from each vendor. More vendors equal more tax money and goods for the town."

"And in return?" asked David.

"In return, new town residents have a say in voting and a certain amount of protection. They also have access to community services."

"Why would we agree to this?" asked David.

"The way I see it is, you will be incorporated sooner or later by someone. Probably Raton or Trinidad, I would guess. If you are part of Weston, you have a friend, now two with Jason, who hold prominent positions in town matters. It's possible I could change the Sheriff's mind, but he's pretty dead set on the idea already."

"I'll talk to him and tell him where he can stick his proposal!" said David.

"That's not a good idea, David. I've seen enough in town to know conversations like that with the Sheriff don't end well. Right now, he has an empty jail and that usually doesn't last long. I'm not saying anything is for sure yet, but if I were a betting man I would say you will be sitting inside Weston territory by month's end. On a positive note, you could trade goods on Saturdays. These kids here have bought pancakes, yo-yos, frozen seafood, and even Chance over here," he said, pointing to the sleeping lab. Fact is, it's not so bad right now, and we even have a restaurant still open and sell them beef from time to time. How would Mark be getting a surgery up on the mountain right now?"

"I see your point, James, and I'll think on it, you have my word. It sounds like you're saying I had better choose sides before it's chosen for me."

"That's how I see it, old friend. You're out of town right now but not far enough, unfortunately. Some cities or towns will be very interested in your group and provisions sooner or later, and at least you know where you stand here."

"Can I get a drink?" asked David.

"Sure, whatever you want."

"A Scotch would be great—probably against doctor's orders, but what isn't?"

"How long are they going to keep Mark?" James asked.

David relaxed a bit, nearly snorting his Scotch through his nose.

"What's so funny?" asked James.

"Kelly."

"Kelly?"

"No...Calleigh, Mark's new friend at the hospital. Doc Walter's girl promised to take good care of him."

"Is that so?" asked James. "She's maybe 16 or 17—about his age, I think. Nice girl and a distraction for more than a few young boys around here, from what I've heard. How many his age up at your place now?"

"That would be none, I'm afraid."

"You may have yourself a problem then, and sooner than later!" replied James.

"I know," replied David. "That I surely do. To answer your question, though, they will keep Mark about three days, they said, with checkups after that."

* * * *

Mark slept, if you could call it that, on his back for the first time he could ever remember. The leg surgery was done and they said it went well. His chest ached, and any sudden move shot a sharp pain into its center. He refused a catheter and was helped to the restroom only once by female nurses not named Calleigh. By morning, he only had three questions. Did she have a boyfriend? How was he going to make it back home up the mountain? And when could he see her again?

"Good morning, Mark," she said, waking him with a hand on his shoulder.

"Ah...oh, good morning, ma'am," he responded.

"They call my mother ma'am," she responded, "but Calleigh is fine."

"Sure," he said, feeling a bit foolish. "They call my dad sir but me... I'm sorry. I was trying to make a joke, and I lost it. Maybe it's the medication, or I don't know..."

"Maybe it's me?" she said, smiling and reaching down to hold his hand.

Mark didn't respond, only stared off into nothing. "Are you okay?" he heard her ask from miles away.

"I don't feel so good," he managed to get out before it went dark.

"All available doctors in here now!" called a nearby nurse down the hall. Word got around quickly, and a team worked on him, mindful of his injuries.

David and Jason walked inside as he regained consciousness, rushing to his bedside.

"What's happening?" asked David.

"It's a side effect of his concussion," said one of the doctors.

"Where is Dr. Walters?" demanded David. "Where is he?"

"He's home resting after a 24-hour shift," said a nurse. "He should be back in...well, any minute now."

David talked with his son, waiting for the one doctor he trusted.

"I have a lot of cases right now," said Dr. Walters, walking in the room. "Mark is a priority patient, as you are a personal friend of the Mayor, but there are others—many worse off than Mark—who also have fathers demanding to speak with me."

David sighed and paused before speaking. "My apologies. I understand your position, Doctor, and I only want what's best for my son... What happened?"

"He had a complication from the concussion and blacked out. I'm going to want to observe him for another day or two. Trust me, he can't get better care anywhere. Once he is released from my care, you will all be back out of town, and I can't do much more from here besides sending you home with meds, unless you can get back down here for regular checkups."

"We're not too far out," said David, as the first perks of in-town living hit him straight in the face. "All we have is the four-wheelers, though. I'm guessing that's not recommended for Mark anytime soon."

"I don't even recommend it for you right now," Dr. Walters responded. "I'm not sure if you're in the market for a truck, but there's a guy, a farmer not far out of town. I've treated his whole family for years and they have a few running trucks for sale. I'll tell you up-front, though, they are not cheap. It's probably why he still has them."

David got the information on the farmer and would talk to Mel about it later.

Mark was back up and talking, just like nothing ever happened.

"It's breakfast time," said Calleigh. "Would you mind coming back a little later, sir?"

David looked at Mark, who nodded that all was okay.

* * * *

"Breakfast is on me," said Jason, taking David to the Weston Grill and Tavern.

They waited inside, as Jason wanted to avoid Cam, the electrical man who failed to deliver on James' chair. He told David the story while they waited inside at the front counter until their breakfast was delivered.

"Let's eat outside," said David abruptly, grabbing his plate and heading straight for the oldest man he could see.

"They call you Cam, right?" he asked, sitting down, with a reluctant Jason still inside.

"Maybe. Who's asking?"

"I'm a friend of Jason's; you know, the guy who paid you to complete a motorized chair for the Mayor of this town. But you haven't done that, have you?"

"No pay, no play!" said Cam defiantly.

"Oh, but you have been paid, and more than once. You don't care either way if the project is completed, do you?"

"Nope, you got me there. Don't make a rat's ass to me what happens now."

"I can understand your point. That steak you're eating there with your eggs, you know where that's from? James VanFleet," he added before Cam could guess. "Jason credits James with saving his life; and now, as of yesterday, Jason saved my life, and my son's as well. That chair you don't care much about is from Jason to James."

"Mayor's already got one," said Cam, seeming bored with the conversation.

"Not from Jason, he doesn't. I hear you're the electric man who keeps this restaurant's generators running in exchange for a meal every day."

"Maybe," replied a disinterested Cam.

"I have a lot of experience in this area, just like you," David continued. "I'll do it for free as a personal friend of the man who is not only Mayor of your town but also supplied the beef to keep this, the only restaurant in town, running. Plus, I'll bet you go into the kitchen a couple of times a week and bang a hammer on something, so everyone thinks you're working. I'm guessing you only occasionally have to do any real work on the generators, and here you are, eating steak. How about you show me around, and I'll take over this afternoon?"

"Now, wait just a minute! I was just a sittin' here minding my own business, and now I've got all this you're bringing me. What do you want?" asked Cam, suddenly realizing he could lose his cushy job.

"I want you to give Jason the chair you promised him. Don't tell me the Judge shorted the deal or anything else; I've heard it already. They have both paid you fairly for something you didn't deliver. Here are four silvers, more than enough to get it done. I'll be in town for two or three days, so what's it going to be?"

"All right, okay. I'll start on it this afternoon."

"Now is good," said David. "I'll tag along, so give me the grand tour...

"Let's go, Jason. Cam's going to finish the chair and has two days to do it."

The tour revealed a half-completed motorized wheelchair, with the rest of the parts strewn about the floor.

"It looks like you have everything you need to get this done," said David. "How about you put in a couple of full days of work and finish it?" he added as he and Jason headed out.

* * * *

They returned to Second Chances Ranch early in the afternoon, following a quick second check on a comfortable Mark.

"I'll admit it," said David. "I might have a change of heart about being inside the town limits."

"Really?" asked James. "How so?"

"Well, doctors and nurses are giving top-notch care to my only son. The restaurant food was crazy good, and I'm concerned about being isolated as a small group in the mountains with surrounding cities on all sides. We could use a good dog like Chance up on the property," he added, petting him on the head.

"He's got a sister almost as big. May still be available; I don't know. What do you think Tina and your mother will think about all this?" asked James.

"My mom is old school; she's lived up there for many years. Tina's from the city and misses it, I know. Maybe this thing you're talking about could give us some of both."

"And Mark?" asked James.

"He's been here a day and is already lovestruck. It is going to be hard to keep him away from town now."

"Can you blame him?" asked Jason.

"No. No, I can't. I just remembered all of the bad things happening with the Sheriff and that Judge you were telling me about, James."

"The Judge is gone now, and I'm second in line to run the town," said James. Sheriff Johnson has a particular way of doing things, I know, but we understand each other. Jason and I have been one step ahead of both the Sheriff and Judge Lowry the whole time...

"Have you seen our still? We have an incredible 360-degree view of the property up on the roof. Let's take a look at both."

"Sure. I just need to get hold of Mel on the radio. Dr. Walters knows a farmer with three running trucks for sale. He doesn't want me running Mark up and down the mountain on the four-wheelers. Here's the info on him," said David, handing James a piece of paper Dr. Walters had written on. You ever heard of him?"

"Makes sense," said James, looking at the paper. "I know him; he's one of my longtime customers. Let's take a ride over there together. What's he want for each of them?"

"Doc didn't know. Just said they were likely expensive."

"I'll bet," replied James. "Supply and demand with everything nowadays."

A quick call with Mel got David excited, hearing Mel was interested in two of the vehicles—with a package deal, of course.

James and Jason hadn't spent much time up on the rooftop deck. None at all, really, since their moonshine lunch a few weeks back that felt like years ago now.

"I have not seen it, but it sounds good," said David. "I'm just a looker today, though. I want to head into town and see Mark one more time tonight. I can take my four-wheeler."

"You'll take a beating on those ribs," said Jason. "We will take a look at the still and James may even give you a bottle to take with you. Then I'll drive you to town in the truck."

"I'll send you home with a whole case," added in James. "My biggest customer was Judge Lowry, and he stopped buying last Saturday. We've got more than we know what to do with now. I'll need your help getting up there, both of you," added James.

"Sure thing. And a case sounds good to me; I can give Mel something he doesn't already own. Put it on my hotel tab, and I'll pay when I check out, if that's okay?"

"It's not like that around here, or up at your place, I hear," said James. "No tabs amongst friends."

David was impressed with the efficiency of the still and complimented James on the construction.

"I had some help with it, for sure," James replied.

"Would you look at that?" pointed James, once they were on the roof.

Four hot air balloons slowly crossed the horizon, heading towards the ranch.

"Should we be concerned?" asked Jason, gripping his rifle.

"Nah," said James. "I recognize two of them. The red one there has the car dealership logo on it and the greenish-yellow one next to it has some hotshot law firm name, if I remember. I think they're just out for a flight, or a float, whatever the official term is. Besides, not a lot of people can fly one of those things."

"They scare the daylights out of me," said Jason. "Always hitting power lines or floating away, never to be seen again!"

"Never?" asked David.

"Just what I heard is all," replied Jason, now thinking it sounded dumb coming out of his mouth. "Everything is found eventually, that's right," he said aloud.

"I'm just joking with you," said David. "Feel free to tell me to shut up!

"Please hand me my binoculars, Jason, and take a look through your scope down at those trucks there," James said, pointing.

"I got them," said Jason.

"Me too," replied David, looking through his own scope a hundred yards away on the road.

"Probably just following the balloons, like they do in case they have to pick them up before the landing spot," said James, focusing his binoculars.

****

Chapter Thirty ~ Weston, Colorado

"Maybe cancel that thought!" James said, as all three saw the beds of both trucks filled with men wearing masks of varying colors and all carrying rifles.

Pop! Pop! Pop! could be heard, as puffs of smoke rose from the trucks, not slowing pace.

"Wait a minute! Are they shooting at the balloons?" asked David.

"Surely not!" said James, watching in horror as the shots fired increased, and two of the baskets rocked side-to-side. "Those people up there are sitting ducks; they can't go fast or high enough to get away!" said James, raising his own rifle. "They're just laughing, the shooters, like it's a round of skeet."

"No, no, no!" called out Jason, looking at a man hanging off the side of the red balloon's basket.

"What's he doing? He can't jump—he'll never make it!" cried David.

Others in the balloon were seen trying to pull him back in. Every time he would gain an inch, he was hit with a random bullet. After a few quickly fired, he dropped, flailing his arms and legs on the way down.

"We can't let these people get slaughtered!" said James. "How many rounds do we have up here, Jason?"

"Uh, hold on," he said, fumbling with the keys to the locked roof trunk. "Let's see. We've got two or three hundred rounds for ours, and what's your caliber, David?"

".223," he replied.

"Okay, we have you covered too."

"All right," said James. "Janice will keep everyone inside when she hears the shooting, but we can't let them get up to the house. Ready? Pick any guy and drop him. They're zigzagging a lot with crazy turns, so lead them just a bit and keep your heads down. Okay...now!" he commanded, opening fire.

The men in both trucks were confused at first, believing it was return fire from the balloons. They kept firing into the sky, but some were now ducking, and both drivers skidded to a stop.

All three men on James' rooftop deck uttered the phrase "Man down" after only a minute.

"We've got loaded magazines by your feet, gentlemen," said Jason.

"Don't let them get up to the house," said James. "I'll shoot every round we've got if we have to."

It didn't take long for the shooters to realize where the crossfire originated. The ones left looked like about ten, including the drivers and half of the original bunch.

"Here we go! Watch your heads!" called out James.

An array of steel projectiles hit the rooftop's outer layer, with more zinging overhead.

"Watch those trucks," called out James. "I don't want anyone sneaking off and coming through our back door later."

The shooters, apparently without spare mags, reloaded all about the same time, picking up random shells scattered about the truck beds.

"They are reloading. Hit them hard!" said James. "Take the trucks out for sure."

James glanced up to where the balloons were and saw only two moving far off in the distance.

"I only see two. There are two," he called out.

Both trucks, riddled with bullets, didn't move. Smoke poured from the radiator of one, and the other crept at maybe two miles per hour.

The remaining heads popped up at nearly the same time, and James with his company did what needed to be done.

"Grab the truck, Jason, and throw my old chair in the back; we'll cover you," said James. "Come pick us up, and let's find those balloons. It looks like we've got good people on the ground."

"I'll get a heads-up to Doc Walters, in case we have incoming," said Jason, running for the truck.

"How are you holding up, David?" asked James.

"Well, I've never shot an AR with two broken ribs," he groaned. "I don't recommend it, but if we saved a life, I would do it again. Will God forgive us?"

"He has directed us to be the protectors of the innocent," said James. "He put us here to fight evil, which would surely have headed for the town next. I see two balloons in the air, so the other two are down, and we need to find them."

Before helping James into the truck, Jason said he told Janice and Lauren to be extra careful and lock up the house tight.

"Help me scan the land," said James. "We have a better chance of spotting the downed baskets from up here."

"Over there!" called out David, pointing north. "It's the green and yellow one."

"Take one more minute," said James. "Let's look for anything red."

With nothing showing up in the scans, they headed for the green balloon, first checking the intruders' trucks. Nearly all were deceased. Gone up or down, depending upon their actions and beliefs.

Both trucks were within 200 feet of each other. Six men, all injured—from grave to recoverable—remained with weapons down and begging to live. David used his rifle to cover two minimally injured men, moving them from one truck to the other and grouping up with the rest. Once he had their attention, he spoke.

"There was a man in my camp only days ago that would have taken all of you out and not missed his next meal. You preying on the innocent for sport is wrong, and he wouldn't stand for it. I don't either, but it's not up to me to decide your fate. You are in the town of Weston, and it's not my call. So, do your best to help your friends worse off, especially him," he pointed to a man in the back truck bed. "Reach for a weapon, and it will be my call."

David held the men he knew were bad until help arrived. It was a truck with one doctor and two of the Sheriff's deputies.

"Should we tell the Sheriff about the new guests?" asked one deputy.

"No, let him fish. He will find out soon enough that we have a jail full," replied another.

* * * *

James and Jason left and found the two downed balloons. Four casualties, all gunshot wounds, with another two injured and the rest frightened but unharmed. Both were able to land safely, having the gunfire diverted by James and his men. They loaded the survivors into the truck, headed for town. We will have the rest picked up and brought to the cemetery before day's end, James promised the grieving family and friends. He arranged for a few more deputies to come and transport the deceased ballooners to town, and he met them there.

"Been a busy week," the funeral home director said to James. "It doesn't pay anything anymore, and you all are taking up my dirt."

"I'll see what we can do," said James, handing him two silver coins. "We can't have our undertaker quitting on us. The funeral is tomorrow?"

"Yes, Mayor. No sense in waiting longer than that. And thank you," he added, holding up the silvers.

"All right, then. We have some more coming; they're the ones who are responsible for killing these fine folks here. Understand?"

"We'll keep them separate, just like we kept those two guys from the gladiator fight away from the townsfolk on the bleachers. And they don't take up valuable ground space next to any good citizens of this town."

James nodded his head, asking what time tomorrow.

"Let's say 2 p.m. Enough time to get the word out?" asked the funeral director.

"Yes. We'll see you then," said James, meeting back up with Jason and David.

* * * *

"I've got Janice on the walkie-talkie for you," said Jason. He had filled her and Lauren in on the details of the day.

"When are you boys coming home?" she asked James.

"A couple of hours, I guess. We have to make a quick stop or two first. You, Lauren, and the kiddos get dressed. We're eating out tonight. Pick you up when we're done."

They stopped by his old friend and longtime customer's farm, inquiring about the trucks for sale.

"Got some beauties still running good," he said, greeting James like an old friend he hadn't seen in a while.

"That red one over there...well, used to be red...now maybe a little pink—she's a '63 Ford F-100 and a workhorse. A new coat of paint and she'll be ready to roll. That other one, the Chevy C10 over there, is a '71. I restored her myself. What do you all think?"

"They look good from here," said David. "Dr. Walters said you had three. Where is the other one?"

"Sold two days back. Got some other folks comin' by later to look at these two. I ain't yankin' your chain, James. Just sayin' is all."

"Can you give us a minute?" asked James.

"Sure, I'll be in the barn. Keys are in both trucks, so give 'em a look over if you want."

"Do you know what you want for them?" asked David.

"I'll know it when I hear it," said the farmer as he walked away.

James, Jason and David checked out the options, starting both up, inspecting the tire tread and under the hood.

"These trucks may be gone later if he really has somebody else interested or they could sit for months. What do you think, David?" asked James.

"I don't think they will sit long," he replied. "Mel and I have a budget of five thousand pre-EMP US dollars between us in silver and gold, but that's for both trucks."

"That's about what I figured," said James. "You want to make the offer now or sit on it a while?"

"I want those vehicles if we can reach a deal. The more I think about it, the more I think they will be gone. The only problem is I don't have any more than a few silvers on me. I didn't think I would need any more just coming down to your house."

"Let's see what we can do," said James, pushing his old chair towards the barn.

The farmer agreed to the package price deal, telling James the price would have been higher if they weren't friends. He didn't want all coins, saying "It's good to have some, but I can't eat gold, if it comes down to it."

David bought two steers from James at the same price the restaurant manager had, minus the butcher fee, and the farmer agreed to the rest in coin.

James produced enough silver and gold in coins he always carried to cover the gap.

"We'll take one truck now. I'll deliver the two steers tomorrow and get the second one."

"Agreed," said the farmer, shaking his hand. "Bring me a case of your best," he said, giving James back two silver coins.

"Are you sure?" asked David, pulling James aside.

"Sure about what?"

"About covering my debt up-front. I'll get you the coin as soon as I get home."

"I know that," James replied. "Can you drive?"

"Sure thing," said David, slowly sliding behind the Chevy's wheel, with a smile as big as Texas.

James almost went home calling it a bad day for the town, but he remembered that age-old tradition of dropping supper off at someone's home when they were struggling.

* * * *

They stopped by the cafe and quickly got the addresses of the families directly affected by today's tragedy. It seemed news traveled faster than trucks nowadays.

"I want twenty-two dinners sent to these addresses tonight. Here's how many go to each address right here," he pointed to the paper he had written them on. "Can you get them delivered?" he asked the owner.

"Sure. I have a guy does that from time to time. But..."

"But what?" asked James.

"Well, it's going to be expensive unless I cut back a bit here and there, you know."

"Full dinners—no cuts—desserts included, and delivered hot in 90 minutes. I'm paying and bringing our entire household here at that time, if you have room?"

"Yes, yes. Of course, we will get right to it. Tonight's special is homemade meatloaf with my wife's almost-famous red sauce, mashed potatoes, green beans, with a side salad and dessert. Unless, of course, you would like to order from the menu?"

"No, the specials will be just fine and throw in a roll with each plate. Can you do that?"

"Oh, sure. They're working on them right now... Who's it from—you or the town?" asked the restaurant owner.

"Anonymous. Just tell them the town is praying for their families. Put everything on my tab, and I'll get squared with you tonight. See you soon."

James wasn't in a celebrating mood, but a dinner out with family and his old friend David helped to clear his mind.

"Oh, make that two more dinners, for a total of twenty-four," he said as they were walking out. Send the last two to the hospital for a Mark Jenkins and Calleigh Walters."

"You're as devious as me," said David, laughing. "Mark would kill me if I did that."

"Young love," said James, laughing as well. "He will surely thank us for it later, I'll bet."

* * * *

David stayed back, visiting with his son until James and Jason returned with the family. The doctors said all looked good and they didn't expect any more blackouts, calming David's mind.

"We bought two running trucks today, Mel and I," he told Mark. "I've got one outside right now," getting an "Awesome, Dad!" from his son.

He didn't say anything to Mark about the dinners but made sure that Calleigh was going to be working tonight.

"She starts back in an hour, Dad."

"She told you that?" asked David.

"Yes, Dad. Now stop!" he said, turning red and lowering his voice, "and you need to be gone before she gets here."

"All right. All right. How are you feeling?"

"A little better. These meds, whatever they gave me, help a lot. Doc said I could leave in another day or two probably but wants me back in a few days, or maybe it was a week, for a checkup."

"Let me ask you something, Mark. We've been up the mountain for a while now, and this is your first time back in any town. What do you think?"

"I think I like living up on the mountain, but it is good to be in town too. I guess I haven't seen much so far, though."

"No, you haven't, but I have. James is taking me along with his family and Jason's to dinner tonight."

"Dinner at home?"

"No—out at a *real* restaurant, the only one open in town."

"Really? What do they have?" asked Mark.

"Just the usual. I guess the special tonight is homemade meatloaf."

"With all the sides?" asked Mark.

"Yep."

"You suck, Dad. I want to go."

"You have to stay. Doctor's orders, but I think James ordered you a plate, so don't spoil your appetite. It should be here in about an hour."

"Ooh, Calleigh is going to be so jealous," said Mark. "Tell your friend thank you."

"Will do buddy; I'll check back with you tomorrow," he said, kissing him on the forehead before he could pull away.

"Dad, come on. I'm almost 16!"

"Yes, that's true, and I almost lost you, my only son. Understand?"

"Yeah. I get it."

"Good. Now get some rest and I'll be back in the morning."

"Dad?"

"Yeah, son?"

"I love you!"

"I love you too," David said, smiling, with a fist bump before walking out the door.

* * * *

He started down the street, driving slowly and getting a few looks from passersby. It was only about a half city block to the restaurant, and he had some time to kill, driving around a town he had never been to before the day. *It's nice*, he thought. *I can see why people seem to like it here.* He parked and waited outside for his party to arrive.

"Hey, mister," called an old man from a nearby bench. "You seen Cal? I saw you talking to him this morning, and now he's missed his card game. He never misses cards."

David smiled. "I guess he's still working," is all he said.

Little Billy and the girls were bouncing off the walls with excitement about the dinner tonight. Candice talked about the biscuits, the size-of-your-face ones, all the way there.

James half thought he might get an earful from Janice about picking up twenty-four extra dinners, but he didn't.

"Does the city pick up the tab for those?" she asked.

"Nope, so we should," he replied.

"You are a good man, James VanFleet, and this town is lucky to have you."

The restaurant owner was thrilled with the silver coins, commenting that he gave a 20% discount and had never sold that many dinners to one person.

"Delivery for Mark Jenkins and Calleigh Walters!" said the delivery man at the front desk of the hospital, now staffed by all volunteers.

"Wait. Who's it from?" she asked.

"Don't know. I just get paid to deliver," he responded.

"Okay, I'll sure pass them along."

* * * *

The family headed back to town late morning for the funerals.

Jason told James about the chair and that David had gotten it back on track.

"Sounds good! Let's take a look," said James.

They stopped in just before 1 p.m., not sure what to expect.

"We came to look at the chair," said Jason to the shop owner. "I'm sure Cam is out to lunch."

"No, he's here. He's hardly left since yesterday morning. Stayed till after midnight and back this morning at 6. Did you all threaten to kill him?"

"No, nothing like that," said David. "What I can say is that the man loves his steak and eggs."

Cam showed off the chair, as if he had never abandoned the project.

"She will be done before sunrise," he announced, looking more at David than James.

"A man in my position can never have too many chairs," said James, realizing how privileged and needy he sounded, all at once. "I'll give one to someone else."

"Jason, can you ask around and see who's most in need?"

"I'm your Huckleberry," said Jason, getting a look from every man there. "What? I thought we were doing a thing? You know—Doc Holiday? *Tombstone?* Come on, guys!"

"All right, I'll give you that one," said James, "and one of my favorite movie lines ever is *You're a Daisy if you do.*"

* * * *

Without the Sheriff on site, James said a few words at the funerals. "Lord," he prayed, "we would ask that you look after our fallen men and women, leaving behind grieving families and friends who will carry their memories forever. It is in your name we pray. Amen."

He was thanked by several family members for the meal delivered last night and was reminded that nothing stays a secret in a town this small.

* * * *

“One more thing,” said James to his group. “David here happens to be quite fond of our dog, Chance. He did have a sister, and I’m not sure what happened to her.”

“I’ll have someone, possibly the librarian, tell me where to find her owner, and we might be able to look her up before heading home,” said Janice, walking off with Lauren.

“Mommy, wait!” said Carla. “We want to come!”

“Let’s let them go,” said Jason to the children. “They could use a stroll around town, just the two of them.”

James and Jason ate a packed lunch with David and the kids in the park, not seeing Janice and Lauren back for two and a half hours.

“Did you know there’s a wine bar down the street?” Lauren asked the men.

“They make their own, and it’s not half bad!” added Janice, with the men nodding their heads.

“Let’s all take a walk and talk to the dog lady. I have her address,” Janice added.

* * * * * * *

Chapter Thirty-one ~ Weston, Colorado

"Everyone hang tight," said Janice, "and stay back on the street. I'll knock on the door."

She talked with the woman for several minutes before waving okay and disappearing inside.

There was a smell; it was the smell that caught her. Not the kennel smell of a home dog breeder but the smell like in her old friend's house—the one she and James scoured to find its occupants dead but not buried.

She looked at the woman's bruised face and neck, Chance's former caretaker, and asked. "Your husband. Did he abuse you?"

The hard woman standing like an oak responded with "For the last time."

Janice nodded, remembering her own mother abused by a boyfriend for years until her stepfather stepped in.

"Show me Daisy," Janice said. Daisy was the sweetest black lab, with a growl that sent most men running for somewhere, anywhere else. She weighed less than Chance, but not much.

The woman put a leash on her and brought her outside. "Come on over and meet her," she said.

"That's okay," said David, not getting out of the truck. "She looks like a great dog."

"You haven't even met her," said the woman. "Now you've come all this way, and she's getting nervous just standing here, so come on out and at least say hi."

James had heard this similar line before from the woman and would not be surprised at all if David bought her five minutes after thinking he wouldn't.

"All right," said David, exiting the truck. Daisy was on him straightaway, licking his hair, face and both hands.

She turned on her leash, pulling to the end of the rope with a low growl, and barked as a man rode a bicycle by.

"What's with that?" asked David.

"That man on the bike was released from prison only two years ago. Did a long stint for attacking an innocent woman," said her owner. "Daisy doesn't like him."

"Well, neither do I," said David, reaching into his pocket.

"Weren't you just saying something about a Daisy, James?"

"Yeah, it was a classic *Tombstone* line, but the coincidence may just be fate."

"I may catch grief for this at home, but how much for Daisy, ma'am...I mean, if she's for sale even?" David asked.

"Oh sweetie, they're all for sale, but only to good homes. They're still my babies. She would go for three-fifty, maybe four, a couple of months ago. What are you offering now? Come over by the house."

David noticed the odor right away and had seen the bruises. "Ma'am, if you don't mind, please tell me who's in that house, and why?"

"It's my husband, and five days ago he beat me for the last time. Six years I've been too scared to leave, and my dogs didn't like it either. This time he beat me, and I mean bad, for overcooking his supper."

She pulled her hair back to reveal more purple and yellow bruises on the back of her neck and lifted her shirt's back, revealing the same all down her spine.

"I would have put up with it, like I always do, but that day was different. The first few times, he apologized and cried right in front of me, swearing he would never lay a hand on me in anger again. Then he would only apologize, and the last couple of years he didn't even do that. The last time, five days ago, he was at it again but the back gate was open somehow. Anyway, the dogs, my dogs, chased him into a corner in the back of the house. I tried to call them off, but he shot two of my babies."

"Didn't anyone hear the shots?" asked David.

"No, it was a crossbow. I was in shock and just watched as he reloaded after killing the first one. After two, I snapped, I guess, and threw a vase—this one right here," she said, pointing to a heavy vase with the top third missing in a shattered pattern. "Hit him square in the eyes, and he fell where he stood. Anyway, I didn't know what to do with the body. I guess you all have the murder weapon and a motive now. What's going to happen to my dogs?" she asked, with tears rolling down her cheeks.

"I'm sorry you had to endure that, ma'am, and I'm not the law but it looks like self-defense to me," said David. "A man who hurts a woman has a special place waiting for him way underground, as far as I'm concerned."

He agreed on a purchase price with the woman for Daisy, including the removal of one five-days-old piece of trash, with both parties happy with the deal.

"I'll pick her up in a few days after I go home and get some money," he said, not wanting to ask James for another loan.

"Oh, nonsense," she replied. "Any friend of the Mayor is good for a short-term loan with me. Take her today, and I'll see you back in a few days."

* * * *

The girls and Billy couldn't wait to reunite her with her brother, Chance, petting her all the way home.

Chance did remember her, after growling at the front door when they arrived. A potty break for both cut the tension. He curled up next to her only minutes later, sharing his bed and blanket, and they never moved until morning.

"If Tina says no, you just bring her back here," said James. "She'll have a good home either way."

"My girls, Veronica and Suzie, will love Daisy. I just know it—and Mark too," replied David.

"Thank you, James, for bringing me by there today. I still owe her a favor, as you heard, but I believe her."

"So do I," said Janice.

"There's no room for abusers in this town," said James. "I'll get it taken care of."

* * * *

David picked up a reluctant Mark with Jason's help, introducing him to his first-ever dog. He was released early but told to stay low for a while.

"Did you get her digits?" asked David.

"Come on, Dad—nobody says that anymore, if they ever did."

"It was a thing we all did," added Jason.

"And what was with the extra dinner for her from 'Anonymous'?" asked Mark.

"That was all James," said David. "Did she like it?"

"Yes, she did, so don't ask me any more questions. She will be working on my follow-up appointment in three days, so let's not miss it. Okay?"

"The appointment or her?" he asked, laughing.

"I'm not even answering that, Dad. Can we just be on time, though?"

"Sure thing, son, as long as there are no bears."

Mark rolled his eyes, but out of embarrassment, not disrespect, and spent the rest of the trip home thinking of her.

* * * *

David insisted that Jason and James follow him home, so they could square up for the trucks. The two stayed only thirty minutes, saying hi and taking a quick look at the greenhouses that James declared looked promising. Mel was grateful for James' loan to David and sent him home with five pounds of freshly roasted coffee beans as a thank-you.

* * * *

Tina, Veronica and Suzie, with Beatrice and Mel, welcomed them home. Daisy was a surprise to all and warmed her way into their hearts straightaway. She slept on Suzie's bed the first night, creating a rivalry of sorts between the daughters.

"Now we're going to need one of those," said Mel, with the children excitedly asking, "Does she have any more?"

"Yes, a few, actually. It seems not too many people volunteer to have another mouth to feed right now, let alone pay to buy one," said David. "Besides, you and I have to make a trip over there in three days for Mark's appointment and to pick up the second truck. We can stop by and take a look."

"Perfect! Our Katie misses Ringo and Mini. She needs a friend," replied Mel.

"That brings me to my next discussion. We're going to need every adult in attendance because it's big news that will affect all of us," said David.

* * * *

They gathered for dinner outside tonight with something simple—chili and cornbread. Every man and woman was eager to hear about David and Mark's adventures and the big news only rumored about.

The children were mesmerized by David's account of his bear encounter, with Tina telling him to tone it down so the kids wouldn't have nightmares.

Mark received sympathy from all and thanked them, but he couldn't shake the girl from his mind. Her smile, the way she walked and talked, the smell of her hair. He was confused, a fifteen-year-old with his whole life ahead of him, living with his dad and new family miles from anywhere. *What if she doesn't like me?* he worried, *or is seeing someone else?* He would see her again in three days' time and vowed not to leave until he had his answers.

David ended the riveting story with James' proposal. "Be a part of Weston now or wait until another town sweeps you in, without a choice."

The vote was nearly unanimous, with David surprised at the enthusiasm.

"We could lose some residents, maybe," he told Mel later, "if they can live in town."

"Maybe so, but not me and my family," he replied. "I'm good to trade on Saturdays and would like to take my family to church on Sunday, but we will be here working for the common good for the rest of the week. We need a safe road down the mountain, though. Both times—with James and Janice, plus you and Mark going down it—someone almost got killed. I don't want that risk for my family every time we head down the mountain."

"That's a fair point," said David, "and I'll bring that up to James. It would be nice, though, to trade wares once a week."

David settled into a routine of sorts, mostly directing the greenhouse plantings with his ribs on the mend. Mark resumed radio duty, being the least physical job in the camp. They planned the follow-up doctor visit and hoped for a safe trip.

* * * * * * *

Chapter Thirty-two ~ Rocky Mountains, Colorado

Lonnie pulled up the map, pointing out the route.

"It's about 80 miles to Grand Lake," he said. "From there, we go up the mountain and then back down Trail Ridge Road. We have a heavy load that's going to be a struggle both ways. The chances of having to unload Bert and drive over before loading him back on the trailer is probable. We keep that trailer in the last spot of our caravan, either way. Grand Lake is not far from Estes Park, and then it's a straight shot down the canyon to Saddle Ranch."

"This is going to be a tough last leg of the trip," I said, "but we need to make time. I'm hoping to be at Saddle Ranch in two days' time. We will only stop for bathroom breaks, any danger or maintenance issues, and a quick lunch today. We will shoot for Grand Lake by tonight and try a shot all the way in tomorrow. Any questions or concerns?"

Nobody raised a hand or had any objections. *They are probably as tired as I am and just want to be done with the traveling*, I thought.

* * * *

The day was long, with only a few stops. Bert sailed us through the occasional barricades without paying a toll and only answering a few questions about our group. Grand Lake was beautiful, even now littered with tents lining its shores. The caravan pulled in late afternoon, making great time through the mountains with mostly clear roads. Lonnie gathered everyone to discuss the plan.

"We have a big day tomorrow," he said, "and I'm proud of everyone today pitching in to get us this far. One more tough day, and we will be home. Let's only unpack what we absolutely need, and nothing more. I'm going to bed early after dinner and will be sleeping except for my guard shift. I recommend you consider doing the same. We leave tomorrow morning at first light."

"Good speech," I told Lonnie, with Jake agreeing.

"I didn't want to come off like I was telling everybody what to do, but every day we are out on the road is another chance of bad things happening," Lonnie replied. "Besides, we need every extra day we can to help them get ready for the Great Battle at Saddle Ranch."

"That's the irony," said Jake. "Us hurrying to get out of the mountains, only to quickly arrive at a battleground.

"We'll try to get the tank up the hill tomorrow," said Lonnie. "But if we can't—Vlad, we need you, Sheila, and you too Jake, to drive it over the hill. Once off the Divide, we should be able to load it back on the trailer and head down in low gear. It will be all downhill from there, so we all need to be careful not to burn out our brakes. There's a reason they have 'Runaway Ramps' up here for the big trucks."

"I've seen it," I interjected. "One came right by us once, honking its horn, and went a good couple hundred feet up the gravel-filled ramp right before a corner in the road that would have flipped it for sure. Let's not try that this time."

The night was calm, peaceful almost, and felt more like a lake campground on any weekend before the day and not the temporary refugee camp it actually was now. There was no gunfire, no apparent danger, only quiet campers who somehow found a way to get along, and hopefully even help each other out.

* * * *

We got an early start. And Lonnie, true to his word, had us pulling out a few minutes past sunrise.

It wasn't long to get to the bottom of the steep hill heading up over the mountain. The old truck carrying Bert struggled to inch up the winding hill in low gear. Steve was driving and stayed at the rear of the caravan. Everyone agreed they did not want to be on the downside of him if something happened.

"It's like that movie," he said—*Final Destination*, where the logs come off the truck up ahead and hit the vehicle behind it. This time it would be a tank and not a log!"

Steve made it halfway up before Vlad called it. "That's enough!" he called over the radio. "This truck won't make it up or down with that kind of weight on it, and we are going to need it on the other side for sure."

Unloading Bert was a time suck and took more than an hour. The time was still early, just before 9 a.m., so the morning wouldn't be lost. Now they would take the lead to the other side.

"Single file, everyone!" called out Lonnie over the radio, once they had reached the top. "Let's give each other enough room to navigate if needed, but not enough to get split up. We're at near 12,000 feet above sea level, so pop your ears if you need to; and if you get a headache, it's normal. This Divide designates which ocean the rivers run into. Some will hit the Pacific, others the Atlantic, and some spill into the Gulf of Mexico—that's a fun fact you may not know. We will stop at the bottom to reload Bert on to the trailer and get some lunch. With any luck, it will be smooth going after that."

With Bert in the lead, we made our way down the back side of the Divide. Taking extra time creeping down the steep grades, we made it to the bottom, stopping for a quick lunch while getting Bert loaded back on the trailer.

* * * *

It was the children who first saw the smoke, asking who was camping so far away. I was helping the best I could with getting Bert loaded, and we all blew it off for a minute.

"Daddy!" called out Hudson.

"Yeah, buddy, just a minute," I said, without looking at him.

"Daddy, there's some smoke way off."

“There are a lot of campsites now, son,” I responded.

Other kids joined, getting all of our attention at once.

“That’s no campfire,” said Lonnie, pointing to the now-obvious plume of smoke off in the distance, to the north.

Some of us got binoculars out but couldn’t see flames.

“I think it’s in a valley,” said Jake, looking as well.

Lonnie already had the Rand McNally map out, as we tried our best to determine its location.

“It’s north and east of us, for sure, but not much,” said Lonnie. “Since we are traveling almost straight east, we should stay parallel to it. I can’t tell which way it’s headed, but I don’t want to get stuck up here trying to figure it out.”

“What about the wind direction?” asked his wife, loud enough so we all could hear.

“That can change in a minute up here,” Lonnie replied. “It’s another reason I don’t want to hang around. I want us to be long past this thing before we lay our heads down tonight.”

* * * *

“We leave in five minutes,” he called out. “Finish your lunches, or eat them on the way.”

We had seen fire firsthand more than once, and this was different than the last time, for sure.

“There are no planes coming up this high in the mountains to put this thing out,” I said. “There needs to be a good rain or this thing will be an inferno in a few days’ time.”

“It’s already getting bigger,” said Vlad, “however, that’s possible.”

I looked up from my binocular’s fine focus, and it looked like more smoke to me too.

"Let's go! Let's go!" called out Lonnie. "We can talk while we're driving," he added, pulling ahead once again. "Any adult not driving needs to keep their eyes on the smoke and report anything new!"

Vlad, Jake and I took turns scanning the area with and without binoculars. Lonnie was making good time and maybe going a bit too fast, but he was in the lead.

"Flames up on top!" called out Vlad.

"Where?" I asked, scanning the ridge in detail.

"Right up there," he pointed, so I could zoom in.

"I got it," I announced. "It's going up the next ridge over—the valley couldn't contain it."

"What's near here?" asked one of the ladies.

"Allenspark, a small town, is pretty close. Estes Park is the one we need to make it through to get where we're going," I said over the radio. "We have two choices to get halfway down the canyon from there, but then we are committed for sure. Right now, we need to keep moving. Don't stop unless it's urgent."

We drove down the windy roads in low gear, saving our brakes and watching the growing fire over our left shoulders for the next two hours.

"We're coming up on Estes Park," said Lonnie—"just about three miles ahead."

"It's a pretty good-sized town," I added, "at least for these parts, so I'm expecting a barricade and some type of passage trade. Let's slow down when we get close. They may take Bert as more of a threat than a curiosity."

"Estes Park—Two Miles" the road sign read. I looked back at the massive fire that before the day would have planes dropping slurry or water on it, picked up from Lake Estes in the middle of town. Not today. The sky was an orange-black, taunting anybody brave enough to stick around.

"Watch the dogs," I called out, holding Ringo's collar.

"Why is that?" asked Joy over the radio.

"That's why," I said, watching the parade of animals coming out of the trees and into the large meadows.

Ringo gave me a 150-pound tug, wanting to jump off the trailer.

"Easy, boy," I said, watching Jake have an easier time with Mini.

Deer and elk poured from the trees, with rarely seen predators doing the same. Black bear, coyotes, foxes, and even a mountain lion could be seen in close proximity to each other.

"There's nothing else up here that will make predators and prey stick so close together without something getting eaten," I said to Vlad and Jake.

"They are all prey to the flames now," added Jake.

* * * * * * *

Chapter Thirty-three ~ Estes Park, Colorado

"Barricade up ahead," called out Lonnie. "We're going to approach real slow."

I stood up, but not too high, to look through my binoculars at the barricade I guessed would be at the Rocky Mountain Park entrance we were coming up on from the other side. It was formidable from what I could see—the most fortified I had seen since Breckenridge. But it was open. Not completely, but enough for us to go through single file.

The town was bustling with people, all hurrying to get somewhere or just standing on the street, pointing at the fire. It no longer took binoculars to see the rising flames. Sirens roared throughout the town, and an old ice cream truck drove the streets with the music every kid ran towards for the last fifty years.

A man called out over the megaphone. "Citizens of Estes Park! Make your way down to the lake in a swift but orderly manner. This is the Estes Park Police Department." He repeated the same message over and over.

It was strange to hear the sound of the truck jingle that drew every child in the vicinity into a mad dash to find some money before he left, contrasted with orders to keep moving and presumedly "Do not get ice cream!"

To my surprise, and the others in our caravan, very few people in town gave us a second look, with even police directing us through the center of town without a single question.

"Keep moving," the officer yelled at Lonnie when he tried to stop and talk to him.

"Yes, sir," he replied, heading our weary group through the center of town and towards the lake, passing near the waterwheel and the carillon clock tower on Fall River.

"There is a walking bridge and wooden deck with stairs that led up to WaterWheel Art Gallery," I pointed out. "The artwork was all by local artists associated with Saddle Ranch between 1975 and 1986. My dad, Bill, managed the Gallery and was one of the artists." The aroma of salt-water taffy that I remembered as a kid filled the air, now coupled with smoke from the fire. Sweet and smoky, reminding me of more than a few camping nights growing up with s'mores and hot chocolate. "Look to your left, everyone!" I said.

"Is that the Overlook Hotel?" blurted out Lonnie over the radio.

"Well, kind of," I replied. "You see, the Stanley Hotel bore the idea for the book *The Shining* and subsequent movies by Stephen King. Filming took place in multiple locations for the original movie, including studios in England and the Timberline Lodge on Mount Hood in Oregon. In the second adaptation with Steven Weber, Rebecca De Mornay, and Elliott Gould in 1997, the three-episode made-for-TV series was shot right here at the Stanley. My mom Sharon was even an extra and can be seen walking down the steps to the front lawn in the opening scene. My dad, Bill, stood in for Elliott Gould, being about the same height and build. Both movies are worth a watch when you get the chance."

* * * *

We stopped just beyond the lake, at the mouth of the canyon.

"Let's take five," said Lonnie, "for a bathroom break only."

He came back to talk to Vlad, Jake and me, asking, "Lance, what's up ahead?"

"It's just over twenty miles to the bottom, and then another seven to go around and enter on the north end of the Saddle Ranch property. There's a quicker route once we get down, but we can't make a bridge turn with the trailers. I don't expect any more barricades, but I'll guide us the last bit when we exit the canyon."

"The last leg is coming up," called out Lonnie, getting a "Wahoo!" out of most of us.

"That's not going to do!" said Vlad. "We're here at the finish line—let's hear it again!" he yelled out.

This time everyone pitched in, including the kids, getting the most looks from townsfolk that we'd had all day.

* * * *

The last twenty miles down the canyon brought up a lot of memories for me. Mostly good, like hiking, camping and fishing when growing up, and some not so nice.

"This is where that Big Thompson Flood happened back in '76—the big one I told you guys about," I called out to Vlad and Jake.

"I can see how so many lives were lost," replied Vlad. The canyon, it's not very wide, and it was at night. I remember you telling us."

Our caravan followed the river down the canyon, passing houses that were spared by the flood, and others rebuilt the next year. We passed by one of my favorite places to stop as a kid, The Colorado Cherry Company—"A Taste of the High Country," the sign out front read. The signature jugs of likely red dye I always thought was cherry cider hung completely around the outside of the quaint one-story riverfront building that had been there since I could ever remember. I had half a mind to see if they were still open before recalling that bad things happened when we stopped.

The canyon, feeling ominous to many with its winding road and high narrow cliff walls, made me comfortable, like an old T-shirt. I had never felt more protected on this whole trip.

"Passing the Dam Store, another popular haunt when we were young, I was filled with emotion. It seemed strange since that wasn't one of my personality traits, but I felt a mix of excitement, exhaustion, relief, sadness for what lay ahead, and a comfort I had not known in some time. We passed right by my elementary school, Big Thompson Elementary, and up the valley just adjacent to Saddle Ranch.

"Let me do the talking when we arrive," I told Lonnie. "I don't want any misunderstandings with the guards.

"Hold tight, everyone!" I called over the radio, pausing only seconds before making the announcement: "We're Home!"

To be continued...

ABOUT THE AUTHOR

Lance K. Ewing lives with his wife, three boys (Hudson, Jax and Hendrix), Ringo, Mini and Bobo (dogs and a cat) in McKinney, Texas. When he is not at work, he can always be found with his family, preferably outdoors. Lance grew up in the foothills of the Colorado Rocky Mountains, with the Rockies quite literally in his backyard.

Families First is his debut novel. Volume six is being written now.

Lance is a Chiropractor in Dallas, Texas. His new *Chronic Pain* quick-read series of books is now available for sale on Amazon Kindle.

He just released a children's picture book, titled *The Great Toy Revolt*, reminding kids that their classic toys can still be more fun than the glitzy electronic ones. It is now available on Kindle, KU and in paperback.

From the author: "As a young man, I was fascinated by the writing of Stephen King. I can still remember getting a used, or sometimes brand-new, copy of classics, such as *The Shining*, *Firestarter*, *Christine*, *Cujo*, and *The Dark Tower* series. One book, however, topped them all: *The Stand*. To this day, that is the book I measure all other Post-Apocalyptic work against, including my own. As I grew older, I never left for a vacation or camping trip without a book by James Patterson stowed away in my backpack."

If you enjoyed this volume, please leave an honest review. In this new age of publishing, reviews are heavily tied to the success of Indie authors who don't have the backing of a large publishing house.

Contact Lance at *Lance@lancekewingauthor.com*.

For those interested in this series, please consider keeping in touch by visiting my website at *lancekewingauthor.com* for upcoming books and projects, as well as updates on what I am up to. Join our e-mail list for news about upcoming volumes and sneak peeks. I will not distribute your e-mail anywhere. In return for your e- mail, I will forward you my Quick Guide e-book (free of charge and not available for sale) with more on the characters of *Families First*, including their backstories, much of which you will not find in any of the volumes.

Visit the Facebook page: *Families First*.

https://www.facebook.com/groups/447305392509202

Author Pic

More Books by Lance K Ewing

Families First A Post-Apocalyptic Next-World Series ~ Volumes 1-7 (EMP) (PG-13)

Volume 1: Families First

Volume 2: The Road

Volume 3: Second Wind.

Volume 4: Hard Roads

Volume 5: Homecoming

Volume 6: Battle Grounds

Volume 7: The Change

Long Road Home ~ a Post-Apocalyptic Next-World Series (EMP) (PG-13)

Book 1: Long Road Home

Book 2: The Plan

Book 3: Turning Point – In Production

2030 ~ An Apocalyptic Series

Book1: In Production

Book 2:

Book 3:

Coming of Age under my pen name Kendall Ewing

Bonze (Bo-nes) – On Pre-sale **(PG-13)**

Fragile – In Production

Children's Picture books (ages 3-8)

The Super Great Adventures of Rico, the Monkey-Tailed Skink

The Great Toy Revolt (Lost Toys Series)

Nonfiction Health and Medical

The 30 Days to a Better Back Challenge

Made in the USA
Monee, IL
21 May 2023